Patricia,
Fast paced this is. Enjoy!

SIX

A Dax McGowan Mystery

JACK HARNEY

This is a work of fiction, and the characters, places, and events are the creation of the author. Resemblance to any person, living or dead, is entirely coincidental.

Available on Kindle and CreateSpace:

The Millstone Prophecy: A Dax McGowan Mystery

Please visit: www.jackharneyauthor.com

Cover Design and Art by Victoria Landis

ISBN-13: 978-1517651251

ISBN-10: 1517651255

Therese Albrecht

Your powerful story never ceases to affect my view of the world.

PROLOGUE

No meaningful amount of snow had yet visited the city, but a biting Polar air mass had taken up residence. Every shelter in the Mott Haven area of the Bronx was filled beyond capacity.

After a hundred late-day meals were served at St. Vincent de Paul's Homeless Shelter, Sister Mary Barnabas helped settle a host of poorly clothed adults and children into an array of cots and floor blankets for the night. The cleanup stretched into the late evening, and as usual, she was the last staff person to leave. Her donated and stained powder-blue overcoat was tightly wrapped around the sweater she had buttoned over her beige-colored habit. She was sure her veil, and an added red woolen scarf, would insure the protection of her neck for the two-block walk home to her apartment.

She peeked out the metal door on the east side of the building. "Oh no," she said aloud. Across the alley, the light bulb over the service door to the neighboring butcher shop was turned off. She had always counted on it to partially cover the fifty yards or so between her exit and the less scary well-lit public street. Police flyers posted everywhere had warned of a psychotic killer who had the entire neighborhood in a state of panic. No matter, she thought. Her weary bones, in need of a warm bed and a loving snuggle from her cat, convinced her that even the worst of men would not venture out on such a bitter night. She would hurry.

The door locked behind her as she stepped down the four cement stairs to the alley floor. Because a blast of wind-swept, stinging cold air greeted her face, she lowered her head, and commanded her elderly legs to shuffle forward as fast as they could.

As she reached the butcher's door, a masked figure dressed in black stepped out from behind the door's waist-high brick stoop.

"No!" she screamed. Halted frozen in place, her grip instinctively tightened around her purse. Her purse never the target, the figure lunged, and through her scarf and veil thrust an elongated hypodermic needle into her neck. The searing liquid caused every vein in her head to bulge and burn with pain. Dizziness engulfed her. As she fell in slowed motion, her eyes caught the ambient light from the street bounce off the jagged edges of a smashed light bulb still screwed into the socket above the meat-merchant's door. Twisting in her descent, her back hit the wall of the stoop and she inched downward from there. Coming to rest with her head propped up, she peered down her strewn body at legs and feet that seemed no longer attached. A pair of alien thumbs held her eyelids open for a time, and when released, they were unable to close. The pain in her neck and head had disappeared. She could see; she could hear, but not move.

The assailant was on her in rapid fashion, using a sharp knife to slit the buttons off her coat and through her sweater, habit, and undergarments. She expected her exposed skin to scald in the frigid air, but she felt nothing.

Was she to be raped? Would her lifelong vow of chastity be broken in the last seconds of her life? She had been careless defying the posted warnings of this danger. Would God forgive her the error leading to this desecration of her body?

She watched as the attacker gradually pulled the knife back and then thrust it between her legs. Paralyzed, the act had no meaning for her at first. A moment later, she saw the faint reflection of what she knew was blood flowing over cobblestones and into a drain in the middle of the alley.

It seemed from nowhere, her limp left arm suddenly appeared before her unblinking eyes, and the back of her hand was pushed in front of her face. At the end of a fear-filled pause, her palm was savagely stabbed with the knife, piercing through several times and twisting in a boring motion. Any attempt to shut her eyes or pull away was futile. The ritual was repeated to her right palm. Would that be the end of it? She prayed that it would.

Not so. The index finger of a latex-gloved hand slid across the top of her left breast, stopping above it and pressed between two ribs. A scalpel-filled other hand then moved in to pierce her torso there in a most delicate fashion. Her fear accelerated. Instinct told her whatever had been sliced below her ribcage was something critical.

Creeping slowly like a crazed lizard over her exposed body, the assailant's masked head hovered above her face. A cloud of aroused hot breath spread like a heavy fog over her nose and mouth. In a flash, the knife was thrust into her left eye, and her mind screamed from its core. The knife was raised again above her right eye, but hung in anticipation, as the fiend lifted the mask long enough to expose a face sneering a look of hate-filled disgust.

"No. No. Not you!" were the last words the nun's mind spoke. What little she was able to see was beginning to fade. She sensed her life ebbing away from somewhere inside her chest as a barely perceptible glint off the knife's blade came crashing through her remaining eye. A few seconds more, the blackness of death gripped her soul, and it was over.

CHAPTER ONE

Monday, December 11

A bitter pre-dawn wind sliced through the barren weeping beech trees dotting the landscape of Woodlawn Cemetery. He wore only a suit with his white dress shirt open at the collar. The frigid air held no sway in Dax's attention, as he stood motionless over Grace's grave. Her loss had taken many tolls, one being shocks of gray had invaded the temples of his wavy black hair where none resided before her passing. Still lithe and muscled at thirty-six, his sturdy six-foot frame stood more as a mere shadow, a ghost in this setting.

He had chosen Woodlawn, known as the resting place of the likes of Juilliard and Pulitzer, guaranteeing his daughter an undisturbed rest to last a time equal to the life expectancy of New York City itself. Its eminence as a non-sectarian burial ground was also well suited given the circumstances of her death. The precocious and gifted child had been presented an irreconcilable choice. Either she continually accede to the sexual desires of a pedophile priest, or he threatened to have God cause her father's death in his danger-filled job as a homicide detective. Grace opted for what she thought the only way possible to escape her serial horror and still save her daddy's life. She took her own.

With only a hint of light appearing from the east, he placed yet another quarter dated the year of her birth on her headstone. Grace had always loved the gift of these special quarters from her father for all the large and small academic successes she had achieved at Lighthouse Charter School. A soft smile crossed his face as he observed all the coins he had placed in the past were still there. New sets of flowers and trinkets from friends and strangers alike greeted his every visit, though the numbers had declined over time and today there none.

The modest granite gravestone's proof of her death at age eleven struck a pain in his chest that he knew would once again last the entire day; though this morning, for the first time, he felt its effect seemed somewhat lessened. Dax had no place in his Holmesian view of the world of an afterlife or communication with the dead, yet he was moved to say aloud, "Daddy loves you, sweetheart. I will always love you."

It took the walk of the many yards down the lane to where his car was parked for the grip of grief to loosen sufficiently for him to feel the need of the overcoat he had left inside.

CHAPTER TWO

"Why today? Goddammit, not this day," spoke the career-worn, burly sixty-three-year-old, and thirty-year veteran of the NYPD. Captain John Pressioso had no expectation of a response from the walls in his office that only bounced back the vibrations of his deep voice.

So much pressure had come down from the top brass on the matter of Officer Teresa Gallagher that the date had slipped his mind. The meeting he arranged for today was also the anniversary of Grace McGowan's death. Another element in the captain's stress level was the third party involved to meet with him and Dax. Dr. Clinton Hogarth, the NYPD's top forensic psychologist.

The captain had crossed paths, or as he would term it, "tangled," with this shrink on numerous occasions, as psychological profiling had in recent times become a mandated procedure in the world of homicide investigations. He had more than once described Hogarth with a hand-over-the-mouth comment as "arrogant as a peacock in a flock of turkeys."

Aside from having to once again deal with the department's diva, drawing his main concern was the nature and purpose of the meeting. The assignment was going to break all kinds of new ground. Hogarth had been given orders to turn over all his notes and diagnoses on Teresa Gallagher, a first-year rookie cop and the daughter of Jeremiah Gallagher, the city's tyrannical Police Commissioner.

The captain's ear to the department grapevine had already informed him that every means had been pursued to determine the cause of her suffering from a sudden onset of unpredictable bouts of confusion and near loss of consciousness. The extremes of Teresa's behavior had finally led her best friend and patrol partner, Larry Destin to report to their superiors that Teresa's deteriorating condition was getting scary and a possible danger to the public. The last straw for him was her failure to back him up on a guns-drawn domestic violence call.

Pressioso was initially surprised at how much Dax knew about the issue when he called him to set up the meeting, though he realized virtually nothing in the machinations of the department escaped the knowledge of his best detective.

"Yes, sir. What I've heard is that after the medical doctors ruled out any physical causes, a number of the best mental health professionals in the city were employed, but no one could finger the source of her condition. Then the P.C. turned to Dr. Hogarth as a last resort, thinking how she was treated as his daughter by her fellow officers was the cause. If I ever needed any such services, I would never consider Hogarth even as a last resort, but Gallagher is getting desperate. I suppose him turning to me makes me the real last resort. This is surely outside my territory. I might even refuse to take this on. Technically, it's a personal matter, nothing to do with my duties to the city."

"Whoa, Dax . . . turning the commissioner down? If you really feel you want no part of this, I suggest you figure out a more diplomatic way to do that. You know his ego doesn't handle refusals very well, to put it mildly."

Dax went on to reveal that his sources told him some of the other professionals had pursued the line of potential delayed reactions to childhood abuse, but then demurred on that diagnosis. Making accusations about the possible presence of such a problem in the politically connected Gallagher family would have been professional suicide. Others were unconvinced abuse was a factor at all. They were more inclined to blame the fact that eighteen years earlier, at age six, she and her older sister, Angela, had come home from school to discover the body of their murdered mother. No one in that contingent of practitioners felt able to claim it definitively, however, as copious interviews on the matter with the young woman left them unsure.

The Captain knew the issue had reached a point where Teresa Gallagher's condition had fallen into the black hole of no one diagnosing anything, and the dilemma had the entire brass at One P.P., One Police Plaza, on edge. Her autocratic police commissioner father made it clear he wanted his daughter treated and back on the job. She was the only one of his offspring left to carry on the more than a century's long lineage of Gallaghers serving in the NYPD. There were no other options.

It was these same department heads who suggested the Commissioner give the city's best detective a shot at figuring it out. Dax McGowan's reputation at divining solutions in what often appeared impossible cases offered at least a safety valve solution for the moment, though all involved knew they were grasping at straws. The suggestion had been called absurd in many quarters, but given the lack of any other option, the commissioner begrudgingly approved. It was well known within the department that the commissioner often saw Dax's public fame as a threat to his own, and the P.C.'s ego getting out of hand was a danger.

The childless Captain Pressioso stared from his office window into the glow of an ice-cold dawn, concerned that *his boy,* his surrogate son, was to be tested in an arena of mystery totally out of his realm. The potential to incur the wrath of an unpredictable commissioner known to lose his temper when things did not go his way seemed inevitable. Adding to the captain's troubled state was having the dubious task foisted on Dax on the anniversary of the most tragic day in his life.

CHAPTER THREE

It was 8:28 a.m., and Dax was expected any minute. The captain could see his finger tapping on the round, four-seated, leather-inlaid conference table in his office was driving Dr. Hogarth to distraction. Sitting across from him, the doctor asked the captain to please refrain, but was met with a glare of disdain instead. Pressioso gritted and bared his teeth at the balding, obese psychologist in his late fifties. "Listen, Hogarth…"

"That's Dr. Hogarth," the doctor hurriedly voiced in the form of a Truman Capote whine.

"Listen, Hogarth," Pressioso began again, "I've already told you I don't like the idea of saddling my best detective with a no-win case like this. But you'd better know something. Today is the anniversary of his daughter's death. If you put him through any of that high-handed shit you usually spread around in meetings like this, I will personally knock all your teeth out."

With an oft-mimicked smartass grin well known in the department, Hogarth answered, "Now, Captain, I could have your entire career crushed in the palm of my hand should you attempt any such thing."

Pressioso stood and quickly pulled into the chair closest to the psychologist, intentionally crowding his personal space. "If you think I can't have you wake up in an alley somewhere with all your teeth missing, with you having no fucking idea how you got there, you are one naïve son of a bitch."

"Okay! Okay!" was Hogarth's response between gaps of heaving breaths.

Returning to his original seat, the captain never took his eyes off the doctor, despite his lieutenant's entrance into the room.

As he entered and observed the two men, Dax caught the conflict in the air, though unable to determine its source.

"Good morning, Captain." Dax nodded and then said, "Dr. Hogarth."

"How are you doing?" the captain asked.

"I'm okay, sir. Doing better than expected today," he answered, taking notice of the special concern in his mentor's voice. Dax seated himself between the two men.

Protocol required an immediate movement to the issue at hand and the captain's next words. "Okay Lieutenant, you and I have already discussed what the commissioner has assigned you to do in regard to his daughter, Officer Teresa Gallagher. As you know, Hogarth . . . excuse me, Dr. Hogarth, has brought us his file on her for your review. I also have here her release, allowing you access to any and all of her medical history from any source should you need it," he added, passing the document into Dax's hands.

"That's good, sir, and thank you Doctor for being willing to share this information," Dax said politely, knowing Hogarth had no choice in the matter.

"Let's get this straight, Lieutenant. I didn't want anything to do with this move, except the commissioner made it abundantly clear this is what he wants. I've been against this drastic and doomed idea from the outset. It's beyond all reason, in my opinion."

"Are you suggesting the commissioner is acting irrationally, Doctor?" the Captain asked.

"Of course not. Simply put, the lieutenant here has no qualifications whatsoever to be involved in psychological diagnoses."

"Listen, gentlemen," Dax said, taking charge. "I'm well aware of the process involved in making this decision, and the departmental political pitfalls everyone is so concerned about. I'm also aware this doesn't fall into the normal purview of my work, but I assure you, a mystery that begs a solution is just that, regardless of its source or its context."

"Dax,-er, Lieutenant," his captain began, "are you saying you now have an interest in taking this on?"

"After considering it more intently on the way in this morning, yes, sir, I do. Officer Gallagher is clearly disturbed by something very real. No person begins to behave irrationally at the age of twenty-four after appearing quite normal all her life without good reason. I want to help her if I can. I expect I will," Dax added, with as much the look of a concerned parent as his detective's interest in the case.

"Listen, Lieutenant, I don't care how good a detective you are," Hogarth began vehemently. "Your involvement in this woman's psychological issues is totally out of bounds. You don't have the credentials."

The extended veins on Hogarth's neck, coupled with spittle reaching far enough across the table to cause the captain to pull back, told Dax the doctor took handing over Teresa Gallagher's case more personally than expected. Not only were the doctor's skills to be scrutinized by someone his ego considered a lesser person, but Dax sensed Hogarth's fear that he might be bested in the process.

"I'm sure the lieutenant isn't claiming he has more education in this area than you," Pressioso said. "It's just that you, and all the other head-case people before you have gotten nowhere, have you?"

"None of that matters," Hogarth retorted. "McGowan here is not going to be able to succeed where others have not," he added with a flip of his hand. "The Gallagher woman has some inherent dread of facing something that lies behind some dark curtain in her psyche, and dissociates as a means of self-protection. For some reason, this well-hidden source of her trauma has taken control of her mind and is currently beyond the reach of the professional psychiatric community. How can your lieutenant possibly do any better in discovering what plagues her, when he lacks the ability? What's he going to do? Supply us with an array of detective-type observations like she trembles and becomes faint at times for no apparent reason? We already know these things." Hogarth raised his arms and flailed his hands in disdain.

When being verbally attacked in the past, Dax always took on the role of the logic-driven peacemaker. He not only wished to arrive more efficiently at needed solutions for any challenges at hand, but in an instinct-driven, almost conscious fashion, it was his way of making the world a safer place for his daughter to grow up. Her death changed all that, and instead the doctor had riled a newly acquired facet in Dax's emotional treasure chest, a controlled but vengeful anger. He stared at the doctor hard, his right eyebrow rising in a

Spock-like fashion. He leaned forward, aiming his extended fingers across the table's surface squarely in the doctor's direction.

"You know, Hogarth, I find people unknowingly give away many things about themselves, often things they desperately wish to hide. I think you would be surprised at what a few observations can reveal about anyone, even you, Doctor, if one knows what to look for."

The thin, dry air of the heated room suddenly took on a degree of weight as a smile of anticipation crossed the captain's face. Dax knew, that he knew, the direction the conversation was now headed.

"Listen, McGowan," Hogarth began, "we've never worked directly together on any case. In fact, I know you've done your best to exclude me from yours. We've sat here, what, a few minutes? What could you possibly know of any significance about me?"

"Well, Doctor, here is what I've readily surmised from those last few minutes. You live well outside the city, most likely on the island. Not the Hamptons, but in a more modest neighborhood not too far from the water. You're not wealthy, but you own a boat. You've been married at least fifteen years, but I would say closer to twenty. You and your wife have recently split up, and like most newly separated men, the first thing you want to do is get laid. You were up quite late last night doing just that. You never made it home, likely slept in your office here in town and rushed to get to this morning's meeting."

Dax watched the doctor's red face of embarrassment take more than a few seconds to exit as the fingers of Hogarth's right hand dug deep smudges into the conference table's leather inlay. "Listen, McGowan, it seems to me that you may be the person around here in most need of analysis. There's only one possible explanation for you to have any knowledge of my personal activities. Were you so fearful of facing me this morning that you followed me last night in an attempt to provide you with some needed advantage during our conversation here today? That's a little fear-filled obsessive, I'd say."

"Wrong track there, Doctor," Dax said, his deep brown eyes taking on the appearance of bottomless caverns. "First, I would say it's only people who routinely seek the need for an advantage who suspect that of others, and this short time together has been more than enough to divine what you've been up to." Dax slid back in his chair, clasped his hands with both index fingers touching, and pointed at his prey. "As to the clues involved, they are quite elementary," he added, with the accent of the Queen's English as emphasis. "Shall I proceed with what you would call my detective-type observations?"

"Go right ahead. I'm sure it will be quite entertaining," Hogarth replied with a stilted confidence.

"It's early December, and the tips of your brown hair are still slightly bleached from the sun. City dwellers get little enough sun, even in summer, and by this time of year virtually all remnants such as bleached hair tips are long gone. Only a Long Islander who catches double doses of sun from the star itself, and its reflection off the water from a boat late into the fall would still show hints of them.

"There's a tiny splash of dried white paint on the outside of your left wrist. I also see dark garden dirt in the deepest parts of your fingernails, both things you missed cleaning this weekend when you were doing some of your own painting and gardening. If you were wealthy, you're the type who would enjoy paying others you consider lesser humans to do such chores.

"Your left ring finger, absent its wedding ring, has an indentation the depth of someone married in a fifteen to twenty-year time period. Take my word for it; I've calibrated the measurements. Your ring hasn't been off long enough to exhibit any of the normal healing that takes months and sometimes years to erase. How am I doing so far?"

"Okay, Lieutenant, but I'm sure there are plenty of detectives who would have picked up on my missing ring, and I'll give you the hair-tint thing as something extra, but these are hardly indications of me hiding anything."

Despite Hogarth's attempt to come off disenchanted, Dax noticed a telltale vibration across the table produced by the doctor whose knee was oscillating up and down off the sole of his foot. Dax went on.

"On your right hand you missed wiping off the entire red hand stamp you received when you paid a cover charge and entered a men's club last night. The Elderly Dragon is a place in Chinatown specializing in getting horny old men laid. However, that only happens after you've bought an underage Asian girl several expensive drinks while you consumed a good many yourself. When you attempted to wash that stamp off this morning, you missed the small star that appears on the tail of a dragon that is the club's logo. I arrested a suspect in there once, and know it well."

Dax watched as his references to getting laid, underage girl, and arrested suspect in conjunction with the psychologist's activities had the doctor reeling. Before Hogarth could respond, Dax continued.

"Clearly you never made it home last night. The right cuff of your white shirt has a smudge of the same red ink where the person who stamped you brushed against it. You're wearing the same shirt you wore yesterday."

"Must this continue? Haven't we heard enough?" Hogarth pleaded.

"But there's more. Your tie has a wrinkle in it I could only describe as having been slept on by a man too drunk to take it off before passing out, probably on a couch in your office. Also, when I first walked in, I observed several wet spots on the end of your tie where you attempted to wash something off."

"What the hell does that have to do with anything?"

"I can tell you, Doctor, those spots on your tie have dried now, and you won't be able to remove the discoloration from those acid burns. That's stomach acid, stomach acid from vomiting, more evidence of your night's inebriation and rush this morning, not to mention the wrinkles on your face."

"Are you done now, McGowan, you smart ass fucking bastard, are you done?" Hogarth spewed his words while rapidly drawing and expelling enough air between his clenched teeth to create a hissing noise.

"Actually, just one more thing, Doctor. I see two places where you pinched your face and neck with an electric razor I suspect you keep in your office for backup. That tells me you normally use a regular bladed razor, which always creates a near-microscopic layer of callouses on one's face that a seldom-used electric shaver will inevitably catch on. Now I'm done." Dax said, straining to prevent a victor's smile from breaking through to his face.

The captain had all he could do to quell one of his well-known Twin Tower coughs from exploding across the table, a huge laugh of his own in waiting, as Dax sat perfectly still allowing the doctor time to gain control of himself.

"Okay, McGowan, so you're good at this shit. So what? What do any of those skills have to do with diagnosing a person's psychological issues? I don't see the connection."

"What you don't see, Doctor, is that unlike you, I wouldn't rely on what a person may say once or twice a week in an office setting, at times even fooling a professional. I travel to observe their living conditions, seek out what challenges they may face daily, and interview the people close to them in their life, a distinct advantage over your methods, wouldn't you say?"

"Listen, Hogarth," the Captain interrupted in a diffusing manner. "I'm sure the lieutenant would be the first to say he may or may not be able to figure out the source of Officer Gallagher's demons, but I do think you've just seen why the brass wants him in on this…even as a last resort," he finished while winking at his lieutenant.

A long heavy breath from the doctor exhibited a short-lived acquiescence to the value of Dax's skills, but it only took him a few more seconds to go back on the attack. "Of course, I have no control over the decisions of the police commissioner; however, I want it on the record. I accept this mandated transfer of my file to you under protest, and if you do anything to mess with this woman's mind or do her any damage, McGowan, I will raise a holy public stink. Your usually positive press coverage could tank quite badly if that happens, especially when any mistakes you make concern a high profile family like the Gallaghers. And as you know, the press is always acutely interested in reporting the downfall of any previously adored celebrities."

"Is that a threat, Doctor?" Pressioso asked.

"No, Captain; it's a promise. If he fucks up, he'll pay for it."

"Be careful, Hogarth. My lieutenant will gladly take responsibility for anything he does, but if you decide to cause him any unwarranted trouble . . . well, we've already covered that, haven't we?"

Left only to display his disgust, Hogarth shoved his file across the table toward Dax and left the room with no further word.

The sunlight through the east window was now overpowering the artificial light of the overhead fluorescents. For Dax, it had the feel of a new beginning, having followed the defeat of a negative influence that had just left the room.

"You know, Captain," Dax said as he stood to make his own exit, "I'm well aware Hogarth is an accomplished psychologist. However, based on the limited contact I've had with him, I get the sense the only reason he entered the profession was so he can get to sit in a room with people so troubled, it feeds his need to feel superior. Bottom line, I don't like the guy."

"I'd say you described the arrogant bastard precisely," Pressioso replied smiling. "So, my boy, I didn't want to get into it with you in front of him, but you're really feeling good now about taking on this crazy assignment? Uh, excuse the crazy reference. You know what I mean."

"Yes, I do. I haven't met Teresa Gallagher yet, but her department file tells me she's been an outstanding rookie, and word is she's liked by everybody, despite the connection to her father. Clearly, she's facing a most unusual circumstance, and I want very much to help her. You know the experience with my Grace..." Dax hesitated in an attempt to control the tightness in his throat, "the whole experience with my daughter has taught me something I'd better pay closer attention when the people around me are experiencing damaging distress. In a sense, if I can help Teresa Gallagher in her unique circumstances, I might discover something I wish I had learned a long time ago."

"Dax, Dax, c'mon. You're not blaming yourself for what that bastard did to your daughter, are you? That priest was a master manipulator. All those pedophiles are, and Grace was trying extremely hard to keep it from you because she was sure she had to, to save your life."

"True, Captain, but it was still on me as her father to have at least suspected something that would have led me to saving her. I know you're being my friend, and to some extent, you're right about the blame issue. But I will never be able to completely let go of what I was not able to do for her. It's just the way it is," Dax said with strong intent to end the issue there, as his trembling hand pushed his wavy black hair back across his ear.

"Okay, my boy, but somehow you've got to find a way of letting that go. Let me suggest you start with realizing that nobody's perfect, you included."

"I know, Captain, I know," Dax said with a small smile. A year passing since Grace's death, imperfection was a concept he was only just beginning to accept about himself.

CHAPTER FOUR

Before Dax could enter his office adjacent to his captain's, his cell phone rang with the familiar ringtone for Special Victims Unit Detective, Janct Meehan.

He discovered she had downloaded a custom ringtone for him on her phone. It was a line spoken by Bradley Cooper from one of her favorite movies, *Limitless*. "I see scenarios, I see fifty scenarios."

He reciprocated on his phone with a ringtone from the movie *Relentless*, where a character states, "*It's an insane world, but I'm proud to be a part of it.*" They once shared hearty laughs over a pitcher of Southern Comfort Manhattans at Coogan's cop bar on Broadway, where they each touted why they believed the movie titles, and those lines fit the other so perfectly.

Dax was picturing his female friend in one of her faux men's suits exhibiting eclectic color combinations, her ongoing protest against male detectives who had preconceived ideas about how female detectives should dress. With her short brown hair, unplucked eyebrows, and no makeup, she would often stand up close to such offenders, daring them to make a comment. Over time, two factors eventually removed that kind of tension from her life. She had been decorated several times as one of the outstanding Special Victims Unit detectives in the city, and it wasn't long into her career before everyone realized she was afraid of nothing and no one.

"Janet, I'm so glad to see it's you calling. How is my relentless fellow officer of the law?"

"Well my brainy friend, I have good reason to call," she began with a muted laugh, but her words trailed off a bit sadly. "Hey, Daxman, today's the day, isn't it? You knew I'd be calling. How are you, buddy?"

The initial joy of hearing Janet's voice faded behind thought-sweeping images of their work together on his daughter's case. He was reminded how his then new friend helped him navigate his desire to push the law aside to focus on murdering the priest who caused his daughter's death. Janet was willing to break all the rules and allow him to partner with her to work on Grace's case, all the time knowing he had never fooled her about his real intentions. She had faith in the man everyone either knew or expected him to be and was willing to confront him with his own principles when it was necessary.

As he settled into his well-worn cloth-covered chair, he responded warmly to Janet's concern. "I'm trying, my friend. I'll never be the same, but I think I'm finally managing better. Visited Grace again this morning. It was almost like . . . I don't know, less pain than before. And yes, I knew you'd be calling. It's been a while, hasn't it?"

"That's the truth. But man, I have reason to think about you almost every day. Let's never let the busy stuff ever get in the way of you knowing I'm right by your side at all times, and will instantly appear whenever you need me."

"I know, but a reminder like this is good to hear," he rejoined, having detected a rare breakdown in the strong voice of his friend. "Busy stuff is part of who we are as detectives, isn't it, J. M.?" he said, offering her an escape from a perpetual affliction of hers, the fear of getting caught showing the gentle nature that was the core of who she really was.

"No shit. We broke so many rules getting your daughter's case solved last year, and even though I was promoted to lieutenant, I've been working really hard to prove to my Captain I ain't gonna overstep like that again. Of course for you, Dax, I'd do it again in a heartbeat."

"That goes the same for me," he said, putting his right leg up on the desk, feeling a fully delighted relaxation brought on by her call.

"Hey, I don't want to forget to ask you, what's up with Rebecca Bain?" Janet asked, referring to the president of Clergy Abuse

Survivors, a Chicago based international support group for victims of sexual abuse by religious clergy. "Are you guys still the major item even the press made you out to be? Man, the last I could tell, you two were so hot for each other I've been expecting to hear you'd be getting hitched."

"Uh, Becca and I are still close, but I'll tell you, my friend, it's going to take a session at Coogan's for me to give you all the details. For now, let's just say our relationship would best be described as both professionally and geographically undesirable."

Aware that Janet had herself experienced the loss of the affection of more than one female partner because living with a cop was more than most spouses and lovers could handle, he was hopeful his next words would end the subject. "We're both married to our jobs, and their specific locations, and we live eight hundred miles apart."

His hint taken, Janet steered in another direction. "Hey, Daxman, the grapevine is tittering that you're taking on some assignment to figure out why the Commissioner's daughter has gone wacko. I hear she's a good kid, and wacko is probably a poor choice of words, but that's the craziest shit I've ever heard. Ask the city's best detective to solve a family's psycho problem? How's he gonna square that with the mayor? And as we both know, and I'd say this only to you, the commissioner is a nut job himself. One of these days, the mayor has got to ax that son of a bitch. Everybody knows he wants to. How the hell did you get roped into that mess?"

Janet's question had Dax standing, pacing back and forth between his desk and his closed office door. "I'll just have to see how he's going to rationalize the city paying me for it," Dax replied, "but I'm sure he'll find a way, the same way he manages to get around a bunch of things that drive the mayor nuts. I've already done a good deal of homework on the Gallagher family. I won't go into it now, but like any other case, it will have my full attention. How goes what you're facing at SVU? What I read in the papers and see on TV tells me you have your hands full."

"No shit! I've got one crazy mother fuckin' serial killer offing nuns, and I'm getting nowhere. Actually, Dax, I wanted this call to only be about Grace, but I'm so stumped on this one, I gotta ask for your help. I've got four murders in the last fourteen weeks, and they rank right up there in terms of weirdness and difficulty to solve. I'm sure you can imagine how the self-righteous hypocrites in the archbishop's office wants to blame us for not nabbing this killer fast enough, but stood in our way when little kids like your Grace were being abused by their own kind. They still won't reveal the names on a list of priests they know who destroyed the lives of little children, and may still be doing so in some unknown locations. Listen, I want this perp because he's killing some of the finest people on the planet . . . these dedicated women who make the rest of us look pretty damn selfish."

For a moment, Dax was reminded of Janet's often callous use of street language, but not in judgment of it. For him, it fit her dedication most genuinely. He also knew his upcoming meeting within the hour with Commissioner Gallagher would likely include an order he drop everything else to pursue his daughter, Teresa's issues. However, saying no to helping Janet was out of the question. "Tell me my friend. What's so weird and different? You know I'll help any way I can."

"Mostly it's just the facts. One thing the press has already made a big deal of is all these nuns still wore the old-fashioned habit. That's a rare group anymore, as most of them wear street clothes now. But here's something we haven't told the press. The killer immobilizes his victims with a syringe full of some element I've never heard of. The M. E., Doc Perkins, says it's a form of saxitoxin. It's some rare chemical shit she discovered because she wouldn't quit testing until she determined what had been injected that left a large needle mark on each victim's throat."

"Whoa, Janet," Dax interrupted. "That definitely gets this into the weird and different category" His moderate pacing now quickened, "I'll tell you what I know about saxitoxin. In its natural form, it's a poison produced by ocean algae and it often ends up being absorbed by bottom feeding shellfish. It's a highly potent substance, and history is full of speculative stories of early human populations dying off from eating those contaminated crustaceans."

"Jesus, Dax, is there any damn subject you don't know something about?"

"You know me. If there's a substance that could be used to commit murder, I've boned up on it. There's more. In the 50s, the CIA began experimenting with it as a weapon until the international community eventually judged it to fall into the category of a chemical weapon. As a result, the U.S. supply was destroyed, but small amounts were licensed to medical researchers for potential positive applications. The real question is how this perp could have gained access to the substance."

"Jesus Christ. Is Homeland Security going to show up at my door now and try to take this case away from me?"

"That's a real possibility," Dax said, a bit hesitant. He found himself in a most familiar position, sharing pertinent information from the vast store of knowledge he had accumulated, but leading him to also be the bearer of bad news and the unappreciated messenger of it.

"Yeah, but man, this guy isn't a terrorist; he's a serial killer. I don't see that playing a part in this at all, and what's H.S. going to do? They'll turn this into a major security case and go off on a wild goose chase looking for some kind of nonexistent conspiracy. That'll get us nowhere when we're looking for some lone sicko roaming the streets of New York, and more of these good ladies will die in the process."

"You may have no choice. I'm sure the substance falls within a listed category that requires an immediate report to the H.S. people. What's your Captain Hughes say about it?"

"Not a word. Uh, because I haven't shown him the report yet. Damn, Dax, I'm positive this case has nothing to do with terrorism."

Dax re-seated himself at his desk as his thoughts became more contemplative. "I'm sure you're right, Lieutenant Meehan. One point that supports your position is this substance, or some hybrid of it, would at least for a period of time, leave the killer's victims in a state of paralysis, but could eventually cause death sometime between two and twelve hours. As we both know, a major part of the attack for many of these sociopaths is to enjoy watching their victims suffer, literally being the interactive spectator of a slow death. That leaves us picturing victims, their eyes wide open, lying helpless, likely on their back, only able to watch and hear the damage being inflicted on them. Very cruel and sad, indeed."

"Are you saying maybe I could keep this information close to the vest and go full speed ahead?" Janet asked.

"Sorry to disappoint, but since you now know what you're dealing with, you're forced to report it. Think about the embarrassment to your captain, the department, and you as well, should the press find out the information was withheld, even if you catch this perp and are proven correct."

"I know, I know," she exhaled.

"And Janet, H.S. is also better equipped to break down the chemical signature of this particular form of the toxin and then maybe identify what medical research facility it was stolen from, assuming that was the source. Is there anything other than the toxin you want to tell me about? I have to head out in a few minutes to meet with the commissioner about his daughter."

"Well, it gets more than a little kinky in how this guy mutilates his victims. There's a stab wound in the palm of each hand, and both eye sockets are pierced. There's a major wound to the vagina, and then a small slit under the ribs to what Doc Perkins calls the aortic arch that feeds blood from the heart to just about everywhere else. It's that little slit, she says, is the actual cause of death. She described how it would have caused a slow bleed out for each vic while the bastard carried on with all the other damage he's intent on doing. Jesus Christ, Dax, this is somebody with a major ax to grind, not some pussy pervert who has a bunch of scars across his knuckles from an old nun's yardstick he's still unhappy about."

Dax switched his listening ear. "Agreed, and it's clear he has more than a fair amount of medical knowledge. Executing such an exact incision to the aortic arch to cause a slow bleed would require a surgeon's knowledge, or at the very least, a good deal of study and practice in preparation. But Janet, I don't see where that makes this crime so unusual. We've both dealt with cases just as gory. Also, you mentioned four murders. I'm aware from the news of only three. When did the last one happen?"

"Just last night and discovered early this morning. Listen, I know you're in a hurry. Is there any way you could meet me at the crime scene sometime this morning? You remember, Ted Laney? He was my partner last year before I was promoted. He's been out there for a couple of hours, and I'm finally headed out there myself. Got held up in the prosecutor's office on another case. If you're there to check things out, maybe you'll catch something no one else would. Hell, of course you will."

"Sorry, but I'm headed to the P.C.'s office so he can browbeat me about how I'm to handle this investigation into his daughter's issues, and then I'm meeting with her on another floor at One P.P. immediately after that. It depends on how long all that takes. What's the location?"

"Hey, I don't care how long it takes. I'll have everything on hold including the body till you get there. The place is Saint Vincent de Paul's Homeless Shelter on Willis Avenue in Mott Haven. You know where that is?"

"Yes, yes, I do," he answered, his eidetic memory recalling a visual of the property, as there were few places in the Bronx he had never been. "I'll call to let you know when I'm on my way."

"Great. Thanks. Damn, it'll be good to see you again, old buddy. Bye!"

Dax sat for a moment, his gaze sweeping around the fifteen-by-fifteen foot room that was his office. Talking with Janet kicked up the thought how much it needed a transformation. Pictures of his ex-wife were to be excised. Plaques or displays of accolades he had considered more fluff than substance had to be weeded out. His desk and credenza set, he often thought current day archaeologists would find of interest, would have to go, even if at his own expense. He knew he needed to create an environment of a new beginning to reduce the constant pull of hurt and despair that had plagued him the last twelve months. Being stuck in the past had to end. For a brief moment, he pictured everything on his walls gone, and a fresh coat of white paint everywhere, an expectant canvas calling his name.

He picked up several files from his desk that he had organized in the event he needed them for his meeting with the P.C. Those few seconds afforded him the opportunity to appreciate that aside from his Captain, and his partner, Dick Daley, Janet had become his closest friend on the force. The loneliness from his early morning visit to the cemetery felt a bit more distant as a result.

CHAPTER FIVE

In 1901, the Governor of New York State, Teddy Roosevelt, established the Office of Police Commissioner for New York City, a person who would be appointed at the will of the city's mayor. Since that year, forty-three different men have held the rank. A quick read of the names leaves no doubt about the dominance of Irish influence in the office. One man named Kelly held the office twice. There were three different Murphys, and the rest sprinkled through time included a Mulroney, an O'Brien, a Monaghan, and other descendants of the Emerald Isle, but no name appears more often than Gallagher. Counting family members all the way down to patrol officers, and going back to Lincoln's presidency, more than 120 blood relations have served the city, with a dozen holding major posts within New York City's Finest.

Descendants have never been at a loss to tell tales of family heroes, stories that over time became ever more embellished with growing elements of legend and lore. There were also well-documented cases of Gallaghers who took bribes, used their rank to award contracts to cronies, and engaged in various dishonorable activities. One Depression-Era sergeant almost skirted going to prison even after an alcohol-induced argument with his wife led to him shooting her in the face.

With the family's tradition of wielding power and no hesitation to use it, those stories were seldom spoken or heard of by department personnel as negative career adjustments could be the result. Those conditions have been especially true under the leadership of the current commissioner, Jeremiah Gallagher, whose arrogance and fear-based management style have plagued the force for the last seven years.

In any organization where the headmaster falls into the category of a tyrant, underlings need some form of release, some manner of getting even. Amongst the whispered put downs behind their boss's back, the P.C.'s staff were able to point to a larger-than-normal visitation of the disease of insanity on the Gallagher family.

While the current number of extended family members living in the city exceeded a thousand, there appeared to be a disproportionate share of kin domiciled in mental institutions. This fact became known when, John Zurich, an alleged, unfairly fired assistant to the commissioner did the research to write a self-published tell-all book exposing a lengthy list of Gallagher family members living in those facilities. What stung most acidly was the author's speculation that the cause stemmed from the fact that the overly self-absorbed Gallagher clan had many times shrunk away from wedding outside their family and chose to marry close cousins instead. While Zurich adequately documented those marriages and the numerous cases of family mental illnesses, no specific evidence was offered to prove any cause-and-effect relationship. That oversight didn't matter. Underlings of the commissioner ate up the information like ants on an abandoned hot dog. A bad assignment or an unwarranted reprimand could be treated to an unseen smirk or the hidden twisting of the forefinger around one's temple as a face saving offset to his despotism.

The current mayor, William Sternberg, had inherited the politically powerful Jeremiah Gallagher as police commissioner, and chose wisely in his early days of office not to rock that boat. Although it's well known there has been no love lost between the two, Sternberg had always despised the commissioner's arrogance and methods. Many in city government were in anticipation as to what he would do with Gallagher now that His Honor was about to enter his second and lame-duck term of office after being re-elected in November.

What happened to the previously fired assistant to the Commissioner, John Zurich, the author of the exposé? He disappeared without a trace.

CHAPTER SIX

The time on the slow moving wall clock in the outer office of the police commissioner told Dax he had been sitting nearly thirty minutes after his appointed time to meet his boss. Based on his experience, this wait was no surprise and knew there would be no apology offered for it. His eyes rolled at the thought of the self-aggrandizing first words he expected to hear out of Gallagher's mouth and was not disappointed in the speculation.

"Ah, Lieutenant," Gallagher began, hanging up his phone and smiling as Dax entered, "it appears the president feels the need to check in with me every so often to get caught up on our security strategies here in New York. I have to say, at least he's always up for learning something new."

Already knowing the president was speaking at the UN when this call was to have taken place, Dax reached across to shake the commissioner's hand over what he always suspected was the largest hand-carved mahogany desk in the city. The walls behind it dripped with plaques extolling accomplishments, surrounded by pictures taken with just the right national and international luminaries as exhibits of the commissioner's power.

Gallagher was a tall, large man in his mid-sixties. With the exception of a stomach that might qualify as a before picture in a diet ad, he had the stereotypical look of a retired Marine drill sergeant. His gnarly salt-and-pepper hair sat on a square-topped head with a jaw that also seemed to turn at right angles. The P.C. always wore his dress uniform, and his broad shoulders book-ended a barrel chest adorned with a large bling of medals. Dax had discovered that some of those medals were earned by past Gallagher family members because this Gallagher's need to impress had no boundaries. Dax once heard the Commissioner had negatively described him as having Hollywood good looks too soft for a homicide detective.

At Gallagher's pointing, Dax headed to one of two black leather guest chairs in front of the P.C.'s desk. He had once observed their legs had been sawed down somewhat. The result was an obvious attempt to create a psychological height disadvantage for any of the P.C.'s visitors. Dax wondered how the president reacted on his visit to New York, when he likely fell into, more than sat on one of them.

Once seated, he began to calculate the amount of time the commissioner would ruffle papers on his desk meant to establish an air of superiority.

Three, two, one . . .

"You've met the president, McGowan, of course," Gallagher foisted, "right after we exposed that plot to assassinate him on his visit to Ground Zero. He was very impressed with the work we did that day," he continued with a look of complete ownership of the event.

"Yes, Commissioner, I did," Dax replied plainly, remembering how hard he fought to convince the Manhattan brass, including the commissioner, he was correct that an assassination plot did indeed exist. There was not a lot of "we" in that adventure.

"Okay, McGowan, let's get right to it, shall we? Just how much background do you have on my daughter's issues?"

"Well, Commissioner, I have all the files provided by Dr. Hogarth as well as the reports from the other professionals who attempted to help her previously. Beyond that, I would say I've already done a good deal of homework."

That last statement brought a noticeable look of concern to the commissioner's face. Abruptly, "Lieutenant, you are to report directly to me about any and all of your findings where Officer Gallagher is concerned. Do you understand? Not to your captain, not to your partner, Detective Daley, not in bed to some woman friend of yours, no one else. Are we clear on that?"

Dax smiled to himself at the P.C.'s attempt to cloak the assignment as department business by the use of his daughter's title.

He also understood how the commissioner had put himself in a box, the kind egomaniacs often do. With the medical community at a loss as to the cause of Teresa's condition, and nowhere else to turn, the commissioner's insistence that his own staff come up with a solution had the P.C. stuck with their last resort recommendation, that he take on the mystery. Dax also suspected Gallagher was being pushed by the certainty that it would not be long before the press would learn of his daughter's unusual condition, and have a field day associating it with Zurich's tell all book related to the family's mental maladies. He was sure his boss hated the whole idea of turning over his daughter's needs to someone he considered his number one competitor for the public's affection, but was stuck with it. There was also the pressure of the family legacy. Was he to be the final Gallagher who was not able to produce an heir to the family's name in the NYPD for over 150 years?

While at the heart of it Dax was not in any dramatic fear of his boss, caution ruled his response. "Commissioner, sir, I certainly expect to be keeping you informed of my progress; however, you know better than anyone, none of us on the job works alone. I will at the very least need to rely on my partner to do some legwork if I'm to solve this mystery in any kind of reasonable time. Your daughter's well-being is of course at stake."

"Yes, yes, of course it is. Where do you get off reminding me of that?"

"I was reminding myself, Commissioner. Your charge has been to get your daughter back on the job as soon as possible. I can only hope I'm able to accomplish that."

The commissioner proceeded more directly. "Frankly, Lieutenant, I'm convinced I already know the source of my daughter's problems. Since no one has been able to nail this down to some past trauma that Officer Gallagher has suffered, then it must have to do with something that's been happening to her recently. Like all us Gallaghers, her whole life revolves around her work here on the force. So, it adds up, that has to be the source."

"But, Commissioner, the professionals haven't ruled out any past trauma, they simply said they were unable to identify anything specific, and at this point her mind is too closed to reveal it."

"That's a bunch of mumbo jumbo, McGowan, excuses because they failed at their job. Listen, despite my popularity as their boss, I'm sure there are a good many of her fellow officers who resent her relationship to me and have made her life hell for it. I've attempted to ferret out who these bastards might be, but everyone's afraid to talk. Hell, Teresa won't admit it to me because she's a damn good Blue Code cop. The reason I've approved your taking this on was because I expect your lesser role in the department will give you access to more insider information on who's responsible for hurting my daughter. I want those sons-a-bitches to pay. And they'll pay big time. Understood?"

Despite my popularity? Really? Dax knew he had to first entertain this notion before he could proceed. "I'll tell you, sir, I have no liking for any mistreatment of any officer on the force, especially if the result is as severe as what I've read in these reports on what Teresa is experiencing. I've seen other female officers burn out for that very same reason. However, should that train of investigation turn up nothing, I'm certain you would expect me to continue down other avenues until I discover the truth. That would involve me looking into her personal relationships more thoroughly than the professionals have done. As you know, the fieldwork we detectives do can reveal a good deal more than what they might discover as they confine their work to within their own offices," Dax said in a matter-of-fact fashion, hoping to gain the P.C.'s approval of that next possible direction.

Watching Gallagher struggle with the possibility of family issues coming to the fore, Dax added, "Of course, sir, I would discuss that with you before I moved forward and only should it be needed." He half stood out of his chair, appearing to adjust the position of his suit pants to add to the less-threatening and routine-sounding nature of his suggestion.

After a few seconds, the commissioner responded. "That'll work, Lieutenant, as long as you follow that procedure with daily updates as well. However, I'm telling you, the answer lies within the department."

Dax's could see his boss was concerned he should come off like he had nothing to hide but realized in the same moment he needed to add conditions.

"Listen, McGowan, if for any reason you suspect this involves my family in any way, I want you to stop right there and report it to me immediately. Do you hear? Immediately."

"Sure, sir. I can do that," Dax answered, still pleased that at least he wasn't now prevented from making such discoveries.

Gallagher went on with what Dax considered a reasonable justification for his last statement and a stern warning as well. "I want you to clearly understand; absolutely no information about my family is to be shared with anyone. Should that happen, it will lead to the end of your career. The Gallaghers have already suffered enough at the hands of one of my past employees writing preposterous lies about our family."

"Commissioner, I have only one goal. I'll do my best to help your daughter, whether it means she gets her job back or gets on the road to some form of recovery. If I discover what you would classify as anything negative about your family in the process, I will present it to you directly."

Gallagher sat stern faced, swiveling back and forth in his high-backed executive chair. Dax was certain the man was attempting to assess if his last statement to the P.C. contained any loopholes. Before the commissioner might deduce what Dax knew those loopholes to be, he went on. "Commissioner, I have a question regarding the professional work that's already been done in terms of Teresa's diagnosis. Your other daughter, Angela, maintains a stellar reputation in the field of psychiatry herself. Am I right?"

"Yes, she's well known internationally. What's your question?" the commissioner asked, adequately distracted as Dax had hoped.

"In my reading of these files, I don't see where she personally did any work with her sister. Is that correct? Also, it appears none of the other professionals ever attempted the use of hypnosis, and I understand Angela is considered an expert in that technique."

"Yes, well, Angela treated her first before any of the other doctors, but with no success. She applied every hypnotic process she knew and informed the others as such. That's why they didn't try it. Listen, it would probably be a good idea to check in with her as you proceed. She has the expertise to explain anything you might uncover and don't understand. In fact, I order you to do that. Other than me, no one cares more about our family than Angela."

Dax took a second to weigh the implication that other family members, Jeremiah and Michael Gallagher, Teresa and Angela's two brothers, might care less. He had already decided that speaking to all of Teresa's siblings was an important step in his investigation, but he knew this wasn't the time to bring that up.

"I'll do that, sir. Maybe it would be best that if I do discover any family issues involved, I should report them directly to her so she can interpret them, and inform me of what I might pursue next." Dax said, taking advantage of the new opportunity his boss had just offered him. If the commissioner agreed, it would allow him to pursue family matters more unfettered than the P.C. was willing to permit, matters he was sure were more likely involved than any hazing within the department. It also meant, should the commissioner ever feel less informed than expected, he could claim he was working with his daughter on any particular issue.

"I suppose that makes sense," the commissioner said. "Angela's involvement would provide me with more in depth information as well. Just remember, McGowan, you are being held to absolute secrecy where Teresa and my family are concerned. You don't want to cross me on this."

"I understand," Dax responded. Observing the time from across the desk on the commissioner's Rolex, "If there's nothing else, sir, I should be on my way. I have my first meeting with Teresa in a conference room downstairs on the third floor. She may be waiting for me now."

"Also, McGowan, I've already instructed your captain to re-assign all your current cases. I want your undivided attention on this."

"Yes, sir," was Dax's reply, but aware his promise to aid Janet on her serial killer case would not be broken.

Dax stood, offering his hand with as friendly a smile as he could muster. With no words offered, the commissioner stared at him hard, holding their handshake longer than normal, the message in his vice-like grip quite clear.

CHAPTER SEVEN

Dax stepped off the elevator on the third floor at One P.P., and as arranged, his partner, Dick Daley was waiting. On the wall opposite the lift doors, Daley was seated on one end of a wrought iron bench, bordered by two large bamboo plants, all positioned under the gaze of a portrait of Rough Rider, Teddy Roosevelt. Dax watched, curiously observing his partner writing feverishly on a white legal pad.

"Good morning, Richard," he greeted, seating himself next to his good friend and portly partner.

"Oh hey, Dax," the sergeant answered with a brief wave holding a pen in his hand.

Dax always thought his partner reminiscent of that eight year old, sandy-haired, freckle-faced boyhood friend anyone could count on to be their best buddy and always met you with a smile.

"I tried to reach you a couple of times this morning, but went straight to voice mail. How are you doing? I mean . . . today. You know--."

Daley had a more personal struggle with the anniversary of Grace's death. It had taken him weeks to get past the nightmares he suffered a year earlier after having been the person who took Dax's wife, Darlene's call at the precinct. In a state of utter despair, she told him she had just discovered their only daughter, Grace, was dead in the bathtub with her wrists slit. Well after tracking down the pedophile who abused Grace and dealing with the suffering that resulted, Dax often found himself asking Daley how he was doing, aware of the long-term effects Darlene's call had on his partner.

"I'm doing pretty well, Richard. Sorry about not taking your calls, I've been tied up virtually all morning."

"No sweat. I'm just glad to hear you sounding so okay."

If there is any partnership that could be described as dedicated, it's the relationship held by paired detectives and officers of the NYPD. In the days after Dax first made detective, Captain Pressioso paired him with experienced detectives of higher grades in an attempt to teach him what any cop with a new gold shield needed to learn. Those pairings didn't work out as he had hoped. Instead, it was hurt egos, as Dax would consistently outthink his elders, causing unintended professional embarrassments. When it came to solving the mysteries of murder, Dax was uncompromising in his pursuit. His peers were not any less dedicated, they simply lacked his skills and finding Dax a true partner in the tradition of the NYPD seemed at first impossible. For a lengthy time, Dax operated alone. However, if for no other reason than Dax's personal safety, Captain Pressioso chose to assign him a partner that would act more in the role of an assistant. Although Dax's senior by nine years, Dick Daley was the perfect candidate. He idolized Dax and bragged about him to anyone who would listen.

"How'd it go with the P.C.?" Daley went on.

"Much as you would expect, Richard. A lot about what results he's expecting and a list of limits on what I can and cannot do to accomplish them. One of those limits concerns you," he added with an ominous tone.

"Me? What? He's upset with me?" Daley asked, noticeably throttled.

"Just kidding," Dax replied with both hands raised and smiling. "He understands I'll need your help, but any skeletons we might find in the Gallagher family closet will have to stay just between us, or we'll both be asked to turn in our shields."

"Oh, that. Okay. Sure partner," Daley said in relief.

"I have to tell you though, the P.C. has no handle on what his daughter is facing. Anyone who has read these medical reports, and clearly he hasn't, would never suggest that her problems stem from any hazing she might have experienced at the One-Five."

"What? I don't get it."

"He thinks she's been under the pressure of some conspiracy in the department to make her life hell because he's her father. He's convinced it's the cause of her experiencing the spells she suffers from. Even my limited knowledge about the possibilities . . ."

"Jesus, Dax," Daley injected. "Anyone trying to give her hard time over there would have to be out of their damned mind. They all know her father would have their genitals mutilated. I can double-check that if you want. But man, it's not very likely."

"I agree, but let's check it out so we can at least say we did. I've always observed that narcissists carry the paranoia that folks are out to get them because deep down they know they piss people off. And this is one of those cases where the paranoid person is more than sufficiently correct. We'd better get moving to meet with Teresa. We're a little late already."

After a conversation-ending fist bump, they headed down the hallway from the corridor of elevators toward a small conference room in the middle of the floor. As they approached, Dax recognized Teresa Gallagher from her department photo in his file. She was seated on a wooden hallway bench next to a white-haired Latina whose arm was around her in a consoling manner. He gauged the relationship between the two as a strong one, years in the making.

As he drew nearer, he could see Teresa's straight-ahead stare was swaying back and forth between alert and somewhat lost. Her shoulders were slouched well past what he considered a normal position of ease. He noted her to be an attractive woman, even in her uniform, which she had chosen to wear despite her temporary suspension from duty. She was blue-eyed with real blond hair, and as her friend helped her to her feet, he estimated her to be five feet, seven inches tall.

"Good Morning, Teresa," he opened with an extended hand. "Thank you for coming downtown to meet with us. This is my partner, Sergeant Dick Daley. Who is your obviously very close friend?"

"Señor, I am Peeta. Peeta Sanchez. I am little T's nanny for many years," was the ready and confident response of Teresa's diminutive and thin-boned matron.

"Very nice to meet you. Please, Ms. Sanchez and Teresa," Dax said smiling and stretching his arm to point to the open door of the adjacent conference room. "Let's sit down and see if we can begin to unravel what's causing all this distress for you."

Before the two women could turn to enter, a group of loud speaking unis--uniformed officers, came walking down the hall.

Without warning, Teresa's eyes rolled up in their sockets, her irises disappearing, only white showing. With her head gyrating erratically to one side away from the boisterous group, Dax thought her actions reminiscent of a scene from *The Exorcist.* Teresa's doting companion quickly pulled her into the conference room, held her hands, and gently kissed her on the cheek.

"Excuse me, Ms. Sanchez," Dax said as he closed the door quickly behind them to deafen the officers' voices. "Does Teresa often react to such disturbances in this manner?"

He felt her look piercing through him, rummaging for trust, calculating what she felt comfortable to say.

"No, señor, it only happens once here, once there…no sense to it," she answered plain faced.

Dax realized he'd already allowed himself to be drawn into talking to this woman as a surrogate for Teresa and needed to change that. He waited as he could see Teresa begin to return to normal before pressing on. The sight of her in this condition drove a spear of pain in him as his mind swayed between Teresa's condition and visions of what he imagined his precious Grace had experienced during her abuse. He took his own moment to recover and proceeded with the easiest of questions.

"Teresa, Ms. Sanchez seems to be about the best friend a person could have. Am I right?"

Almost miraculously calm now, she responded like a cop, if not a bit weakly. "Yes, sir, Lieutenant. She is my rock, sir, my rock. She's been a second mother to me since my mother died when I was seven."

Dax reacted thoughtfully. "I see . . . Please, Teresa, Peeta . . . may I call you Peeta . . . let's sit." Dax had already decided to defer any discussion about her mother's death to a later time until he had the opportunity to research it in more detail.

"Si, señor," Peeta replied to his request.

In front of them was a long, dark brown wooden conference table with a dozen well cushioned, color matched leather chairs surrounding it. The square room's walls were covered with portraits of past NYPD leaders and police commissioners. Gallagher faces dominated the scenery, assuring Dax that his boss had in some manner played a part in this particular room being reserved for their meeting.

Just as he began to pick the chair at the head of the table closest to the room's entrance, he saw Teresa stop in her tracks, looking both left and right across the room. Hurriedly, she moved from the right side of the table to sit to his immediate left. Peeta then followed Teresa to sit on her left side. Wondering what Teresa's actions meant, Dax made a small note of them on one of the files he was carrying. Daley chose to hang back finding an orphan chair not far away against the wall near the exit door. Dax appreciated that his partner sensed a more intimate interview by one person would be less intimidating to the vulnerable young officer.

"First let me start by saying this. I have only one goal in mind, and that's to help you, Teresa. I have no interest in department politics or any concerns where this investigation will take us. I am committed to finding out the source of your problem with the single purpose of it leading to your recovery. Period."

He was pleased to observe his statement was taken as truth based on the satisfied smile across Peeta's face, and receiving a similar response from Teresa, who said, "Lieutenant McGowan, sir, those are the kindest words I've heard so far through all this mess. I mean, my sister Angela's been just wonderful, but everyone else has picked at me with question after question that I have no answers for. It's all been pressure and more pressure. And sir, I know how difficult my father can be. He had all the other docs . . . er, I know you're not a doctor. He had them all scared shitless to even be talking to me. Uh, sorry about that slip, sir. No disrespect intended."

"None taken, and since you've brought up the subject of intimidation, let's clear up something else. Have you been experiencing any form of hazing, or had any undue pressure brought on you by any of the staff at your precinct?"

"Did my father tell you that?

"Well, yes, and he seemed quite convinced it's the source of your problem."

"Sorry about that. I don't know where my father comes up with this kind of stuff sometimes, but the answer is no. I mean, sure, I got some ribbing when I started there, but less than anyone else who was new to the One-Five. The fear of my dad, ya know."

Despite but a twelve-year difference in their ages, Dax smiled at her much as he would have his daughter. "Teresa, please understand fear has no play in this for me, and I would like you if you are able, to set aside any and all pressure on yourself where this investigation is concerned. It's my responsibility to carry that burden," he said warmly, placing his left hand over the back of her right hand nearest him on the table. "But I do have a couple of basic questions I need to ask today to get us started, and please, let's dispense with the formalities. Please call me Dax.

"Thank you, Lieu, I mean, Dax, sir. Sure, ask away."

"I've read all the reports of the doctors who treated you, but I want to ask you when you first began to experience this problem, these spells? Also, I should say this so it may bring you some confidence. Whatever you may not be able to tell me could be as helpful as what you can tell me."

Teresa sat motionless staring down at her lap, in a clear attempt to reach for something specific to say. She looked up disappointed and shaking her head. "I can't. I'm not sure; it's all just such a blur."

"That's okay. No problem." Dax said calmly. He looked to Peeta, assured she knew the answer.

Without hesitation, she offered, "It's been three, four months, Señor McGowan. They start at home first, then her job," she added, reaching to clasp Teresa's other hand in her own.

Dax went on. "These reports speak of you unexpectedly falling into a confused state and describe what we just saw you experience when those officers passed us in the hallway. Do you feel anything coming on when this happens? Do you know what it is that sets you off? Are you even aware you're in such a state when it occurs?"

Teresa slowly pulled both her hands free from their friended grasps to sit more erect in her chair and place her elbows on the table. "You know, sir, I'm a good cop and really want to get back to being one. I know I gotta get this figured out, but the only thing I can tell you is that there is this dread, this great fear that comes over me, and the next thing . . . well . . . nothing. I've only had Peeta and Desty, my patrol partner, tell me what happens next. You saw how I looked and acted, but I don't have a clue about any of that. When I come out of it, like now, I just feel drained and tired. Damn, does any of what I'm saying make any sense?"

"Yes, it does, a good deal," Dax answered, smiling assuredly. He stared for a moment looking down the length of the table in an effort to organize his thoughts. "Peeta, have you noticed any pattern as to when these episodes come about? Are you aware of any triggers that might set them off?"

"No, señor. They are random. T could be watching television and it happens, or just now, in the hall. And, señor? We had to stop shopping. Too many times they happen then."

Quickly sitting up, Dax asked, "You mean these episodes come on more often when the two of you are out in the stores?"

"Si, mostly clothing stores, señor."

Ignoring a distant chuckle from Dick Daley, Dax responded immediately. "Now, that's particularly noteworthy," he said, folding his arms and placing his right thumb under his chin with his forefinger straight up across his lips. "Tell me, Peeta, has anyone, or any of the doctors who treated Teresa questioned you about this? Have you mentioned to anyone that these spells occur so often in clothing stores?"

"No, señor, you be the first."

"I thought as much," he said, leaning farther back in his chair. "Okay, Teresa, Peeta, this is all the information I need for now. As I said, no more pressure on you. It's all on me. I'll be getting back with you now and again, but in the meantime, just know I am on your side. Short of a full-out promise, I expect to get this figured out for you."

"Señor, that would be a wonderful gift for my little T."

"Oh Mama Peeta, I'm no little girl anymore, but I am so fortunate to have your love." Teresa turned to Dax, "I know all about your reputation, Lieutenant. So I will choose to be confident you'll help me get my life back."

"That's the plan," Dax responded nodding his head to the side sharing the widest of grins.

Feeling this new information was an excellent starting point for him, Dax wished to end the meeting, but stood slowly so as not to appear abrupt and extended his hand in Teresa's direction.

After she stood to return the handshake, he noticed her shoulders were now in a more normal posture as she headed for the door. Peeta next used both her hands to grab the sleeves of his suit jacket in a muted hug. Tears welled above her lower eyelids as she blinked a sign of her approval of him. He smiled back and managed to gently squeeze the fingers on her trailing hand as she moved to exit with her charge.

Daley stood quickly to present the women with a final wave as they passed and then moved to where Dax was standing near the conference table. Dax chose to sit again and Daley sat to his right.

"I heard you say what Teresa told you was helpful. What's your take, Dax? I wasn't so sure we learned anything new."

"Richard, the first thing I wanted to clear up was Teresa's commitment to getting her job back, and that this wasn't just a case of pressure from her father to meet some Gallagher family legacy goal. Our conversation certainly left no doubts for me that her head is in the right place on that score. I also hoped to get some kind of handle as to the source of these spells. These doctor reports are no more than a bunch of sterile observations followed by a substantial use of the term inconclusive. And did you catch the importance of Ms. Sanchez's point about these spells occurring in clothing stores?"

"Yeah, I guess I did. It sounded pretty funny though."

"Also, Richard, there is nothing in any of these reports where any doctor has diagnosed her as bipolar or with any underlying condition of depression. In other words, she's not experiencing these episodes because she is depressed to begin with. It appears the only depression she suffers revolves around the fact these damned episodes are ruining every aspect of her life."

"Hey, that was some weird shit out in the hallway," Daley said. "Just some loud cops walking by? And actually, partner, the clothing store thing only confused me all the more," he offered as a confession. "How could those unis possibly be linked to any of that?"

"That, Mr. Daley, is what we are going to figure out."

"Okay, buddy," Daley said standing. "What say we grab some lunch and you tell me our next moves?"

"Can't do that now. I'm headed out to a crime scene in Mott Haven on a promise I made to meet with your old partner, Janet Meehan. She asked if I would help on her serial killer case. The media and the brass downtown is driving her nuts to make an arrest, but there is something I would like you to check on right away."

"Sure, and say hi to her for me. That looks like a doozy of a case. Man, someone killing nuns? That's got to be a straight-line trip to hell for somebody. What is it you want me to do?"

"Based on a smattering of research and a subject that has come up in many of these medical reports, a very young Teresa and her older sister, Angela, came home from school one day to discover the body of their murdered mother. None of these doctors were able to claim any conclusive link to that life-changing event and her current symptoms, but it doesn't mean we should discount its importance. I need you to pull everything we have on that old case. There may be something in the interviews with Teresa and her older sister taken by the detectives at the time that might reveal something these doctors were never privy to reading."

"Okay, partner. You know, that old murder story popped up in that book about the P.C.'s family, as if the murder was somehow tied in with the family's crazy issues. Do you know the name of the perp who killed their mom?"

"Yes, a Miguel Diaz. He's serving life without parole at Sing Sing. I've already gleaned a portion of the information on the case from the public side from the Internet and microfiche of old newspapers. The commissioner was just a detective first grade at the time, but they already lived in the Gallagher family's palatial estate in the Hamptons. Diaz owned the landscape company that did all their gardening work. The story goes that in a fit of rage over how Mrs. Gallagher had treated him over a long period of time, he stabbed her several times. It seemed odd to me, Richard, how thin the newspaper stories were on the details. What you pick up in that old case file should fill in the rest. Oh and be prepared that the file might have a hold on it of some kind, given the fact that the writer of that book may have used the file as a resource. Any new inquiry to view it is likely to get back to the commissioner and set off some fireworks. Just stay adamant to the officer in storage about needing the file. I'll handle the P.C."

"Okay, as long as you've got the P.C. end of it," Daley said making a cross with his fingers as if fending off a vampire.

"Oh, and Dick, while the Southampton police on the island should have had jurisdiction over the case back then, I'll bet for obvious reasons, the file was somehow transferred to the basement of this building where the P.C. could keep his eye on it. I'd check there first."

"Uh, all right. That makes sense, but I'm famished, so I'll start right after I grab a quick bite to eat. Check you later."

CHAPTER EIGHT

As Dax exited One P. P., he walked with his head lowered. Flurries from fast-moving overhead snow clouds were traveling sideways and accelerated by the tunnel effect of multi-story downtown buildings. After leaving the NYPD parking lot on the Avenue of the Finest, he headed seven miles north up the 9A and pulled his black Lexus sedan into a maintenance-shed area in Central Park. He had chosen this relatively isolated spot once before for the privacy it afforded his rather unique, self-indulgent form of an exercise in logic. Like his partner, Dax also felt the pangs of hunger, having eaten nothing before leaving in the early morning for the cemetery. The need to engage in his tried-and-true method of organizing his thoughts about any tough case, however, had the upper hand. He left the car and heater running to keep the cold at bay and made sure no one was in immediate sight.

"So, Watson, how do you assess our progress thus far in the case of our troubled officer friend, Teresa Gallagher?" he began in his best mimic of Basil Rathbone's voice, his favorite icon for Sherlock Holmes, a skill he had developed as a young teen.

"Please, Holmes, you know I've fretted over this predicament from the very beginning. Your visit with the Gallagher woman hasn't minimized my concerns in any fashion," was the reply in the voice of actor Nigel Bruce's portrayal of Dr. Watson.

"I understand, Watson. However, I found the words and emotional manner of both Ms. Gallagher and Ms. Sanchez quite revealing. Earlier this morning I expressed the expectation of these kinds of results rather clearly to the good Doctor Hogarth."

"Hmph," Watson returned, "I find your use of the word good in regard to that cad as quite charitable."

"Nonetheless, he made one point I believe our meeting with the two women confirms. Miss Gallagher appears to be quite normal except for the fear of a remembrance of some person, persons, or event that lies in the recesses of her mind that she wishes to avoid facing. However, an unknown element has lately begun to trigger a reminder which sets her off into a state of what appears to be a defense mechanism her mind employs as an avoidance. It never ceases to amaze me, Watson, how resourceful the human mind can be in its efforts to protect itself."

"But Holmes, this young woman must eventually face those fears if she is to have any chance to return to a state of normalcy. And I must say my friend, as skilled as you may be as a detective, I hold my own medically influenced reservations as to your abilities to resolve this woman's issues."

"Indeed, Doctor, but clearly, discovering what triggers these episodes could at the very least lead us to the cause of her distresses. How best for her to address them would then be more readily determined."

"Sherlock, it appears these episodes are so random it indicates the possible cause to be the proverbial needle in a haystack. How can you possibly narrow it down, when the young woman is unable to supply you with any clues and the professional medical community is baffled?"

"Well, Watson, as to narrowing it down, that requires a simple exercise in deductive elimination. We must first determine which of Ms. Gallagher's five senses produces that reaction. Taste and touch are out of the question, as they played no role in the passing of those police officers in the hallway. Smell is also ruled out, as it clearly had no effect in their presence either. I would have detected any unusual odors, my formidable skills in that regard, as you know.

"It leaves us with the senses of sight and hearing. It is possible any specific thing said by one of those officers could also be heard on the telly and possibly, once or twice in a clothing store. However, the officers were laughing as one of them was describing having dealt with an irate citizen over a parking ticket. The chances the reverse is true, seems quite remote that during multiple trips to clothing stores, as reported to us by her nanny, Teresa would have encountered the very same heavily laced police jargon those officers employed. I believe we are safe to conclude it is the sense of sight as the culprit here. From there, we are left to discover just what common element one might observe on the telly and in a clothing store that would directly relate to the extremely limited set of visual elements we fortuitously observed in the hallway at One P.P. It is certainly not the police uniforms or something as ubiquitous as shoes or fad induced hair stylings, or poor Miss Gallagher would be in a constant state of catatonia. No, Watson, it has to be something much more obscure, unique to all three of those settings. Yet, I suspect we will determine it to have been quite obvious once we discover it."

"Well, Sherlock, I'll give you that it appears you have driven the large number of possibilities down to a more manageable figure, but finding the common element you say must be present, still leaves you with a good deal of just guessing, it seems to me."

"Watson, you bring up an element just now that may be worth my pursuit going forward."

"What was it I said, dear boy?"

A sharp rap on his car window startled Dax, and he turned to see a woman in maintenance garb bent over, peering through with a look of "What are you doing here?" Having prepared for this contingency, he tapped his Bluetooth earpiece to appear he had just ended a cell phone conversation. He flashed his gold shield, changing the look on the woman's face to an "Oh, sorry," matched by a friendly salute to him in her retreat. After a small smile and his return salute, he put the car in drive and headed out of the park to his next intended stop. He would travel farther north into the Bronx and the Mott Haven neighborhood. There would be an illegal double-parked stop in front of a street vendor just outside the park, however, to buy a large New York City boiled hot dog on a sourdough bun with a generous serving of yellow mustard and sauerkraut.

CHAPTER NINE

Fifty thousand people crammed into one square mile would be enough to make any inhabitant's life intense. Because the densely populated Mott Haven area of the Bronx is the home of some of the poorest residents of the city, it's also one of the more dangerous places to live. Any large city's practice of folks avoiding each other's eye contact or showing any conspicuous interest in anything other than one's own business was a norm not to be defied in Mott Haven. Though, an expensive late-model Lexus wending its way through this poverty-stricken community would always make heads turn. Pulling up as close as Dax could to the yellow police tape cordoning off the alley adjacent to the homeless shelter had him smiling that even his car itself felt a bit safer as a result.

"Dax!" was the exclamation he heard as he exited his car.

"Hey, Ted. How're you doing?" Dax greeted Ted Laney with a hearty handshake.

"Janet said you'd be checking in with us on our latest psycho. It's good to see you again. I wish I could stay longer to talk, and continue to freeze my ass off out here, but I've got to get back to the precinct. She's inside talking to the director of this place."

"Okay, thanks, Ted. You take care."

After arm-bending his way through a few leftover paparazzi bobbing up and down to stay warm while balancing cups of hot coffee, Dax took the time to generate a respectful salute to a couple of units stationed on each side of the twenty foot wide alley where they stood as sentries. When he slipped under the taped barrier, chants of questions to him from the press began in earnest.

"Lieutenant! What can you tell us about these murders?" "Dax, are you on this case, now? Has this been transferred to homicide from SVU?"

He turned from looking down the alley to raise his hand to quiet them. Because he was considered a friend of the press, they usually obliged this signal.

"Hey Candice, hey Willy," he said, smiling. "I'm just here as an observer, and don't have anything to tell you, you don't already know," he lied.

"C'mon, Dax," Candice Emmons of the *Daily News* began. "No way Dax McGowan is here and it doesn't mean something important is in the works."

"Really, guys. My good friend Lieutenant Meehan asked me to take a look and add anything I thought might help. This case is totally in her capable hands. I'd visit with you more, but I'm on a tight schedule today and only have a few minutes to confer with her. I'll catch you all later somewhere else, eh?" he said half-smiling, knowing they weren't buying what he said.

To the sound of new questions he was drowning out of his head, he peered down the full length of the crime scene. Other than the well-covered body of the victim to his right some thirty-five yards away and spread out at a right angle from and against the bottom of a brick stoop, the alley appeared as he expected it would. Trash of all forms lined the walls of the buildings on either side, as any constant wind flowing through alleys always caused that phenomenon. A series of five drains he counted down the length of it were all half-covered with pieces of trash caught in their metal webs, the effects over time of rain and melting snow carrying them to those lower points of gravity. At the very back, making the alley a dead end, was a standard ten-foot cyclone fence. Lined in front of that metal barrier were two large green dumpsters with their covers bulging with black plastic bags announcing trash pickup was most likely very soon. The sun, though never in an overhead position in December, provided enough light for Dax's eyes to take an eidetic mental photograph, pending a closer inspection with Janet.

As he began to open one of the double metal doors at the front of the shelter, he felt a tug from inside. It was Janet attempting to exit.

"Oh my God, I was just coming out to see if you were here yet, and there you are," she said, chuckling.

She pulled his overcoat sleeve to drag him into the shelter's open entry, pushed the door shut, and put her arms around his chest, hugging him strongly enough to make him exhale a noticeable, "Humph!"

"Well, hello to you too," he said in a pleased fashion, wrapping his arms around her shoulders, instinctively kissing the top of her head.

"Damn, it's good to see you, Dax. I can't believe we've stayed out of touch for so long."

"Same here, my friend. It's so true that you don't know how much you've missed someone until they're all of a sudden right in front of you," he said looking at her full face.

As their hug began to dissolve, he watched a large tear roll down her cheek.

"You know, Daxman, some nights I lay in bed thinking about all you went through last year with your daughter and how you managed to somehow solve my sister's murder at the same time. You even arranged for me to cuff the son of a bitch who murdered her. I still go through all the old pain because of her loss, but now I feel some satisfaction as well thanks to you. I'll always owe you big for that."

Dax met Janet for the first time the previous year. The sexual elements of his daughter's case required it be assigned to the Special Victims Unit. In the process, he became acquainted with the reason Janet had worked so hard to become an SVU detective in New York City. While in high school in Michigan, her much older and beloved sister, Karen, was sexually assaulted and murdered in Manhattan. The killer was never identified. Despite his single-minded intention at the time to track down and kill his daughter's abuser, he found his new friend's need to resolve her sister's cold case murder impossible to ignore. His skills made short work of it.

"Janet, solving that for you ranks right up there as one of the most important ever for me. And don't ever feel like there is any owing for anything. What we both did for each other last December puts us even forever in my book."

In typical Janet Meehan style, a quick sniffle and the wiping of her eyes led to her saying, "Okay, enough of this crying shit. We have a case to get into."

"Sure, sure," Dax said, laughing out loud, her sudden mood

break affecting him like the punch line to a good joke. "What do you have for me, my friend? Shall we visit the alley?"

"Yeah, but let's go out the side door to the alley so we can retrace our victim's steps."

In short order, the two navigated past several volunteers and staff members still cleaning tables in the large open mess hall after the meal served that morning, and readying for the meal that would be served later that day. Into the kitchen in the back, scores of recently cleaned, glistening pots and pans were littered across brackets hung from the ceiling from one end of the room to the other. As Dax and Janet headed for a door on the right side and to the rear of the room, Dax became distracted. "I don't know how these people, including the ever-so-committed nuns who now have our immediate attention, can manage to face all the work they do here every day and at every shelter like it in the city. I doubt I'd have the patience for it. They are the best of human beings, wouldn't you say?"

"I know. I feel the same way. I just accept the fact that compared to these folks, I'm just not that nice," she quipped. Pushing the alley door open, she went on. "Okay. According to her fellow workers, this is the door our saint, Sister Mary Barnabas left from every night about ten o'clock."

The cold and clear late afternoon sunlight bouncing off the opposite alley wall caused both Dax and Janet to squint and move into the middle of the cobblestone corridor, out of its reflective glare.

"So, Janet, tell me what else I should know about these deaths that the press hasn't been privy to."

"Sure, but as a review, all these nuns still wore the old-fashioned habits. All of them were stabbed in both hands, both eyes, and in the vagina, and slit in the aortic arch around their heart, causing them to slowly bleed out.

"Saxitoxin was used as the disabler, and yes, I've given my captain the M.E.'s report. He's already been on the phone to the commissioner who demanded he be the one to call the mayor and Homeland Security. So the shit will hit the fan anytime now, and my office will soon be crawling with long overcoats and sunglasses requesting I turn over all my files."

"You've made copies of everything for us to work with, I assume?" Dax asked.

"Roger that."

"Okay, what else?"

"Well, the only MOs I could discover here or nationwide for killing nuns anything like this go back to the seventies and eighties, and I couldn't find anything close to the kinds of ritualistic wounds inflicted on these current day women. This is a new killer, not any kind of copycat that I can tell.

"Another important piece of information I haven't told you yet is that none of these bodies were dumped. The killer managed to attack each woman in some planned and predetermined isolated location and left the body there."

"That might tell us a few things, but in that regard, were the location of these crimes limited to this area of the city?"

"Well, yes and no," she said, pulling from a file she held, a Google Earth satellite photo of the one square mile that was Mott Haven. "This latest, Sister Mary Barnabas, was killed here, not far from where she lived, and the first vic was murdered at an isolated prayer station behind a Saint Bonaventure Church also here in Mott Haven, not far from where she lived. However, another nun was killed along a running trail in a park in nearby Harlem, and a third was murdered way out in Lake Ronkonkoma on the island. She was a birdwatcher, and out in that area a lot, according to interviews with friends. The tie in was that all these nuns had local jobs and were involved in different social activities in the neighborhood . . . kids, soup kitchens, you know, what you'd expect in this part of the city. They all lived within a pretty tight radius of the center dot in this satellite photo of Mott Haven," she finished, handing Dax the printed picture.

After a speedy view of it, Dax said, "This perp certainly resorted to a good deal of stalking and planning to pick the perfect place to catch these women alone, in one case a great distance from here. That is rather odd, but doesn't preclude him from living in or close to Mott Haven. It seems likely he may have had direct contact with all his victims through the various service organizations they worked for."

"We thought so too, but so many of the folks getting help in these places are people coming in and out of the neighborhood, and these organizations keep only limited records on their identities. We're still following up on all the names the different administrative people have given us, but we haven't been able to find anything close to nailing down a realistic suspect. We're also checking out all the staff people who work for these nonprofits. Hell, half of them have been homeless long enough themselves that they have no official identification to prove who they are.

"Canvassing has produced nothing. Nobody saw or knows anything, and it's not the usual fear thing about talking to cops. Everyone is scared shitless of this guy and wants to help, just has nothing to tell us," she said, throwing her hands up in disgust. "This evil devil is really good at staying invisible."

"I assume you already checked out every known sex offender and felon in the area?"

"Yeah, but no keepers. We managed to pick up some perps on a couple of outstanding warrants, but that's it. There's something else, a piece of major evidence we're keeping really close to the vest. In addition to the knife wound to the vagina, this guy had sex with all the victims after they no longer had a pulse. The M.E. confirmed post mortem damage to their vaginas. And Dax, get this. We have the perp's DNA."

"Really? So Janet, you're telling me this rather clever and methodical killer has made the error of leaving his DNA at the scene? In what form?"

"I know, I know, and it's not just hair or skin. We're talking semen, man, in all of the last three cases, and I suspect this one as well. Crazy shit, huh?"

Dax was already finding the clue recognition and compatibility program in his head running into glitches with the addition of each new aspect of the case. Certain of the answer to his next question, he asked, "And, you're going to tell me a match is nowhere to be found?"

"Correcto mundo. There isn't an available DNA database I haven't had checked at least twice."

"Of course," Dax began, folding his arms, but pointing toward the corpse sitting still a good many yards away from them. "I'm sure our fiend would have known he was safe in that regard, wanting to throw it in our faces as a dare. However, it could also indicate some form of underlying desire to be caught eventually so he can take credit for what he considers the most perfect of crimes. You know how these guys think."

"Yeah, but until then, we're nowhere and have no idea when he'll strike next. There's no time pattern with this asshole."

"Clearly, all the stalking he's committed to doing based on each victim's personal schedules has the most bearing on that. So we have a very patient, narcissistic, highly intelligent ritual killer with necrophiliac proclivities, who uses a potential weapon of mass destruction to disable his victims, but may also want to be caught. And, I should add, has a substantial degree of medical knowledge. That puts this guy in the top tier class of serial killers, a Ted Bundy or worse, a Jack the Ripper. Who, as you know was never captured."

"Yeah, that's what worries me about this one. Jesus, Dax, I'm worried this might be a case even you--sorry man, just rolling that possibility around in my head," she began, lowering her head.

"That thought, dear Janet, never enters my mind until I've exhausted every possible clue, and it's only happened twice in fourteen years. I'm just getting started on this one, am I not?" he asked smiling to let her know he took no offense at her words.

"Why do you think he goes to all the trouble to murder these women in sometimes far-off places?" she asked.

"Good question. Your first three victims were all murdered in a place that provided them some form of solace, something they experienced personal joy doing--praying, running and birdwatching. It's possible the perp picked those locations to add even more hurt to the psyche of his victims. It may be this last victim had no such special avocation other than the joy of her work at this homeless shelter.

"But there's another reason to consider. Breaking into anyone's home to commit murder in such a densely populated area like Mott Haven would substantially increase the risk to be seen or captured. Isolation is this man's best friend. Getting back to the semen that's been retrieved, has the M.E. been able to give you any determination about the age of our killer?"

"Shit, I almost forgot about that. Doc Perkins said that sperm can stay alive inside a woman's vagina from three to five days. Since all the vics were discovered well within that time period, she's had a lot of the little buggers to run tests on. After the second body was found, and it looked like we had a serial killer on our hands, she took it upon herself to have the semen analyzed at a fertility clinic, thinking they might be able to narrow down some information for us."

"Doc Perkins is a lot like you, Janet, relentless."

"No shit. So the report comes back from the clinic stating the samples contained a very high quality of semen, but the sperm count was unusually low. The doc called the clinic to ask what that meant in terms of the age of our suspect. They told her the semen would likely have come from a relatively young man, though in some rare cases, it could be from a man older then twenty-five. As to the low sperm count, that could be the case for any male at any age. The conclusion is our perp is probably younger that twenty-five with an underperforming set of balls. There isn't any way to nail a tighter age range down. But hell, it also means our perp could be as young as a high school kid. It's scary thinking anyone that age could be this cunning. See what I'm facing here, man?"

"I do. Glad you called me in on this one. If you'll excuse the pun based on where we're standing, it's right up my alley. If there's nothing else, let's proceed to see what we have here in front of us."

"Right. Well, it's clear our Sister Barnabas got about halfway to the street and was attacked in front of that door stoop. It belongs to a butcher who's been bitching all morning that we've chased away all his customers. So Sherlock, it's time for you to do your thing."

Dax began to run the scenario of the victim's walk and attack in his mind like a movie trailer, his favored form of reflection. "She must have been the last one to leave if the body wasn't found until this morning. Who found her?"

"One of the homeless guys who sleeps in a park not too far from here. He was looking to dumpster dive for some food early this morning. It was about six o'clock."

"Did our guys show up before the butcher got here? I'm asking if the scene was compromised by anyone before you arrived."

"No, as far as we know, no one else has been back here since the murder except the guy who found her. He knew the nun because he eats at this place and totally wigged out seeing a naked nun, especially in the shape he found her. After Ted calmed him down, he was adamant he didn't touch a thing. I've even held off the CSU people so you could get first crack at this."

"I suppose they objected."

"Not when I told them why," she said.

"Okay, Ms. Meehan, let's see what this crime scene has to tell us," Dax said, donning a set of latex gloves, and taking on the face of a man absorbed beyond distraction. He walked at a snail's pace in the direction of the body, stopping at times to bend down to view the ground more closely. "There was no rain or melting snow last night, so most of these alley drains probably contain nothing of interest. But we can see by the blackened substance leading away from our vic's body, the drain closest to her was the recipient of her blood. Better have CSU check it out in case hair or any other trace of our perp travelled with it."

"Noted." Janet replied.

As Dax bent over the right side of the corpse, he kept the direction of the street at his back to reduce the number of long-range photos the press was taking of him.

"Has the M.E. been here yet?"

"Oh yeah. She showed to view the body for a quick check, knowing you were coming. She verified the basics that match all the other murders, the wound placements, et cetera, and made a stab at time of death. Oops, sorry about that. It was pretty easy she said, even with the body being frozen, already knowing the nun's habits and when she usually left every night. She'll make the TOD official later after she gets the body back to the morgue."

Nodding, Dax started to pull back the department blankets from over the nun's head and winced in a way he hadn't done in a long time. Although he had witnessed many a gruesome corpse, the horror of the sight of this victim exceeded the self-imposed and necessary apathy he attempted to bring to the cases that any homicide detective must learn to do. He later understood his reaction had been to the combination of the deep black holes of her eye sockets, and the frozen blood around them, surrounded by the adornment of a clerical veil he had always identified with some of the finest human beings he had ever met.

Steadying himself, he slowly pulled the blanket down to a place just above her naked breasts. There he observed a puncture wound to the left of her sternum just below her second rib. His self-taught medical knowledge told him it was the gateway to slit her aortic arch.

He was stuck. He couldn't bring himself to pull the body cover any lower. A lump formed in his throat as his whole torso shuddered as well.

"Hey man, you okay?"

"Sure, sure, I'm all right." He hesitated again and said. "You've seen everything. I mean the wounds to her hands and the one between her legs? Anything different to report?"

"No, man, it's all the same as the others. We can wait till Doc Perkins gets us the enlarged photos of all that later. Are you seeing anything around the vic or nearby that catches your interest?" she offered.

The gesture had Dax slowly looking up across the body to where Janet was standing. He smiled and said. "You know . . . you trying to distract me? You're more of a softy than anyone thinks you are."

"Yeah, yeah, yeah," Janet threw back, a blush giving her away.

Dax stood. "Do we have any reason to believe the assailant was waiting for our victim from inside this butcher shop's door?"

"No. We cordoned off the area inside the door on that possible theory, but there was no sign of forced entry into the shop anywhere and no evidence that would indicate any stranger waited inside. We've already checked the alibis of the owner and his only employee, his son, for last night during the time of death, and they both held up. Actually, they were both with witnesses for several hours around that time. They're clean."

"The only other place to hide then, Janet, is behind this stoop. It's tall enough for someone to crouch behind, especially considering how dark it must be here at this point in the alley. I can immediately tell you two things for certain. Our killer is left handed, and the switch inside for the light over this door is in the on position."

"Uh, okay, how?"

"There are pieces of broken light bulb glass strewn over the right side of this stoop, and down these steps aimed toward the street. That means our perp would have taken the time to walk up the steps past the door to the stoop railing and busted the bulb above the door from that side using his left hand, forcing the broken pieces to fly in that direction. Of course, he wouldn't have bothered unless the light was on. As you can see, the base of the bulb is still screwed into the socket. It also continues to prove he knew just where and when to attack this victim as he did all the others. Be sure CSU checks those shards and the socket in case our killer used a glove or something else that left traces of anything to follow up."

"Gotcha. Good catch, Mr. Holmes," Janet said seriously.

Gathering himself, Dax squatted and closed his eyes, and

allowed his head to hover over and around the chest and head of the nun while breathing in deeply. He then opened his eyes to the smallest of slits to locate the edge of the blanket to cover the sister's head again.

"I was just checking, but with the body frozen, I didn't expect I'd be able to discover any unusual scents of anything that might give us a clue, but would you ask Doc Perkins to see if she can detect any unusual odors when the body thaws back at her lab? You never know. Even the most intelligent killers have quirks, like wearing too much cologne or some exotic oils. Remote, but worth checking."

"Sure. You got anything, anything else at all?"

"No. Unless CSU discovers something I've missed, this crime scene only confirms what we already know. This killer is very talented in terms of avoiding capture. I'm guessing he wears very dark clothing, likely some form of leather or athletic material, to allow him the most ease of motion and least likely to shed any kind of trace evidence. I'd speculate he wears some head covering or a mask, even a hair net, to prevent us from discovering his hair color, which might give us some good guesses as to eye color as well. He already knows the DNA from his semen is unable to help us out, at least not yet. We're going to have to add really smart son of a bitch to the sick descriptors for this guy."

"That's what I was afraid you'd be saying," Janet said, with her near brain-frozen words slurring a bit. "Can we go inside, now? I have no feeling in my toes anymore."

Dax shook a bit himself, as Janet's request jolted him from his focused thinking and had him recognizing his own body's reaction to the cold wind slicing through the alley.

Once inside, with the exception of an occasional person sliding in and out with things to put in a cupboard, Dax and Janet discovered the kitchen to be relatively quiet. They sat on a couple of vinyl-covered stools in front of a large triple-bottomed, stainless steel sink against a sidewall.

After shedding their overcoats and laying them across a near spotless food prep counter, they both vigorously rubbed their individual hands to generate some warmth.

Dax spoke first. "I think the frustration we're both experiencing lies in the fact that this case has so many aspects that don't fit together. Each element of this perp's actions appears to present a profile in conflict with the others, which has to be a clue in itself."

"Absofuckinglutely, why I called you in," she said.

"Clearly, your people continuing to work the neighborhood is the best thing to go on for now. Me? I'm going to have to spend more time thinking on this. Would you mind if I take the rest of that file you're holding with me overnight? I'll drop it off on my way in early tomorrow. Sorry, I don't have more to offer right now."

"Well, I suppose I can't beat myself up too badly," Janet began in a half-kidding tone, "if the great Dax McGowan is as stumped as I am."

"Ah, my dear Lieutenant, please refrain from the use of the word stumped in the same sentence with my name in it. An unsolved case is plainly a short term dilemma where all the pertinent facts have yet to be uncovered, only to eventually succumb to the appropriate applications of logic and reason."

"Hah! You know, Daxman, sometimes you come off like some character in a centuries old novel, and I totally love that shit when you do it."

Before Dax could form any look of satisfaction, his phone rang. He answered with the usual, "McGowan," but already knew from reading the caller ID to hold the Droid a distance from his ear.

"Who the fuck do you think you are, McGowan, ordering up the case file on my wife's murder? I'll have your head over this you stupid fuck."

Janet placed both index fingers in her ears wincing in empathy, having recognized the commissioner's high-volume voice coming from Dax's phone.

The strong reaction Dax expected had arrived, though its level of ferocity was more intense than he had imagined. Instinctively knowing to avoid any fear-based apologies the P.C. was so expert at extracting from everyone else, he went completely the other way. "Commissioner, do you want your daughter to have a chance at a recovery or not," he retorted sternly.

Janet's fingers dropped from her ears. Her face changed to one of total disbelief at hearing the strident words of her friend.

"Listen," Dax continued in a crescendo, "I've already eliminated that any hazing took place at Teresa's precinct as the cause of her problems. I'm looking into every other potential source, and has it ever occurred to you there's a reason I solve more cases than anyone else in the department? Has it? I do that because I make sure I don't miss even the tiniest of possible clues. That means I check out every goddamn thing, including, as in this case, what the professionals said they couldn't nail down about the effects of your wife's death on Teresa."

"What . . . er, what--," Gallagher began; unable to react to what Dax knew was a response the commissioner had never encountered from his minions.

Dax allowed him no footing. Maintaining a strong voice, but with the decibels now trailing down, he said, "For me to ignore such a life-changing event in your daughter's life would border on detective malpractice. Just because a group of shrinks may not have been sure of its effect on Teresa, or had some fear of broaching the subject, doesn't hold any water with me. Doesn't it make sense that the detective's interviews of your daughters at the time of their mother's death might produce some new, critical information the doctors would never have thought to investigate? I've solved cold cases before where some off-the-cuff comment made by a bystander of no apparent importance broke the case wide open. Don't I owe Teresa the very best of what I can do, sir?" The *sir* was a calculated acquiescence to the commissioner's authority.

"Listen, McGowan, no one gets off talking to me like that," the commissioner said, but in an unbalanced tone.

Dax hoped implying the commissioner's interference might get in the way of helping his daughter would damp down his ire some, but he knew major damage control was still needed.

"Then I'll apologize. It's just that once I bite into a case-- you see, I have now met and discovered what a beautiful person your daughter is, and I am going to get very possessive of any information I believe I need to help her, sir."

"Well, yes . . . uh, she is special," was the commissioner's hoped-for reply. After a long pause, he said, "Okay, McGowan. I'll have the file released, but let's be very sure about something. This is not, I repeat, not some cold case that requires your interest. We had the killer red-handed, and your clearance to inspect the file is to remain only on how the event may have affected my daughter's mind. Are we clear on that?"

"Yes, sir."

"And let's be sure about something else. I'm going to let you off the hook for now on your insubordination. We'll be discussing that again . . . later. And Lieutenant?"

"Yes?"

"This conversation had better stay just between us."

"Yes, sir, of course," Dax responded as he glanced in Janet's direction, knowing what he just said was already too late to be true.

The commissioner hung up immediately. Dax put his phone back in his coat pocket. After sitting silent for a few seconds, he bent over slightly to adjust his position on the stool. He sat more upright and crossed his legs. Slowly he raised his head to look more directly at Janet.

"Holy fucking shit," she started, extending hers arms, palms up. "My heart is still pounding a mile a minute, and you look like you're just sitting there waiting for someone to serve you a cup of tea."

"Don't let the façade fool you," Dax said, his voice noticeably shaken. "That was a close one."

They both sat a few seconds more, assessing the damage and its possible implications.

Dax snapped his fingers. "Janet, I've got to head out and call Dick right away. He was trying to retrieve that old case file."

"Sure, we can talk later. I'll wait to hear from you. That's if you're still working for the NYPD," she said with a look of concern, "and be sure to say hi to Dick for me."

"Will do," Dax said, winking confidently for the sake of his friend, who he knew had attempted to say something that sounded normal for his sake.

CHAPTER TEN

Already heading back down Willis Avenue toward Manhattan, Dax issued a voice command for his car system to call his partner. "Hey, Richard. I hope you haven't left One P.P. yet."

"No . . . still here. I'm in the main lobby, up from the basement where the old case files are kept. But I gotta tell you, some major shit hit the fan when I asked for that evidence box."

"I'm sure it did."

"I mean big time, Dax. I started out having a great conversation with an Officer Keegan down there, who turns out is the younger brother of a guy I roomed with at the Academy, so he was ready to help me and all. But after he made a call to the commissioner's office, because there was a hold on the file as you predicted, what seemed like a new friend I'd made, came back scared shitless and not too happy he'd made my acquaintance."

"I'll bet. You should have heard the content of my call with the P.C."

"Damn, Dax. Are we in a load of trouble now?"

"No. I managed to calm him down, and you can go back down and pick up the file. Gallagher should have already called and cleared it. I'll fill you in on the details later, but all is good for now."

"Okay, if you say so. Hey buddy, I like being your partner, but you sure drag me out near the edge of a cliff sometimes," Daley said.

"I know, Richard. I know. But so far, we haven't gone over yet, have we my friend?"

"No, not yet, and we sure have kicked some bad asses, asses, in the process," Daley finished with a trembling laugh.

SIX

It was late enough in the day that Dax saw no need to stop at his precinct, especially since all his other cases had now been re-assigned on the commissioner's orders. He decided he would take Janet's file home to review and wait to hear from his partner about any discoveries he made after reviewing the case file on Margaret Gallagher's murder. He accessed the map of the city in his head, located his current position, made an unlawful U-turn, and headed northeast toward his home in Throgs Neck.

CHAPTER ELEVEN

The approaching winter solstice had already spread its early onset of darkness, and Dax's mind was still in full work mode as he crossed the Throgs Neck Bridge, and drove on to Lafayette Avenue in Queens, the location of his red brick walk-up. His home was no longer a place for him to seek a form of psychic relief as the ghost of his daughter still permeated every aspect of his life within its walls. He was constantly torn between a desire to move away in order to free himself of the near disabling grief that overtook him as he turned the doorknob to his home, and wanting to never leave because he felt the move would somehow be a form of abandoning her. He often wondered if he should have sought counseling after Grace's death, but the rigidly independent mind that defined to the world who he was would never allow it. He would rather struggle alone than admit to anyone, especially himself, there was anything he couldn't handle on his own.

Walking the long hallway from the front door to the kitchen in the back of the house, Dax threw Janet's serial killer file on the food prep island. He reached for a glass out of the cupboard even before shedding his overcoat. Getting ice from the fridge and retrieving the Southern Comfort and sweet vermouth from an adjoining cupboard were to be his next automated moves.

Reaching a little too quickly for the alcohol are we, Dax?

He stopped to shed his overcoat and blazer and walked back to the front door closet to hang them up. He returned to the kitchen and re-organized Janet's file into a sequence he would prefer to use.

While well aware these exercises were part of a fool's errand to convince himself he had some control over his need of it, he then poured the longed-for Manhattan.

He took two full gulps on his way back to the front of the house to a large living room off the foyer and nestled into a cushy L-shaped upholstered couch that faced a small, whitewashed fireplace topped off with a large flat-screen TV. He instinctively reached for the remote sitting next to him and began to aim, only to let it drop from his hands back to the cushion. "No more stimulation for now," he said aloud.

He took a searching deep breath and reached for a thought to distract his thinking. Janet's remarks earlier reminded him how much he reveled in being considered the Sherlock Holmes of the NYPD. With the exception of his partner, he never shared with anyone how much he had fashioned himself to match the qualities of the iconic nineteenth-century detective in order to reach his lifelong dream to become the city's best homicide detective. Even though armed with an eidetic memory, and an extensive education in all things criminal, Dax was well aware of how much he struggled whenever his personal feelings came into play in any investigation, an imperfection the dispassionate Holmes rarely experienced. It was not easy, when shortly after Grace's death he had to admit this weakness to himself and how it played a role in his missing the signs of the sexual abuse she was enduring. He wondered if he would ever be able to strike a workable balance.

Sitting in his living room in a near dead silence, he pondered the question of whether he would have to teach himself to somehow eliminate all his emotions. At the same time, he considered why would he wish to devolve into the near loveless, full-time stoic that Holmes was portrayed to be? Now divorced from his hot-tempered wife after their daughter's death, was he never to fall in love again or have more children? Part of him was sure he didn't want to pass up the opportunity if the right woman appeared in his life. Yet, must he learn how to turn his emotions on and off so drastically to do his job and still have a home life? He could only agree with himself that any answers to that dilemma would have to be put off to another time. Facing the anniversary of Grace's death this day, an interview with a troubled young woman that only reminded him of his shortcomings in protecting her, the commissioner's ego so flat in his face, and

Janet's serial killer case, that was now his as well, was all he could handle. These thoughts required two more large gulps of the sweet dark liquid and a trip to the kitchen for another.

On his return to the couch somewhat later, he was shed of any clothes of his profession. It was underwear, a robe, and a third drink after dispensing with the memorization of Janet's file. He turned a tableside lamp down to form only a glow of light over the pale white painted room. His mind sufficiently loosened, he sent it to a place he felt most comfortable.

"So, Watson, quite the day we've had, wouldn't you say?"

"Indeed, Holmes, indeed." Watson replied, "But, dear boy, I find it my duty to bring to your attention what seems to be a dangerous need of yours of late to imbibe in excessive amounts of alcohol."

"Well my friend, it was the first two concoctions of this magic elixir that brought me to this conversation with you. Worth the cost, I would say."

"Hmph. Unfair of you…that ploy. I say, unfair."

"I offer then a small apology, but let us discuss Janet Meehan's case, shall we"?

"Ah, Sherlock, a case I would title "The Dreaded Loss of Good Habits."

"Aptly put, Watson. The world surely mourns the loss of these fine women. But alas, to prevent the loss of any others, we must find a way to stop this fiend. The facts are most unrevealing. They are disjointed and have come together to form a puzzle where the pieces do not fit. The various skills possessed by this apparently young killer are quite formidable, yet when added together, they seem not likely to be possessed by only one person. This could indicate there is an accomplice, yet my instincts tell me some of the elements in these murders have likely been contrived to throw us off this perpetrator's identity."

"Actually, Holmes, I was about to suggest the accomplice idea myself. What is it that sways you from accepting that possibility?"

"The M.E.'s reports on the first three victims I had Doc Perkins send to my phone on the way home are quite specific in describing every wound inflicted on each victim to be a near exact copy in every case, even the results of the boring motion committed on both the right and left palms of their hands. The medical knowledge involved, in particular the slit made to their aortic arch, would at least suggest a person somewhat older than the very young person the DNA results would indicate. Would someone as methodical and skilled as this killer appears to be bring along a younger, necrophiliac accomplice for the sheer purpose of having sex with each victim after they expire? I think not. This is a mystery within the mystery. That is, until I divine it.

"I must admit, Watson. I have been sufficiently distracted by other matters today and feel I'm not at my best at this moment to give this case a proper effort of my skills."

"Understandable, Sherlock, but it is also the alcohol. Maybe a good night's rest would make for a better companion tonight than I. Let these torturous stabbings and young Teresa's dilemma escape your attention for the next few hours and get some sleep."

"The stab wounds, Watson, and your use of the word *torturous* brings to mind a thought worth consideration. It raises the question of why the hands, eyes, vagina, and of course the heart were chosen for destruction. What horrible misdeeds might these parts of the body have committed in the mind of our killer that he feels they must be punished in such a fashion?"

"What I see Holmes, is that you have a start to begin your day with tomorrow, as I also observe a set of eyes that are struggling to remain open. Goodnight, my friend."

Dax began to slip sideways to lie down on the couch as his exercise in duality trailed off. The right side of his face lay atop his extended right arm, while his left hand set his glass containing only melted ice now on an adjacent coffee table. By instinct alone, he pulled his legs up onto the sofa and closed his eyes. Contained in his robe pocket, his phone would ring twice, but go unanswered until it rang once again early the next morning.

CHAPTER TWELVE

Tuesday, December 12

"Hey Dax, how soon before you get in this morning?" Daley asked.

It was 6:50 a.m., a good hour before any appreciable light would make its appearance in the city.

"Good Morning, Richard," Dax said, yawning as he sat up on the couch looking to clear the fog from his head. "I see you tried to reach me last night, but I was out cold after a long day yesterday." He yawned again. "I also see my phone is about dead, and I'll be plugging it in all day trying to stay ahead of its dying battery. Actually, Richard, I have an appointment at nine with the P.C.'s daughter, Angela, the psychiatrist."

"I met her once. Not professionally, of course," Daley added with a small laugh. "She seemed like a nice lady. I mean, I almost expected her to be, you know, a little off like the rest of the clan. But no, a normie."

"I hope so," Dax said, yawning yet one more time. "I'm counting on getting at least some insights from her on Teresa's condition." He let his robe find its way off and onto to his left forearm while listening to familiar creaks of wood as he headed upstairs for a shower.

"Hope you do, but I called because this case file on her mother's murder? It's a big nothing. Just eager to get your take on it."

"What about our main concern?" Dax asked. "The notes taken by the detectives on the two daughters?"

"I think we should wait till we get together later. It's weird how little there is here. Even the simple stuff that's missing doesn't make any sense. How much after your appointment do you think you'll get into the precinct?"

"Not sure. I assume Dr. Gallagher is a very busy woman and can afford me only a limited amount of time. Her office is in the new chic area of South Harlem. I'd estimate I'll get in about ten-thirtyish."

"Sounds good. See you then," Daley said.

CHAPTER THIRTEEN

Angela Gallagher's office was located in what was a high-end modernized office, part of an upper floor in an old tire storage warehouse. While a lot of the grounds and portions of the old relics of buildings still looked distressed in this section of Harlem, the bones of the structures were solid, and developers were picking them up as fast as their financing would allow, turning them into real estate gold, all part of a fast-moving gentrification of the area.

As Dax approached a secured door at the building's south entrance, a friendly voice called to him before he could press the doorbell. "Is that you, Lieutenant McGowan?"

"That would be me, Dr. Gallagher," he responded, looking up into a security camera placed high enough on the two-story building to prevent any easy destruction of it.

"Good. Please come in," she replied as a loud buzzer and door release almost drowned out her words.

He entered into a large street-level open area that looked like it would eventually be a fashionable waiting room for several businesses, except for now the doors to those potential establishments were set up in a circle around the large room and protected by open iron cages like flexible doors on elevators. To his left was a stairway he surmised would lead to the psychiatrist's office and easily deduced she was the building's first tenant. Another buzz at a door on the second floor and he was in.

Angela Gallagher moved quickly across a wide-planked, lacquered wood floor to shake his hand. "Welcome, Lieutenant. I've been looking forward to meeting you. After seeing your picture so many times in the press and reading of your exploits, I'll have to admit to feeling a bit star-struck."

Dax was caught off guard by more than the compliment. Before him was a woman who looked nothing like her father, and she hit a nerve going back to his childhood. The Irish neighborhood where he grew up had its share of beautiful young girls sporting a special hair color its inhabitants referred to as Irish Red, a shimmering representation of the primary color that almost appeared to be on fire. The girls blessed with that shade who received the most attention, at least from him, were the ones whose eyes were also described as Irish Emerald Green. Angela Gallagher had both qualities, and in his estimation matched well with her classic Western European face of beauty and an appealing long, slender body. The sudden encounter had him doing double takes he hoped were not being noticed.

Gaining control, he responded, "Well, Doctor, I'm like a good many other so-called stars in this city . . . just another kid from the Bronx who's done well."

"First thing, Lieutenant, please call me Angela. Of course I counsel a good many women on the dangers of being overly star-struck with any of their male acquaintances, but I do get a kick out of it when I experience it myself." She smiled. "Please come in. Would you like some tea? Or I could make you a single brewed cup of coffee."

"Coffee with a little milk or cream would be great, and please call me Dax, Angela," he responded while hearing a text come in on his phone.

"Okay, Dax, a coffee with cream coming up. Please have a seat anywhere on the couch."

Stopping for a moment, he scanned the text from Janet. "Call me when you can." He texted back, "Tied up in a mtg. will call later."

Before advancing farther into the room, he turned back to look up at an open loft he expected to see, based on a metal circular staircase he observed to his right when he entered the door. Through a waist-high, open guardrail, he saw an expensive quilt cover over a king-sized bed dominating the space. It was surrounded on the back and sidewalls covered with various pieces of artwork of different genres he expected were of the kind you only bought at auction. Off to the left of the nightstand was a door to a good-sized walled area he assumed to be a master bathroom. *Great place to stay overnight should work run late.*

He had already determined from driver and voting records that Angela Gallagher's main residence was still the Gallagher home in the Hamptons, which she shared with her father and her sister, Teresa. Her father had never remarried, but was often photographed wearing wide smiles while in the company of very attractive women, as was said by many to make him look to be a better fellow than he was.

He moved farther into the expansive area, and facing him to his left, occupying one-half of the room's space, was a cozy semicircle couch he estimated to be ten feet long. Its fashionable gray cushions created a comfortable setting as the couch faced a teakwood coffee table, along with two high-backed matching chairs separated by a tile inlaid service table. A large gold lamp with a gray shade sat atop it. Though never a visitor to a psychiatrist's couch, Dax was sure this setup must be the state of the art set for a homey setting to help patients in need of her services.

Directly behind the chairs, occupying the right side of the room was Dr. Gallagher's modest-sized, wooden desk. The entire floor's illumination came from a large array of skylights and the kind of track lighting you would expect to see in a remodeled warehouse. Dax observed the skylights contained louvers that were apparently remotely controlled. At this early morning hour, and likely set for his visit, was what seemed a perfect amount of light splayed uniformly over the couch area, while the office portion of the room to the right was more darkened. Dax was further impressed that the entire setting was appropriately matched with a flavor of classical music. It seemed that no matter where he stood he felt as though he was standing in the middle of an orchestra as its conductor. He deemed the setting perfect for the kind of meeting they were expected to have dealing with the concerns about young Teresa's distresses.

The finishing touch, covering the entire back wall to the ceiling, was shelves containing his estimate of several hundred books.

"Excuse me, Angela," he called to where she stood in a small kitchen and supply room set off the main room to his extreme right. "Do you see all your patients here?" he asked to fill the silence.

"I do now. I closed my downtown office a dozen or so weeks ago. I wanted to create the best environment for my clients to feel as comfortable as possible. This property gave me the opportunity to design from scratch what I hope achieves that. Besides, having an office out here in Harlem provides a lot of my patients a greater degree of anonymity they weren't getting entering and exiting my office downtown, where many of their friends live and work." Her voice took on a playful purr to color her next words. "You may already know that my practice is primarily with people, that in addition to suffering from conditions that plague everyone else, have lives that are complicated by being endowed with considerably too much money."

"Most folks think they would like the opportunity to have to deal with that affliction," he said, kidding back.

"True, but they'd be naïve to the potential evils lurking in the world of excessive wealth," she replied to the clink of a teaspoon and a china cup.

While waiting on his host's preparations, he began to scan her library wall, choosing to pull out several books of interest. He allowed the attention of his memory to absorb all the titles, editions, and copyright dates he could take a mental note of. When Angela headed with a tray to the coffee table with his java and a cruet of cream, he moved to sit just to the right of the most centered middle cushion of the couch. He assumed she would sit nearly directly across from him to the left of it after she retrieved an already poured cup of tea from her desk, and she did.

"That's a sizeable library, Dr. Gallagher, uh, Angela. I was especially impressed with a signed first edition copy of a book by the famed Dr. Theodore Sarbin's works on hypnosis. Based on the signing date, you couldn't have been more than ten when he gave it to you."

"He once attended a party at my parents' house, and someone, my father, I'm sure, let him know about my early interests in all things psychological. But Dax, I'm not sure what I'm more impressed with, your interest in me enough to know and compute the age I received that book, or that you have some degree of knowledge about the work done by Dr. Sarbin."

Dax almost blushed and said, "I read a lot. I'm also impressed to find out you're one of those people who identified the life work they wanted to pursue at such an early age," he said, surprised at how personal he was getting with someone he had just met.

"Well, thank you very much," Angela said with a small laugh, tilting her head side to side.

After a moment to properly allow for the niceties of each other's words to be enjoyed, Dax watched as Angela attempted to shift her seating into a more upright professional position.

"So, Lieu . . . excuse me, Dax, we are here to talk about my sister. Let me first say, I can understand the pressure my father has likely put on you to discover why she is suffering the way she has of late. Do understand; he does have a very real concern for her. But please, I wouldn't want you to feel the slightest bit of guilt if you're unable to succeed at this. As you know, the very best, and if I may say, including myself, have had no success either. I want to help you any way I can because I love my sister as much as is humanly possible, but I'm also in a position to know what challenges you're facing."

While her words were a tinge patronizing, he appreciated them in terms of their positive intention when compared to those of Dr. Hogarth's the day before. Despite the now more officious nature of their conversation, Dax was also feeling a bit entranced by the beauty of her soft, angular legs lounging out from under a short light-colored aquamarine dress that matched her eyes. Her red hair, emerald eyes, her legs, plus the music and the lighting played havoc with a considerable portion of his testosterone. He reached hard for the Sherlock Holmes in him. "I would be the first to admit my shortcomings in the field of psychiatry, Angela, but I do believe good detective work might produce some fruit. We'll see. But tell me, on the particular point of your expertise in the use of hypnosis, would you share with me the results of treating your sister with that technique?" He asked, expecting she already knew he held Teresa's medical information release.

"Of course, happy to. The results with my sister boil down to some well-known facts about hypnosis. First, if no one wishes to be drawn into a hypnotic state, it won't happen. While Teresa was more than compliant, like anyone else, if she holds a secret that her very essence wishes not to be revealed, hypnosis will not expose it. I attempted five different approaches with her under the most ideal of circumstances, including in this my masterpiece of an environment, but I got nowhere," she finished by extending her arms pointing around the room as if it were a consenting partner in her practice.

She then uncrossed her legs, leaned forward to place her teacup on the coffee table, and in the process spread them sufficiently to give Dax a view to the edge of her light-green silk panties.

The more unflappable nineteenth-century Sherlock Holmes was now in a heated battle with the aroused twenty-first century Dax McGowan for control of his words. "Maybe the best question I can ask is, if you had to offer a theory as to what Teresa's problems might be centered around, how would you state it?"

"Well, I've read all the same reports you have, and find myself in agreement with Dr. Hogarth. Teresa fits into that category of persons who refuses to reach inside to discover the source of these spells because she fears what she might find there," Angela described, using her fingers as quote marks around the words *might find there*. "I'm sure you're aware of the devastation both she and I have always struggled with after coming home as a couple of young kids to find our mother murdered by that landscape contractor. I'm certain the memory still plagues her, even if she comes off as if it doesn't. It still plagues me. I understand better now than I did then that my mother wasn't always the sweetest woman in the world, but she didn't deserve to be murdered. And the difficulty may be that it's not just that single event in Teresa's past that's the source. It could also be that as part of her job on the police force, she's had to deal with humans at their worst, seeing children tortured and lives destroyed. That set of conditions, coupled with the circumstances of our mother's death, may have accumulated to a point where she just can't handle all of it anymore. Her need to dissociate so severely may lie in the fact that she can't define its source because it encompasses an entire scenery of issues."

His host's instructive clinical descriptions drew him well away from the spell of her beauty. He proceeded more on point. "Thanks, Angela. What you say certainly gives me a broader perspective to consider. But let me ask, would it seem strange to you that the cause or ignition for Teresa to fall into these trances might perhaps be tied to a single form of stimulus?"

After a pause, "I'm not sure what you're asking, Dax. I don't believe that any of her doctors have concluded that a single stimulus is the cause; neither was it a conclusion of mine. Have you discovered something we all missed?"

"Not really. I stayed in the *perhaps* area because it's only a theory I'm attempting to work on for now . . . probably a dead end," he added, wishing to avoid having to reveal anything more of his thoughts on the point.

He watched her observe him in a deep, peering fashion similar to his own when sizing up a person of interest, but then she turned her look to one of pure friendliness. "Please Dax, if you find anything you think would help, let's be in contact about it. Maybe combining our specialized skills, we might be able help my little sister. It's really what all my thoughts centered on in anticipation of our meeting today."

Dax smiled to himself at the thought of possible new encounters with this woman.

"Angela, I would definitely look forward to having any reason for the two of us to see each other again." *Jesus, did I really just say that?*

The resulting rosiness in her cheeks only accentuated the beauty of her Irish countenance for him. She responded, "Good. I wasn't kidding about that star-struck thing earlier. I've always wanted to meet you, Dax McGowan. When the professional side of all this ends . . . well, let's get to know each other better, shall we?"

Okay, that couldn't have been more direct. That thought was accompanied by a nod of his head with a look of all the charm he could muster.

Knowing the time was right, as their personal connection had moved faster than maybe it should have, they both stood in unison. After he thanked her for the visit and the coffee, she escorted him to the door. They shook hands, sharing a lilt of glint between them, interrupted by her passing him a card with her personal cell phone number on it.

The experience had him gliding down the stairs feeling the flush of sexual attraction, though rushing out the building's door to be hit by a blast of a cold wind pushed his thinking back to the task at hand. He thought it both intriguing and flattering that no one who worked with Teresa, including her sister, had discovered there may be a specific catalyst setting off her spells. He stood at the door of his car deciding he wouldn't yet reveal to anyone but his partner that he believed he had already made that discovery. He decided he still needed more research into Teresa's background to verify the validity of that deduction, but it then hit him he needed to respond to Janet's earlier text message.

CHAPTER FOURTEEN

"Goddammit, Dax, I want this son of a bitch bad," Janet started before he could offer a greeting of any kind. "The M.E.'s full report and all the interviews are in. Wouldn't you know his latest victim was a poor old nun who had just spent her last twelve hours helping a slew of homeless folks? And then the bastard puts her through the same unimaginable horror he has with all his other victims. Sorry. I know you already know all this. I just can't get it out of my head."

"It's okay, Janet. I'm all in with you on that score," Dax said, listening to the caring and heart-wrenching torment he knew Janet always felt for the victims she swore an oath to protect.

He was sitting in his car outside Angela Gallagher's office waiting for the defrost fan to remove the icy fog on his windshield that had formed as a result of his body heat hitting the cold, dead air waiting for him inside. "Hey, my friend, you texted me. You have something new?"

"No, nothing," she lamented. "I was hoping you had a new slant on things. And shit, I now have the top city security folks combing over all my files on the saxitoxin thing with the promise the FBI is going to be right up my ass by the end of the day. You got anything for me yet?"

"Sorry, I've just met with the commissioner's other daughter, Angela, and I'm on my way to review an old case file with Dick. My head's been dealing with all that first thing this morning. However, after one too many Manhattans last night, maybe more than one too many, I did have a thought. You know that old graphic of chimpanzees? Hear no evil, see no evil, et cetera?"

"Yeah, what about them?"

"You and I both know the perp is picking particular parts of these victim's bodies to inflict punishment on them for a reason. It's likely he was once on the receiving end of some form of sexual abuse as a child, perpetrated on him by some adult who may have also been a nun. It's like a take-off on those chimps, except proactive. The palms of their hands may have touched in an evil manner, their eyes saw things they weren't supposed to see, and the vagina experienced evil pleasures. You with me on this?"

"Yeah, yeah, I get it," Janet responded in a slowed fashion. "I mean, I've seen rage with forty stab wounds inflicted on a victim of course, and the occasional major destruction of a vagina, but this would be my first case where body parts like hands and eyes were chosen so specifically. And Dax, I've covered the rare cases of nuns committing sexual abuse, but those are extremely small numbers compared to the thousands of times priests did the assaulting. In fact, I can't believe I haven't seen a dead priest with his dick cut off yet," she added with a smirk Dax could picture over the phone.

Janet's conjecture hit a note about thoughts he had when tracking down the priest who abused his daughter, but he went on. "Those small numbers may make this idea relatively easy to track down. If we take the M.E.'s assertion from the perp's semen, that he's likely a relatively young man, it might lead us somewhere. Maybe a review of abuse cases in the Mott Haven area over the last ten to fifteen years where there was even the slightest possible involvement of a nun abusing a young boy might lead us to a young man who was the victim. It's a long shot, I know."

"Well buddy, it's at least a new direction to go from the nowhere we are now. I'll get Ted on it right away. How's the deal with the P.C.'s kid going?"

"I'm making progress, though the biggest questions are still in front of me. But remember, your case is also a big priority for me. I'll get back with more soon, I hope."

CHAPTER FIFTEEN

While Dax cleared a large portion of his desk, his partner sat across from him with his hands reaching into and through an evidence box on his lap.

"Oh hell, here's the whole thing, what little there is of it," Daley said, placing Margaret Gallagher's case file on Dax's desk.

Dax pulled it toward him, noticing how light it felt in the process. "So the uni in storage said this is all there was?"

"Yep. He mentioned how short the contents seemed even to him, even for such an easily solved murder."

"Okay, let's see what's not here," Dax began. "It looks as if there's a complete M.E.'s report. Pictures of wounds to the chest. No blood-spatter report, though eighteen years ago it wasn't the science it is now."

"There was mention of blood on the two girls," Daley injected. "You'll see it when you get to the flimsy set of notes taken from one of the investigating detectives."

"Blood on both girls? Did they come in contact with their mother? A hug, or something after they found her dead?"

"Yes, the older one, Angela was seen crying and holding her mother. The younger one, Teresa, appeared to just have a few smears here and there, but the detective, a guy named Vovolizza, wrote that Angela had been hugging her sister on and off as well, to comfort her, so they presumed the blood transferred."

"Richard, I don't see any crime scene photos. That's insane. None of the body, how she was dressed or undressed, and no pictures of the girls? The murder weapon, the large kitchen knife is here. Is there anything in the detective's notes about the stab wounds? This isn't an evidence file. It's a box with a name and a number on it that just basically says, 'By the way, a murder took place on such and such a date.' This is ridiculous."

"You're telling me? There aren't any notes on the stab wounds, but do check out what we were looking for on the interviews with the girls. There's at least some basic information there."

Dax reached in to find two palm-sized spiral notepads. One was marked under the name, Detective Second Grade, Emmanuel Vovolizza, and the other, Detective Second Grade, Edward Fitzgerald.

"So Richard, does it strike you as strange that as much pluck as the Gallaghers have had in the department, going back to the Civil War mind you, that a couple of second-grade detectives would be assigned to this case? No aspersions cast on second grades, of course."

"I thought that too. The only explanation I had was that they caught the guy at the scene red-handed with his prints all over the knife. You'll see, as we already know, this Diaz guy was the Gallagher's gardener. There was also plenty of proof from interviews with neighbors that he and the victim were always arguing about something. Who knows what protocol was back then? I guess the detectives just saw it as an open-and-shut deal, and thought they needed to just clean up the details."

"But Dick, those facts wouldn't have come to light until after a more senior detective would have been dispatched to the scene, and then maybe reassigned the details to someone else. There's no mention of any of that here. I just can't see a call from the highly influential Gallagher family reporting a murder would have resulted in what appears to be a rather weak response. Again, not putting those two guys down."

"Hey, totally agree," Daley said, twisting around in his chair.

"Who called the police?" Dax asked in exasperation. And hell, it should have been the Southampton police who had jurisdiction, not two city . . ." Dax stopped to look inside each notepad more closely. "Damn it, Richard, these guys were Manhattan cops."

"Yes," Daley began to explain. "The notes read that the older daughter, Angela, called her father first, and nothing else is mentioned about how the two guys from downtown got the case from there."

"Okay. Now it's clear. The Gallagher machine was in complete control from the start. How our current police commissioner, then only a detective, arranged getting around the jurisdiction issue would be most interesting to find out, though that's not a call I'll be making to the P.C. any time soon based on my latest conversation with him. In any event, give me a minute to read the rest of what's here. Let's see . . . "

Daley adjusted his seating position looking to get more comfortable.

After several moments, "That the trial transcript you have in your lap?" Dax asked pointing to a relatively thin tie-bound booklet of legal-size paper with court stamps on the outside.

"Yeah. You wanna see it?"

"Not just yet, but I'm going to assume from these notes that at trial, young Angela testified that she and Teresa walked into the kitchen and found Mr. Diaz standing over the body holding the murder weapon."

"Yes."

"The fingerprints were irrefutable. The volatile history between the victim and the perp was well substantiated, and the jury returned a guilty verdict in less than an hour."

"Yes on that too."

"Okay," Dax went on. "Vovolizza's notes say that at the time of the murder, he verified that both brothers, Jeremiah, age sixteen, and Michael, age nine, were at home. They were at the far end of the house in their bedrooms and were unaware of what went down until Angela, age fourteen, went to find them just before the detectives arrived. I've been to their home a couple of times, Dick. The place is huge. The kid's bedrooms might even be in a different zip code from the kitchen where this happened."

"I've heard," Daley said, smirking with eyebrows raised.

Dax continued, "Detective Vovolizza further reports that Angela was in a constant state of grief and, as you mentioned, hugging her little sister repeatedly. Teresa was virtually unresponsive till they turned her over to her father after he arrived about twenty minutes later. The P.C. told Vovolizza he'd already called the family psychiatrist to come and help both girls with the shock they had experienced. In addition to some unbalanced-sounding answers to his routine questions, the detective recorded that Angela, in an obvious state of shock, continuously repeated the words, "He did it. He killed my mother." Those words were intermittently spoken between also telling her little sister everything would be all right. Shit, Richard. That's all we have to go on. The other detective's notes, Fitzgerald's, deal only with talking to the neighbors, who corroborated the enmity between Mrs. Gallagher and Mr. Diaz. One of Diaz's employees said the same thing. Diaz hated Mrs. G."

"That's it," Daley agreed once again, "but the case was so cut and dried, I'm not sure it matters."

A part of Dax had an inkling to accept his partner's supposition, but then he discovered some refuse left in the now empty case file box. He reached in with his fingers to retrieve it.

"Look here, my friend, see these?" he asked, as he opened the palm of his hand to expose several tiny pieces of yellowed, oddly shaped paper.

"Uh-huh. Some note paper pieces?"

"Yes, Richard, too many of them. While leaning over this box, someone pulled out several pages from each of these notepads, producing these triangles of paper you always get when you yank pages from a spiral binder. A rather dumb error if you're trying to hide what you've done."

Dax was now faced with some form of coverup too blatant to ignore, and his obsession to know the facts jettisoned him into a next thought. "Richard, I might get my head chopped off for this," he said standing and walking around his partner. He began to pace behind him. This caused Daley to shift his head around back and forth from his seated position to follow his path.

"I'd like you to track down those two detectives, if they're even still alive . . . of course not alerting anyone to what we're doing."

"Sure, but do you think those guys might have anything to add to what we already know about Teresa's problem that exists now?" Daley asked as an obvious next question.

"I'm not sure, but certainly at least soemthing more than this file is telling us," Dax responded, not revealing that his interest was as much directed at the murder case itself. He considered the potential dynamite that could end up exploding in his face and his partner's, if they were to travel down that new path of inquiry, but chose not to let on to Daley until he could learn more. The guilt of that decision led him to a revelation before Daley would exit his office for his new assignment. "By the way, Richard, I still have one more thing to check out to be certain, but I believe I've figured out what's triggering Teresa's spells."

"Whoa, no shit? Tell me, tell me."

"You know me, my friend, I have to nail it down first, but I should know by the end of the day and I'll tell you the minute I know for sure."

"That'll be so cool. Hell, I knew you'd do this. You know, show up those head shrinkers," Daley said, his freckle-faced boyish smile accenting his response as he stood to leave the room. "Catch you later there, Sherlock."

CHAPTER SIXTEEN

Still in his office an hour later, Dax sat phone in hand, as the person who had returned his call had him on hold while searching to find the information he had requested. His expectation of the result would cement his theory about the catalyst setting Teresa Gallagher off into one of her spells. While in that wait mode, Daley pushed Dax's office door open, but seeing him on the phone he motioned if it was okay to continue in.

"It's okay, Richard, I'm on hold."

"Good. Listen, it was easy tracking down Vovolizza and Fitzgerald through our pension people. Fitzgerald is long dead five years now, but Vovolizza is in a senior care home on the island in Amityville. You want we should head out there?"

"I might do that one myself. He's an assisted living resident there, right, not nursing care?"

"Yes, I made sure, and managed to get him on his room phone. He's not the most pleasant guy, but he's just fine to talk with us, uh, you, any time the rest of the day."

"Great. Something else has occurred to me. As thin as this case file is, we shouldn't rule out that maybe Teresa's two brothers, Jeremiah and Michael, might be able to tell us something worth our time. We know they supposedly had no idea their mother was murdered until Angela alerted them and the detectives showed up, but see if you can track them down for at least a phone interview. You never--," Dax halted and raised his index finger as the universal sign his call was back in play.

Daley mouthed the words, "On it," backed out, and closed the door.

"So everyone you checked?" Dax asked. "Good. Thanks Bill. That's a big help. One day soon, I'll catch you up with the details as to why that's important for me to know. I owe you one," he said. An insider friend at the Police Academy had just shared a critical piece to the puzzle that was Teresa Gallagher, information that would normally require a signed release to obtain.

Okay, that's settled. While a triumph in terms of so quickly making the discovery of the trigger for Teresa's near catatonic episodes, Dax realized the reason why that specific catalyst was the trigger was now a new mystery. He decided he should quickly pull Daley in to give him the news as promised, retrieve the address of Vovolizza's residence facility, and head out there while his partner tracked down the two Gallagher boys. He felt he could justify Daley's assignment if asked by the commissioner as Teresa's brothers might shed some insight into her state of mind the day of the murder. He also knew traveling out to interview one of the old detectives on the Margaret Gallagher case, if his boss got wind of the questions he would be asking, would set off huge fireworks with the P.C., and the chances of surviving another such encounter would be nil. Going by himself would at least keep his partner protected, if it came to that. He hit a button on his desk phone. "Richard, I have that information we spoke about earlier," he reported in a matter-of-fact tone for anyone in the outer office who might have heard what he said over Daley's speakerphone.

Dax stood when Daley rushed in, swinging the door closed fast enough to catch the edge of his nose in the process. Dax tried not to laugh. His partner smiled falsely to cover up the obvious pain he had inflicted on himself. Daley, apparently realizing he was hiding nothing, spoke quickly to get the attention away from his mishap and get to the heart of the matter. "Okay, spill it. What's up?" he said, trying not to grab at his injured nose.

"Richard, the cause, or I should say the catalyst triggering Teresa Gallagher's spells is, get this . . . it's the number six."

"Wait. What? You mean the actual number, six? I don't get it. Just a number? I believe you, of course, but you're going to have to explain that one to me."

"Sure. I kept going over and over in my head what connection there could possibly be between the three venues we knew for sure where Teresa devolved into one of her spells . . . watching television, while shopping in clothing stores and what we witnessed when those unis walked by us at One P.P. I'll explain later if you like, but I was able to eliminate her senses of smell, hearing, taste and touch as the cause. So it came down to something she saw that set her off. After much thought, I was able to also eliminate any event, person, or inanimate object, common to those three venues which led me to look for something as simple as a number. Then it all fit."

"What made you think of a number? I . . . I would never have reached for something so remote as that," Daley asked palms outstretched.

"Richard, sometime I'll have to tell you about the kinds of conversations I have with myself, but that's for another time. Here's the connection. I estimate that for fitting purposes, Teresa would wear a size six or seven. That would mean she would be encountering that number in large font sizes on clothing racks every time she went shopping. Of course, the number six appearing on television could be from many sources, like the *Six O'clock News* as an example. The clincher was the number of unis making all that noise in the hallway. There were six of them. The ruckus got her attention, and she immediately counted the source.

"Once I focused on the number six other clues came immediately to mind. Do you remember when met Teresa and she spoke about her mother's murder? She described herself as being seven at the time? As we know, she was only six. I was willing to let that go at first, despite it seeming strange that anyone who had survived such an ordeal would ever state that fact incorrectly. Also, I don't know if you noticed, but when it was time for us to be seated at the table for our meeting room, Teresa suddenly exhibited a mild form of tension, and while I was pointing her to sit on the right side of the table, she quickly moved to the left side. You may recall there were six chairs on the right and only five on the left. It was as if she automatically, I'd say unconsciously, shied away from the right side for that reason. While it all fit so well, I wanted more, and that phone call I just finished nailed down my added suspicion that she's had a problem with that number going back a very long time."

"Okay, I guess I'm seeing it now," Daley said. "Wow. Geez, there you go again coming up with a solution that I swear nobody else would have thought to even consider. What was the deal on the phone call?"

"When it seemed logical to me that just a simple encounter with the number could affect her so drastically at this point in her life, it also seemed likely it was a source of trouble well before that. After some thought on how I might discover if that was true, I contacted an old friend of mine, Bill Tucker, at the Police Academy. Richard, on every test Teresa took at the academy, guess which question she skipped every single time?"

"Holy shit. Question number six."

"Exactly. Not sixteen or twenty-six, or any other number with a six in it, just six."

"Ooh, that's eerie, but do you think it's that number because she was six years old when her mother died?"

"That's not very likely. I entertained the same thought at one point, but only briefly. My research tells me a trigger for the kind of extreme physical manifestation she presents is most often linked to a much more tangible element of an actual traumatic event. One's actual age at the time of such a happening wouldn't appear to be a factor of any significance unless that event happened in the middle of a child's sixth birthday party or something inexorably tied to their age. We know that wasn't the case here, as Teresa's sixth birthday had passed months earlier."

"Okay, but if she's always had some quirk about that number, why is it causing her to go into spells now?"

"That is still our mystery. I'd speculate that up until these last weeks, she's been unaware of her own aversion to the number and has unknowingly avoided it with little or no thought. It's also the kind of thing no one in her company, family, or friends would easily deduce; hence even the psychiatry professionals. But some current-day event has awakened in her the very source of her fear of that number, and now, every time she runs into that number staring her right in the face, she checks out, as with those six unis walking down the hallway. It seems most likely the death of her mother would be the prime event involved. We just can't be sure yet."

"So," Daley began to say in slow motion, "we know what brings on her spells, but we still don't know why."

"Yes. We now have a major clue, but we're a long way from home plate on providing her, or a good psychiatrist like her sister with the information needed to treat her to make these spells disappear. I'd say we're only rounding first base on this right now."

CHAPTER SEVENTEEN

Still an incorporated village within the town of Babylon and despite its proximity to the most significant city in the world, Amityville had always maintained much of its quaint, centuries-old characteristics, particularly along the water's edge on the island's southern coast. Set back four blocks with a distant view of the water, overlooking an array of pastel single-level cement block homes, was the three-story, Joseph Palmer Senior Care Facility where retired detective Emanuel Vovolizza was a resident.

As expected from previous visits to similar facilities, odors related to aging bodies and disinfectant mixed with a faint smell of urine met Dax at the door. He sat in an open guest area while waiting until a staff person had the elder detective brought down to a meeting room on the first floor. He found himself wondering which of the many male residents walking by best represented what he might look like at such an advanced age. He decided with the strict regimen of exercise he adhered to and the advances medical science would make over the next forty years, he would never look as old as these men. The Holmes in him, however, reminded that his current overuse of alcohol might play a role and questioned whether his assumption might contain a good degree of denial as well. A moment later he was waved on to proceed down a short hallway for his meeting.

Already in his early sixties at the time of Margaret Gallagher's death, Vovolizza was more than eighty now, but appeared a good deal older. Dax easily concluded the man's face of deep lines and burst skin veins were sure signs of too many cigarettes, too much booze, and the hard life of a rather unsuccessful career as a cop. The old detective was slumped over in a wheelchair and slid under a shiny metal table. The room was small and sterile containing one matching metal chair and walls covered haphazardly with unframed resident-produced artwork. Dax grinned a small smile, recognizing the man's still very thick, wavy white hair containing numerous dark black streaks, a positive trait often attributed to pureblood Italian men in their old age.

"Detective Vovolizza, thank you for agreeing to see me on such short notice," he opened, sitting in the lone chair directly across from him.

"Yeah, like I got so many appointments I had trouble fitting you in," was the hoarse and graveled response. "I ain't no detective no more either," he added.

"Well, Detective, I like to consider any career cop as always a cop."

"No thanks, McGowan. That might be okay for a famous guy like you. Me? Being a cop wasn't all that fucking great. So what does a hotshot like you want with me anyway?"

Okay, Dax thought, *No surprises here.*

It was imperative to gain a degree of camaraderie for their conversation to produce any valuable information and have any chance of it also remaining confidential. Based on what appeared to be grievances Vovolizza clearly had with the department, Dax knew where to begin. "So is it Manny you go by?"

"Yeah, that'll work."

"Manny, I'm working on an old case that might involve some scary shit with the Gallagher family," Dax started in street language more comfortable to his respondent.

"Those motherfuckers? I hate those motherfuckers. Every fucking one of them found a way to stick his heel on my neck."

Dax avoided his next impulse to jokingly ask the detective to tell him how he really felt about the Gallaghers. "Well, Manny, I'm not sure, but I might be onto something that could cause them a great deal of grief," Dax offered, continuing the ruse. "Can I count on you to keep this conversation confidential?"

"Listen, McGowan, if I can help you nail them bastards on anything, sure, I'll keep it quiet."

"Good. It involves the murder of Margaret Gallagher that you were assigned to, the current commissioner's wife, when she was murdered at their home."

"Assigned? Yeah, I'll say assigned. Me and my partner Eddy Fitzgerald got a call from the Chief of D's. You know, the Chief of Detectives. Do they still call him that?"

"Yeah. Same title."

"Okay, so the Chief of D's orders us to hustle out to the island, where we didn't have no jurisdiction to be, because a Gallagher got murdered in the Hamptons, the rich motherfuckers. The Chief of Ds at the time was this current P.C.'s grandfather. He tells me we're to report only directly to him on the case and not even to our own captain. How about that for balls? I couldn't get one question in edgewise before the bastard just tells me to shut up and get out there. Hell, I'm old and forget some shit sometimes, but I'll never forget how that all went down."

Dax was finding the elder detective's words encouraging. "The case file on this murder is extremely thin, Detective, more than you would expect. Did you ever get the feeling there was any kind of cover up going on at the time?"

"Uh, I don't know…maybe…yeah. First off, the Southampton boys were really pissed when they found out we'd scarfed up all the evidence ahead of them, and so was my captain when I told him the Chief of Ds said I couldn't tell him anything. It really pissed me off that my boss, who didn't have much of any good opinion about me anyway, was so torqued about the deal. But shit, you know what can happen if you cross one of them Gallaghers."

"Yes, I do. So the two sons at home, Jeremiah and Michael, was it true they had no idea what went down before you arrived?" Dax asked to test the detective's memory and possibly dispense with that detail's likely lack of importance.

"Why you asking about them? Yeah. I had no reason to question what they said, and we had the Mexican dead to rights. Blood on him, and the Gallagher girl telling us she saw him bending over her mother with the knife in his hand. But you know, the guy never even tried to escape. He was waiting for us to arrive and pleading large he didn't do it. Anyway, it all added up after the interviews with the neighbors. He and the Gallagher woman hated each other's guts. I thought you said you had something that was gonna get one of those pricks in the family in trouble here. What's going on?"

"Manny, the bottom of the old case file box contains a bunch of torn off pieces of paper because someone ripped out large portions of the notes you and Fitzgerald took at the scene, and all the crime scene photos are missing. You have any idea why?"

"Shit, I have no idea, unless it has to do with the vic. She was wearing one of them nun habits when she was killed, veil and all, a black one."

Dax swallowed hard. "Uh, I didn't know that." His memory went to the medical examiner's report describing a blood-soaked bathrobe as what the victim had worn as a solitary item in a couple of pre-autopsy photos. "Manny, was the M.E. ever on the scene with you during your time at the house?"

"Uh, no, I don't think so. Yeah, that was strange, wasn't it? Hell, we got one call after another from the Chief of Ds asking us if we were done interviewing everybody like he wanted us to hurry up. When I finally said yes, he told us to get our asses back right away and show him our notes. He's probably the guy who tore up what we wrote…the son of a bitch."

"What about a crime scene photographer? Did anyone show up to take pictures? There weren't any in the case file."

Vovolizza shrugged his shoulders. "Not when we was there. I heard the department photographer did show later, but a Gallagher grabbed him when he got back to the precinct and took his camera. I suppose that tracks with why Eddy and me were told we weren't supposed to tell anyone what we saw out there. And McGowan, I was only at the trial testifying for less than ten minutes, and wasn't asked to corroborate any photos. I was in and out…boom…so was Eddy Fitz. You suppose they got the guy convicted without using any photos?"

Dax's mind was racing. The possibilities of any number of scenarios exploding in his head. He took a second to plan his next words to stay in sync with the direction of their discussion. "Yes, I suppose it could be easily enough done. There was plenty of fingerprint and witness evidence to convince a jury, and all the prosecution had to do was show photos of the stab wounds taken during the M.E.'s autopsy later. By the way, the photos the M.E. took were only of the vic's chest wounds, none of the rest of her body. However, the report described six stab wounds, but the pictures show only five to Mrs. Gallagher's chest. Where else was she stabbed?"

"Oh, yeah, she was mostly stabbed in the chest. I don't remember the exact number, but there was also one to the face, in her eye. An ugly one, man. I mean big-time ugly, and all that eerie shit with her being dressed like all those hard-ass nuns I had in school? I was cringing some about it."

Dax sat for a moment pondering the similarity to Janet's serial killer case.

"So, McGowan, you think somebody else killed the mother, maybe a family member, and the whole clan was trying to cover it up? Hey, maybe it was this guy who's the commissioner now, you know, the husband? Hell, it's always the husband," Vovolizza added, seeming for a second to drift into thoughts of old clichés. "You know, I remember now thinking about that at the time. The landscaper, Diaz, said that he heard the husband and his wife arguing when he and his crew first showed up, before any of the kids got home from school. One of the Mexican's employees confirmed that. That could mean the husband did it, and the mother was already dead when Diaz found her later. The daughter never said she seen him actually stab her mother, just said he had the knife in his hand when she and her sister walked in. Of course, there was no fucking way I was gonna bring up that idea, and sure as hell not to the Chief of Ds, but I did put what everybody said in my notes."

"Those particular notes are nowhere to be found," Dax said. "There was also no mention in the trial transcript by the defense that the P.C. had been home that close to the murder. So, that portion of your notes likely never made it to defense counsel in disclosure either. It's even possible the rather inexperienced and young court-appointed attorney representing Diaz decided not to offer that as a possibility, even though his client would have brought it up. I would venture there might have been some intimidation brought down on the attorney by the Gallagher family on that particular point. Attempting to offer then-detective Gallagher as an alternative murder suspect in the city of New York without absolute proof? We can only imagine the possible fates in the offing for such a lawyer. Honestly though, Manny, the case file being robbed of so much of the evidence sure has cover-up written all over it."

"Yeah, McGowan, but what about his wife wearing that nun's outfit? I never did see or hear about that coming out in the trial. Like

I said, me and Eddy Fitz were in and out, bam, bam, but Diaz must have told his attorney about that too."

"Well, Detective Vovolizza, this is sounding more and more like one giant railroad job. I'm sure you're right about Diaz informing his attorney. The only way his lawyer would have been able to introduce it as evidence, however, was to produce crime scene photos that didn't exist or put his client on the stand. According to the transcript, he never did. He couldn't have handled his client's case anymore poorly.

"Before I decided you and I should visit on this, I checked on the whereabouts of this attorney as a possible lead. Unfortunately, two weeks after the trial he committed suicide jumping off the Tappan Zee Bridge."

"Shit, McGowan, you think he had remorse over the whole thing?"

"Either that or he was pushed. Is there anything else you can remember that might help?"

"Let me see. Yeah . . . to back up his story that he didn't kill Mrs. Gallagher, Diaz said one of the little girls, the youngest one, what's her name?"

"Teresa."

"Yeah, her. He said she called him into the house to meet with her mother. That was the only reason he went inside. Diaz said he found her bleeding on the kitchen floor. Then the girls walked in on him leaning over her body…you know, like maybe the P.C. must have killed her earlier? The perp claimed he only pulled the knife out of her eye trying to save her life and even put kitchen towels over her chest and eye to try and stop the bleeding. There were bloody towels next to the body. Maybe that's what really happened, and it was the husband," Vovolizza said nodding his head.

Dax added his own nodding in a more muted fashion because he also had to consider that if Diaz was guilty, he may have tried to stop the bleeding to avoid a murder rap after committing an act of passion for which he was already suffering remorse. Diaz not fleeing the scene, though, and even waiting for the police was an extremely strong element in favor of his innocence. Vovolizza's comments left one last detail to clear up with the ancient detective.

"Did you ever ask little Teresa if she had called Diaz into the house to meet with her mother?"

"I don't remember if I did, but she was really messed up, had that kind of a blank stare you'd never forget. You know what I mean? But hell, McGowan, if you can nail that motherfucker Gallagher for this, it'll make my day, and I could sure use a good day around here once in a while."

"Tell you what, my friend," Dax said. "I'll stay on this till I get it figured out, and I promise as soon as I have something to run with, you'll be one of the first people I tell. And detective? You have to promise me you'll keep all this to yourself, so we don't scare anybody off. Deal?"

"Yeah, sure," Vovolizza answered with a smile that said he felt he had been given access to the inner circle of a new big-time case that needed his help. "You know, McGowan, I didn't mean to be giving you such a hard time when you first walked in. I always wanted to be the kind of detective you are. It's just, I never seemed to catch a break. Ya know what I mean?"

"Sure, I get that," Dax said, out of respect for a man who he knew worked at a time and place in NYPD history when even the most honest of men had difficulty dealing with some of the culture inside the department.

"You'll be hearing from me soon, Manny. You take care of yourself, you hear?" Dax left the room with the old man sitting up a little straighter in his wheelchair than when he first arrived.

As Dax headed out the door, he thought how fortunate he was to be working in a substantially different atmosphere in the NYPD today. *At least an asshole like Gallagher is the exception now, even if he is the Commissioner.* He appreciated how the work of many of the top brass and the last three mayors had created the environment where his kind of integrity could thrive. He smiled a smile of mischief at his next thought. *Now it's time to get rid of that asshole exception.* He knew though that trying to prove this Police Commissioner was the killer in an eighteen year old murder had the term *land mines* written all over it.

CHAPTER EIGHTEEN

Dax waited to reach the Cross Island Expressway on his trek back to the Four-One before he called his partner, wanting to take a degree of time to process all the possibilities his interview with Vovolizza had stirred in his head.

After tapping his Bluetooth, he said, "Richard, you're going to be more than a little surprised at what I just learned from talking to Detective Vovolizza. But before I get into that, did you have any luck tracking down the Gallagher boys?"

"Not really," Daley said. "The older one, the screenwriter, he was easy to check out from all the blurbs about him on the Internet. From there, I was able to track down his agent, told him who I was and that I just had some simple questions to ask about a case we're working on. You know, just trying to keep the conversation nonthreatening."

"No luck?"

"Nope. The guy said he'd talk to Jerry. That's what he called him and someone would get back to me. Yeah, right."

"And the younger brother, Michael?"

"Well, we're gonna have to find out where he is. The info we have on him says he's in Phoenix working as an EMT, but the regional boss he worked for there said he left with no forwarding address several months ago. I also searched every possible social media outlet, other city addresses in Arizona, and every database I could think of. He seems to have vanished. Should we ask Teresa if she knows where to find her brother?"

Traffic from the island over the Whitestone Bridge into the

Bronx had come to a sudden stop, a probable accident as the cause based on the number of emergency lights Dax could see in the distance. The pause allowed him the chance to consider an alternative to his partner's suggestion.

"You know, Richard, I'll contact her sister, Angela. I don't want to take the chance that Teresa may not be aware her brother's location is unknown and stress her out unnecessarily," he said truthfully, though the opportunity to reconnect with Angela held just as much value for him. "Besides, I have another assignment for you that I believe could end up being quite revealing. I'd like you to track down everything you can find out about their mother, Margaret. Her maiden name, where she grew up, worked, and how she ended up married to the commissioner."

"Jesus. Really? What for?"

"I have a good deal more to reveal to you later, but Vovolizza told me that when he got to the murder scene, Margaret Gallagher was dressed in a nun's habit, an all-black habit."

"Holy . . . what, more crazy shit? But wait, that doesn't jibe with the M.E.'s report. It said she was wearing some kind of bathrobe, didn't it?"

"As it turns out, Richard, the M.E. at the time never made it out to the crime scene. It appears one of the Gallagher family members arranged to have her body picked up and brought in. If her torso was covered in a bloody bathrobe, the M.E. could only assume she was wearing it when she was killed. The whole process was so far outside of protocol, there had to be Gallagher pressure put on Hodgins, the M.E., to handle the case the way he did."

"Jesus, Dax, if she was wearing a nun's habit, then the only thing that makes sense is that it was the commissioner who changed her into that robe, and probably sopped up enough blood with it to make it look legit. Why would he do that, unless for some reason he didn't want anyone to know she was wearing the habit, or he had something else to hide."

"Exactly, Richard, exactly."

"Also, why would anyone have a set of clothing like that in the first place? Do you think she used to be a nun?" Daley continued.

"That's a distinct possibility; however, our interest must go beyond that. The pertinent question is what was she doing wearing a black habit in the late afternoon, in the heat of the summer, with

Halloween yet months away." Dax added as a toss at levity.

"Partner," Daley said, breathing out loud, "that whole clan? Jesus, it's one thing after another with them. I'll check all this out right away; can't wait to see what turns up next. You got any theories about what this all means?"

"Yes, I do, about ten of them, but none of them will have any legs until you gather all the facts for me. In the meantime, I'll work on tracking down the Gallagher boys. I've rubbed elbows with some Hollywood folks at parties connected to the mayor's office and I think I know a guy who might help us reach Jeremiah Junior."

"Great. I'd rather be the one to check this new shit out," Daley returned. "Geez Dax, this is actually getting to be more than a little fun, finding out our Mad Hatter of a boss is even more the nut job than we've always thought him to be."

"Hmph, true that is," Dax said laughing out loud. "But watch out where you dig. I don't have to tell you to be careful where you step, who you talk to, and how you gather this information."

"I know, I know."

CHAPTER NINETEEN

Before calling Angela, Dax shuffled around his office for a few moments to gain the mindset he felt he needed to make sure he wouldn't come off like a smitten teenager after the obvious *dance* they had engaged in earlier. He sat down and reopened a file on his desk that he had retrieved earlier from within the department. He had already committed it to memory. It was on her brother, Michael. The facts made it easy to presume that Michael Gallagher was likely considered the black sheep of the family, having failed in his attempt at a career in the NYPD. While he followed family tradition and joined the force, his two-year stint was scarred by numerous violations involving brutality, followed by stints of mandatory anger management classes. Dax was certain the altercations had accumulated to a point where he should have been fired. He was also sure Michael's father overrode any such action, though the sheer number did eventually lead to a pressured resignation. *The old man probably got tired of the embarrassment.*

From there, Michael entered an EMT program with the fire department. He passed the necessary FDNY exams to gain his certification, but that job lasted only six months. The only information available was a report that beat around the bush, but came down to describing his behavior as not playing well with others, and the separation was a mutually agreed upon result. Dax saw no value in pursuing the obvious details for now. That event took place well over a year ago, and his file noted the move to Phoenix, but as Daley reported, he was now nowhere to be found since that endeavor blew up.

"Angela, I was expecting to go straight to voicemail based on how busy I expect you must be with your patients," Dax said after her, "Hello."

"Actually, Dax, you caught me at one of the research labs I have access to here at Columbia. We never got into the subject earlier today, but I've cut my patient load considerably of late to engage in a research project I was fortunate enough to receive a grant for from the National Institute of Health. I'm pleased to hear from you again. So, what prompts your call to me so soon after our meeting this morning?"

"Well, I'd be very interested to hear all about this new research project," he expressed, as much because his intellectual curiosity demanded it. "However, my call concerns your brother Michael."

"Michael? How is Michael related to my sister's issues?" was her off-putting response tinged with an element of fear Dax picked up in her voice.

"Just being thorough. We're going to contact your older brother, Jeremiah, as well. If, as you suggested earlier, I'm unsuccessful in getting any answers to your sister's problems, I want to be able to report to your father we left no stone unturned in terms of who we interviewed. Of course, that should include all her siblings, am I right?"

A long pause without even the sound of her breath left Dax clueless, but it was followed by a more reserved response. "Sorry, Dax. Yes, I see what you mean. Are you familiar with my brother's history . . . I mean with the NYPD?"

"Yes, I am. I have the pertinent reports, and his difficulties are pretty much general knowledge within the department. My call concerns where to reach him. He's gone off the grid it seems."

Another lengthy pause introduced her next words. "Lieutenant, it's clear your investigation will take you into some rather uncomfortable information about our family, and I think it's imperative you get the real facts. Doing it on the phone is certainly not the place. I'm tied up here for a while yet and have to get back to my office later to finish up some dictation. Is there any chance you could meet me there later?"

"Sure. What time?" he said, pleased at the suggestion.

"Let's see. It's about three now, and I should get there around four, need some time for those notes . . . say about five-thirty?"

"Considering the hour, should I bring Chinese or something else to your liking?"

"As much of a health freak as I am, I do love Chinese once in a while. If you can find me some tasty kung pao chicken, I'd be totally delighted. I'm suffering from missed-lunch hunger already."

"Then that'll be two tasty kung pao chicken dinners, one of my favorites as well. Anything to drink?"

"I've got a small selection of whites and reds there. Will one of those work?"

"Absolutely. A little end-of-day alcohol always works for me," he said, biting his lip, wondering how an astute psychiatrist would interpret the words he just blurted out so incautiously.

"It's settled then, Lieutenant. I'll see you at five-thirty," were her final words, said with an inviting lilt, and pleasant to Dax's ears.

CHAPTER TWENTY

The entire open area on the second floor of the Four-One was in a sudden state of organized chaos. After hanging up from his call with Angela, Dax stood in the well of his office door watching most of his brethren don Kevlar and gear up to meet with a SWAT team destined to storm the residence of three gang members responsible for the murder of an innocent bystander. The victim was a child in a recent drive-by shooting on East 151st Street. Normally he would join them but for his current assignment to which he had pledged his full attention. A number of his colleagues, including his partner, sent a salute his way as they exited on the stairway down to the street.

In only the second day on this case, the revelations both discovered and deduced had become most intriguing. Added to the mix was a strong attraction to a woman he had met in the process that had set off a myriad of physical and emotional stirrings he had not felt for a long time. The short-lived whirlwind romance he had experienced the previous year with Rebecca Bain, during the hunt for his daughter's abuser, had ended where he later admitted to himself he thought it would. Dating the world leader of a survivor's group for sexual abuse victims, who, like him, was obsessively dedicated to her work, but was living in Chicago, had "inevitable end" written all over it. After the hot and heavy need-filled experience, the loss of his precious Grace began to take on its full measure. The potential for any female entanglements had been left by the wayside of his life until this morning's awakening.

He stepped back inside his office, closing the door and locked it for privacy. It was time to organize his findings before leaving for his next encounter with Angela. He headed for the chair behind his desk while looking down once more at the yellowed and near moldy trial transcript of the case, "The People of New York *vs* Miguel Diaz."

"So, Watson, it's clear the commissioner, while somewhat a jitter at exposing his family to my investigation, was not prepared that a man of my skills would uncover such a host of secrets that he would never wish to come to light."

"True, Holmes; however, while that may be the case, it is also clear you may be headed toward a disaster that could end in the elimination of your career in the process."

"But Doctor, it's impossible for me to ignore what it is I shall discover. Am I to cast aside relevant information in the very task he has assigned me? And what of the particular revelation that Margaret Gallagher was clothed in a nun's habit at the time of her murder? What of the major family undertaking to cover up that fact?"

"But Sherlock, is it necessary to investigate a decades-old murder that may have nothing to do with poor young Teresa's distresses?"

"You use the term may Watson, because you are also intrigued by its potential relevance for her. Let's also not forget that Detective Vovolizza reported the Gallagher woman had been stabbed several times, including one to the woman's eye. While the court transcript speaks often to six stab wounds, only pictures of the five wounds to her chest were presented as evidence at trial. While the number of times she was stabbed could be considered the source of Teresa's allergy to that number, I have very strong doubts."

"Really, Holmes, I suggest you cast your doubts aside, and there you'll have it. You've solved the mystery as to the cause of these spells. Simply report your findings to the commissioner, and your task shall be judged complete. Please Sherlock; end this now before it's too late."

"Not that simple, my friend. I could accept her mother's murder as related to Teresa's aversion to the number six if only I were convinced she was aware her mother had been stabbed that number of times. Not only would any six-year-old, upon discovering the murdered body of her mother, have been in a terrible state of shock, you know as a doctor that the pool of blood on her mother's chest would have turned a much darker color as it came in contact with the oxygen in the air. With that pool of blood sitting on a nun's black habit, being able to discern the individual stab wounds would have been nearly impossible. As well, one can only imagine the additional trauma visited on the poor child to have observed what was no doubt a horrendous puncture to her mother's eye, forcing her to want to look away.

"In fact, the trial transcript reports only that her older sister Angela testified. It makes no mention of Teresa giving testimony in court where she would have possibly heard the number spoken the many times it was referenced. It's more likely she was shielded from all the courtroom proceedings. I'm convinced she was unaware of the number of her mother's wounds, and every effort was made not to burden her with the information. No, Watson, the number six has some other play in all of this."

"Alas, Holmes, I should have known the folly of suggesting you should agree to my easy solution to the matter."

"Watson!"

"Yes, Holmes?"

"Of course. It stands right in front of me. I can't believe I was so slow to see it. Where did Peeta, Teresa's nanny, tell us her spells began, and what was its source?"

"It was at her home, I believe," Watson said, expectantly.

"Correct, and was it not her viewing the telly as the cause?"

"Yes, it was."

"And my good man, what story has been dominating the news these last many weeks, bringing on Teresa's first episode? It was likely the first murder of one of these nuns, Janet Meehan's case. While the press was not permitted pictures of the unclothed bodies of those poor women, the media created its own animated versions of habit-clad females torn to shreds at the hands of this killer. How could Teresa not experience at the very least the greatest of traumas at such a reminder, and then the stories repeating ad nauseam, as three more murders ensued? And Watson, the words "Six O' clock News" appearing just below some of those animations."

"But of course, Holmes! You've solved the case your commissioner has assigned you. Oh my friend, I am so very relieved. In quite the most satisfactory fashion, I might add, you have reached the solution, saved your career, and allowed to hold your nose quite high in the presence of the psychiatric community. Hah! Most satisfactory. Most satisfactory, indeed."

"Not so fast, Watson. It seems that all we've accomplished is turning this mystery upside down."

"Upside down? Please, Holmes. What does that mean? Must you complicate what appears to be a most acceptable solution here?"

"Dear Doctor, you know better than to use the word *acceptable* in my presence. Think, my good man. We were pleased to deduce that the number six is the catalyst for Teresa's spells, assuming all we had to do was link it to some event as the cause. It appears we may have now discovered the continuous telly broadcasts reminding Teresa of her mother's death as the original causal event, but we are still at sea as to why the number six is the trigger for these spells. Having eliminated the number of wounds suffered by her mother as the catalyst, we find ourselves now upside down on this, old boy, upside down.

"But Holmes, if you've discovered it is her mother's death revisited by these news reports, it creates an avenue for her to begin a series of treatment. The issue as to why the number six triggers her spells could then be discovered over time."

"Over time, Watson? Let's remember, my friend, I promised Teresa I would do everything in my power to help her gain her career back. It's possible she will continue to be plagued with these spells no matter how intense the therapy might be as she continues to be confronted by this evil number that torments her psyche...that has tormented her psyche nearly her entire life. If left to the vagaries of the psychiatric community to eventually discover the connection between the number six and her issues, she may never wear her NYPD uniform or see the inside of a patrol car again. No, Watson. It's all on me. If she is to ever have that second chance of a complete recovery, a diagnosis of all her issues is required."

Dax sat motionless for a time, filtering the results of the most helpful exchange between both personalities acting out within his mind. He always wondered if there were any other detectives on the planet with his skill level, and if so, had they ever used a similar technique, playing one hemisphere of his brain as the devil's advocate against the other's deductions until his frontal lobe made final decisions about what he considered relevant. He knew most talented detectives adhered to the usual process of bouncing ideas off their fellow sleuths, but he had to admit to his own trait of conceit believing the only detective worthy of such an exchange was himself.

With himself as a mentor, though, he thought, *Richard seems to be getting closer every day.*

CHAPTER TWENTY-ONE

Dax's phone read 4:12 p.m. He computed he had the time to make a call to California before leaving to pick up the Chinese food and make it to Angela's by 5:30. The time being three hours earlier on the West Coast seemed ideal as well. He turned to look out his window to ponder how he should approach this acquaintance he hadn't spoken to in over two years. Watching snow flurries caught in the updraft between buildings flying in every direction like a swarm of confused white insects, he decided planning his words had no value and proceeded to dial the number.

"How about that? It's one of my favorite American heroes. How are you, Dax?" were the first words he heard after being transferred by an assistant.

"Hello, Mr. Weinstein. I was unsure you'd still remember me," he replied to one of Hollywood's most influential moguls.

"Remember you? Hey, you saved the life of one of my best friends," said the man, referencing Dax's prevention of the assassination of the president at Ground Zero. "I'd never forget you. What can I do for you, Dax, just ask, and please call me Harry."

Dax's thoughts went to the mayor's party they attended celebrating his saving of the president, and the half dozen times the producer kept putting his arm around him and shaking his hand.

"Thanks, Harry. I know you're busy, and I will get right to the purpose of my call. I have a case I'm working on, and I'm having trouble reaching a guy, Jeremiah Gallagher, a screenwriter out there in your neck of the woods. We need a statement from him as soon as possible, and his agent deferred to the old ploy of telling us he'd see about his client getting back to us. Do you know how I might reach him more immediately?"

"I've never worked with the man, though I hear he's pretty good. What I can do is make sure he calls you. Is this the best number for him to reach you? Would you be available within the next fifteen minutes to half hour?"

"Uh, yes . . . and yes, of course," Dax responded, taken aback by the immediacy with which his request might be fulfilled.

"Good. If it's going to take any longer, my assistant will call you back. Let's give her a few minutes to track the guy down, and I'll call him. Is there anything else I can do for you, buddy?"

"No, Harry, that'll be a big help. Thank you very much."

"You hang, my friend. You'll be hearing from this Gallagher guy as soon as I can make it happen." The phone disconnected before Dax could finish his final thank you.

He sat at his desk unprepared to face a period of time when, rather than having his mind in high gear, he was caught in a full wait mode on Jerry Gallagher's potential call. *Does Weinstein really exert that much power?* He noted it took only a bit over seven minutes for his phone to ring. He answered, "McGowan."

"Yes, Mister, or I should say Lieutenant, this is Jerry Gallagher. How may I help you?" was the man's solicitous response.

"Mister Gallagher, I'm working on an assignment given to me by my police commissioner, your father. It concerns your sister, Teresa. Can I assume you're familiar with the difficulties she's been facing lately?"

"Actually, Lieutenant, I'm not. I've had little communication with my family since moving out here a good many years ago, but what's up with Teresa? Is she going to be okay?"

"Unfortunately, your sister has been experiencing what can be best described as spells of near unconsciousness that have adversely affected her job as a rookie cop. There's been speculation that the cause may be some kind of delayed response to your mother's death when she was quite young. As part of my investigation, I wanted to ask if as her older brother, you have an opinion on that. Also, is there anything you could think of that might be the cause of this psychologically based condition she's suffering from?"

"Frankly, officer . . . excuse me Lieutenant, I heard my sister was attending the academy but wasn't aware she'd joined the force as yet.

I meant it when I said I've been out of touch. As to her mental state as a result of my mother's death, all I can remember is that she seemed to come out of it fairly well. I thought my sister Angela took the whole thing a good deal harder. As to anything related to her mental state, I have no idea. What puzzles me is why this isn't in the hands of the medical professionals. Excuse me, but an NYPD detective? I don't get that."

"It's a long story, Mr. Gallagher. Let me spare you the details and just say that your sister's issues have already traveled down that road with my skills as a detective a last resort effort."

A lengthy pause preceded the screenplay writer's next comment.

"Listen, this whole thing sounds like some crazy shit my father would cook up, though I'm surprised he would allow anyone to be digging into family issues, on the chance someone might discover what else was happening that day. There was a helluva lot going on in our house that super prick needed to address and never did. Excuse me, but I pulled myself out of an important reading session in deference to Mister Weinstein, and I must be getting back. Is there anything else?"

"What do you mean by what else was happening that day?"

"Listen, Lieutenant, I'm not sure any of that matters now, and I have no idea how, if at all, it may be affecting my sister this far into the future. If it does, I'll leave it to you to figure it out. I really must be going."

"One last question. Have you had any recent contact with your sister Angela?"

"She tries to check up on me every so often, but it's been a while since I've felt interested in taking her calls. I would say, she's the one bright spot in the family, always making sure everyone is doing all right. Little Teresa was always a darling, but with our substantial age difference, we never were close. Anything else?" He asked with a hint of exasperation.

"Okay, I'll let you go," Dax said. "I assume I can reach you at this cell number should I need to at some point?" Dax asked while committing to memory the caller ID information on his phone.

"Yeah, I suppose," was the commissioner's son's answer followed by a simple good-bye.

Dax slouched in his chair, swiveling side to side, thoughtful it was no surprise the Gallagher family engaged in a good deal of dysfunction. He was sure he needed to find out why a well-established successful adult child of the commissioner would refer to his father as a "super prick" to a perfect stranger on the phone. Obviously, some very old wounds had not yet healed. The reference to unaddressed issues and "what else happened that day" left yet another wide-open door to be stepped through. More on that subject would have to wait, as he stood to get moving to pick up the evening's meal on his way to see Jerry Junior's sister, Angela.

CHAPTER TWENTY-TWO

"Twice in one day, Lieutenant. How nice, and the smell of that food in your hands is making my mouth water. I'm famished." Angela smiled and gently fingered the sleeve of his overcoat as a more personal invitation into the specialized environment she called her office.

"Me as well, and I had to breathe in all these great aromas on the way over here," he responded with a similar pleased smile.

"I've set us up at the coffee table with, sorry, plastic forks." She pointed at the couch where they sat earlier in the day. "I pulled one of my office chairs over to make it more of a dining experience," she added with a giggle. So, white, or red for you?"

"I suppose convention would call for white, but I prefer red most often. Listen, I'll sit on the chair," he offered seeing it was enough higher than the coffee table, it would require a degree of leaning over, maybe a bit uncomfortably.

"Oh no," she said. "You're my guest; you sit on the couch. Besides, you bought dinner."

"Okay, lady, this is your turf," he said, watching her fine form walk to the office kitchen to retrieve the wine.

He looked around, doing an automatic replay of what he always called "his tapes," noticing that virtually everything was in the same place as this morning except for a few new items and some missing ones from her desk. He further observed a change in the lighting best described as an ambience for evening café dining. The lighting, in addition to a barely heard flow of a Boyz II Men album, seemed to him a perfect match of stimulation to the senses, given his interest in this new woman's acquaintance. He was once again of two minds. He was aware of and enjoying the effects of the surroundings in terms of a potential relationship, and at the same time wished to advance his knowledge as a detective. He chose first to open a conversation about a shared interest, science.

"So, Angela," he began with a raised voice, "you'll have to tell me all about the research you're doing at Columbia. It must be something pretty groundbreaking for them to allow you access to their facilities, access so very much in demand."

Also raising her voice to be heard from the kitchen, she said, "You know about their screening process, Dax?"

"Not from any personal experience, but as I've said, I read a lot."

"Of course," she answered. "Well, as soon as I get over there with the wine and these glasses, I'll fill you in. If you'll excuse the pun, I'm really psyched about the work we're doing."

In another minute, she arrived with two large wine glasses, a small plastic ladle to scoop food from the takeout containers, and a bottle of cabernet which she handed to Dax for pouring duties. In a jest-filled hosting style akin to some noted chef personally serving an expensive entrée at table, she picked up the rice container with her right hand and served it with the other onto two heavy-duty white paper plates and continued the entertainment with the mixture of kung pau chicken. She topped off her performance with the self-deprecating action of licking the ladle and swooning at the taste of it, as might be done on the sly by a hungry waitress in a roach-infested diner.

Dax could tell she was pleased, when his broadening smile had turned into full-on laughter. "So, Angela, your impish side is showing."

"I only let it show when I feel it's safe, Dax McGowan. With my highfalutin reputation, some of my patients would never understand. I'm betting that in many ways, you feel that same pressure, a celebrity cop known for being so brainy."

"Guilty," he said with a new grin.

The meal ready to be consumed, Angela settled into the office chair she had moved across from him, leaving her at the raised height he expected it would. She sat and leaned over to place the ladle on a napkin. Unable to make any modesty adjustments to her already short dress, she inadvertently gave him an ever more revealing view than he had the benefit of earlier.

Okay, there's a distraction I wasn't expecting.

Before he could take any measure of whether she might have arranged the seating for that very purpose, she jumped in with, "Dax, I'm assuming a man of your many interests, you're no doubt aware our science knows a good deal about how children who are physically, emotionally, and verbally abused suffer from the results most of their life. All too often, they become repeat abusers who continue the cycle of violence that was visited on them. In some of the worst cases, we've discovered actual damage to a child's DNA when abuse occurs at various stages of their early development."

"In my case, Angela, I've found that subject of particular interest because it's related to my work. I'm often dealing with the results of that abuse, except I'm coming from the direction of trying to capture those damaged kids, now adults, after they've committed lethal acts on others."

While interested in what Angela had to say, Dax was still struggling to maintain a more stoic attitude akin to his imagined mentor, Sherlock Holmes, and a commitment to keep his eyes on Angela's, well above where Dax McGowan was most tempted to be looking.

"I'm sure," Angela went on. "I don't envy your dealings in that regard, and I appreciate the danger you put yourself in as part of your work. What we're trying to discover now is how the DNA damage affects its victims, and what gene expression may come into play, on the theory that if we can identify those elements, we may be able to develop better methods of treatment, maybe even eventual interventions."

"There's a discovery where I'd be happy to find my caseload substantially reduced. How goes the progress?" he asked, saluting with his wine glass in her direction.

"Slow, very slow, because we have to approach this issue through the back door, so to speak. As you might guess, we're unable to easily identify and test young children currently experiencing abuse. Getting abusive parents to allow us to work with their children becomes impossible because it would be an admission on their part that they're committing a crime."

"I get that," he said, swallowing hard to prevent his words from coming off garbled from the food in his mouth. "Hey, you need to eat and talk too," he added sincerely.

"I know." She sighed. "But let me tell you the good news. We've been able to recruit a sufficient number of paid subjects who have suffered some very severe abuse. They range from younger children who have been completely abandoned, their parents nowhere to be found, to sixteen-year-olds who have been legally emancipated from their parents, to older young adults searching for answers to their difficulties. We introduce one group of them to some very intense psychotherapy, give advanced drug treatments to a second group, and a third group receives both. Our control group consists of participants who receive no treatment at all. We take everyone's DNA early on, map it, and then take it again at specific intervals to see if their maps reveal any changes and where."

Dax sat enjoying Angela exhibiting her enthusiasm with a positive up and down motion of her shoulders. Her words and actions were almost a distraction from looking up her exposed thighs.

"I see. That's quite the reasoned approach. Very impressive," he said, a slip of the Basil Rathbone in his voice. "I could imagine a whole menu of interventions, maybe at some point even in the womb, to strengthen the genetics of all children not only from parental abuse, but from other attacks they might face later in life, like bullying from their peers."

"Whoa there, Mister Dax. Aren't you the future thinker? We haven't yet allowed ourselves to consider those possibilities, though yes, that might be a logical next step," she replied. Bobbing her head side to side, she said, "Let's just hope we have some real success at this level first. Right now, we're too early into our program to expect any results. " She leaned back into her chair, crossed her legs, and held her wine glass up to her mouth to finish its contents. "More wine, please?"

"Of course," Dax stood and poured the balance left from what had been a half-filled bottle to start. "Aren't you going to eat something? I thought you were famished."

"I was, but there are other things on my mind."

"Okay, where would you like to begin?"

"I'll clear up this mess, open another bottle of wine, and let's sit here and talk about my brother Michael, shall we?"

"Sure, let me help you," he offered, pleased to be saved from having to broach the subject of her brother himself.

CHAPTER TWENTY-THREE

The meal cleanup completed, Dax moved the office chair back to the desk area for Angela, and at her suggestion, they settled in to relax on the couch. A fresh bottle of Cabernet sat open on the coffee table, lessened by the amount to fill both their glasses, and found Dax sitting on the end of the more curved center cushion of the couch where he was seated earlier in the day. Angela sat this time in the middle of the curved cushion, considerably closer to him on his right.

Holding glasses already sipped down a good bit and feeling the effects, they sat in more laid-back positions, occasionally glancing at each other to share a friendly grin. Dax was most aware that the looks they were exchanging were not of the kind usual to a couple who were perfect strangers just a few hours before. He had no problem with that, no problem at all.

Angela then offered a broad smile and sat more upright to speak. "Dax, I should tell you that my brother Michael is back in New York, has been for months now. My father, my sister, they don't know. He left his position in Phoenix because it didn't work out for him for the same reasons he failed here in New York. He has substantial self-control issues. After reaching the verge of a homeless existence in Arizona, he called me about four months ago asking if I would help him if he moved back to the city."

"Sorry to hear that," Dax said, choosing to say no more, to allow her to continue.

"I'd been trying to reach him for months before; really frantic about how he was surviving so far away without my help. I've always tried to be there for him, no matter what he was accused of doing. I was elated to finally hear from him, and I told him I would do anything, anything he needed to help him get his life turned around. I could tell from our first phone conversation he was at a point where he may be a danger to himself, maybe even to others.

"I'll be honest. Besides not wanting to worry my sister, who is quite used to her brothers not staying in touch, I had even stronger reasons to keep from telling my father. The way he treated Michael growing up, the damage that did? Frankly, it was a major influence in my taking on my current research project with abused children. Michael is a very lonely man, Dax, very lonely."

"Again, sorry to hear that. It seems, Angela, you've become the person some families need to maintain some semblance of order among its members, but that also makes you the one to carry all the burdens that position carries with it."

"I appreciate your understanding. You're the first person I've shared this with. It feels so good to let it go," she said, her free hand sliding down from her face to her lap. "We psychiatrists need our sounding boards too, you know. I hope I'm in no way burdening you with this, but I also had no choice, since I'm sure you would eventually track Michael down."

"No burden. I also appreciate being let in on this history. It may help in terms of what I might accomplish for Teresa," he added, feeling some guilt he wasn't telling her of the discoveries he had already made in terms of Teresa's condition. Early in his career, negative experiences taught him not to reveal anything about any case to civilians until he had the entire puzzle solved.

"Dax, this is why your interviewing my brother would not be a good thing…at least not right now. While I've been counseling him for a time, and we're making some progress, he's still like a frayed nerve ready to break at the slightest provocation. Talking about the past, my mother's death and Teresa's problems, which he knows nothing about, could set him off and set him back. Can you understand my thinking? Sorry, of course you do."

Dax had to admit he already had a decent picture of what it was like growing up in the Gallagher household. It was also likely Michael played little or no factor in Teresa's reaction to their mother's death. While his head was nodding in agreement to Angela's request, he had an inherent need to know the details of what specific abuse produced Michael's psychotic behavior. He also wondered about the mysterious comments Jeremiah made just a couple of hours ago and how they played into this new information about Michael's abuse. Yet, this very beautiful woman, an expert in this field was requesting that he back off. "Okay, Angela. At least for now, holding off with Michael is not a problem. But may I ask, was it primarily some form of verbal abuse Michael suffered that has him in this state, or was there anything else involved?"

"He is also my patient, so I can't get into the more specific details, but I can give you a bit of background if you promise to keep all this confidential."

Dax offered a gentle nod for her to assume his agreement.

"My older brother, Jerry, for similar reasons to Michael's, left home at eighteen to go to film school at UCLA and has never returned. There was no love lost between him and my father as well. He won't even take my calls sometimes, when I'm just trying to make sure he's okay. The Internet has helped a bit, and it appears his career is quite successful, though I'm still left unsure of how he's feeling about himself. It keeps me awake at night."

"Well, Angela, I was going to tell you that I had a chance to speak with Jerry just before I left my office to come here."

"You reached him?" she asked, visibly stunned. "Uh . . . how so easy?"

"I have to confess I tricked him somewhat into calling me," Dax started, putting the best spin on his methods for her sake. "As you might expect, I have connections that I can call on to help in situations like this." He offered a short squeeze of her hand as emphasis.

"Oh," was all she said, with a blank stare for a response.

"He did speak about his avoidance of family ties," Dax said.

"What details if any did he share with you? I'm curious," she asked in an academic fashion, but also sat up more rigidly.

"No details really. He was in a hurry. He spoke only in general terms."

Like a candle's gentle glow at being first lit, a soft smile spread over Angela's face. She inched up closer to Dax. A look of yearning was present in her emerald eyes. The move caused her perfume and pheromones to fully invade his senses. The effects of the evening's wine were also playing a part in a form of mental imbalance for him. She took her wanting gaze away from his only to lay her head on his shoulder. "I wonder at times, Dax, what would become of my family if anything ever happened to me. The pressure overcomes me at times."

Her expression of loneliness led him to gently move her away just enough to free his arm so he could put it around her shoulders and drew her back in. To his surprise and enjoyment, she reached across his chest to lay her hand on the top of his shoulder. His intent was to comfort her, but the power of the feel of so much of her body against his took over. He felt unable to fight the urges invading his thoughts, and an uncontrolled swelling between his legs was the result. He watched as she lowered her head, confirming she was aware of its presence and then looked up at him. He read her eyes to be asking would there be more than the embrace they were engaged in.

No, Holmes! Not yet, was Watson's plea in Dax's head. *Impatient gratification often contains the seeds of remorse.*

Dax leaned his head back against the top of the couch to view the open beams of the warehouse roof still barely visible in the muted light. Cold steel, the thought of ice cold steel, helped him reach a mental edge where he told himself this encounter was going all wrong. She was in an extremely vulnerable state, and the potential for unintended consequences was too great. He pulled his arm from around her shoulders and reached down to gently hold both her hands. The action caused her to sit up with a look half of disappointment and ready for whatever he would say at the same time.

"Angela, if I don't leave right now, I'm guessing we'll find ourselves up in that loft of yours doing something I'd very much want to be doing, but shouldn't right now. Are you with me on that?" he pleaded.

She stared at him blankly at first and then slowly leaned forward and slipped around to the right side of his face to kiss him on the cheek, her lips brushing across his as she pulled back to present a new look of understanding. "It's something I would want to be doing as well, Lieutenant McGowan. We did agree this morning we'd pursue something later when this whole investigation thing was over, didn't we? Thank you. We lost ourselves there for a moment, and I apologize for not being my professional self. You really are the very fine man the people of New York say you are."

"Oh, I don't know, Angela. If you could have seen the pictures in my head of what I was thinking thirty seconds ago, they might even shock you, my psychiatrist friend," he offered as an attempt at being funny, his hormone levels beginning to subside.

"I don't know. I've been told some rather extreme imaginings in this room, Dax McGowan," she said playfully. "Just promise me when the time is right, you'll describe those pictures in your head back to me so we might engage in the realities of them."

That statement caused his softening loins to pause and reconsider a change in direction, but only briefly. A few moments later, a fierce hug, a small kiss, and he was out the door.

After a judgment he was sober enough to drive with the windows down, he set himself in the direction of home. The frigid air racing through his open window was just the stimulant he needed. He promised he was going to allow himself to daydream every day about how he expected Angela might look totally naked with her fiery red hair swaying back and forth as he gave her all the pleasure she could handle. While the thought brought a huge smile to his face, the brash air had him also noting that in terms of gathering any useable information regarding Michael Gallagher, or of the specific troubles that plagued his boyhood home, the evening had been a wash.

Traffic was normal for seven o'clock on a Tuesday night, and he expected to arrive home within a reasonable amount of time. *Might have a Manhattan for a chaser,* he thought. *Maybe not,* he thought next.

CHAPTER TWENTY-FOUR

Wednesday, December 13

Being the first detective in the office on any given morning was not unusual. Dax was pleased to be facing a new day without the effects of excessive alcohol from the night before. Wine never put his brain in pain the way three or more Southern Comfort Manhattans had always done. He thought it yet another plus of the time spent with Angela. Reviewing the events after leaving her and arriving home, he was surprised at how much he enjoyed watching an archived interview of Robin Williams by Charlie Rose. He found himself laughing out loud at the comic's antics in a totally relaxed manner he knew he hadn't experienced in more than a year. *It's amazing what a little joy time spent with a beautiful woman will do for your outlook on everything.* The rest of the evening was spent in carnal imaginings about this new Irish lass in his life and the eventual physical release of a tension that could not be ignored.

As he sat quietly in his office, he told himself he would take his time with the budding relationship. He ended on the high note of thinking, *The hell with any idea of never falling in love again. This feels too damn good to pass up at least giving it a chance.*

Employing the usual shaking of his head as a tool to change the subject of his attention, he reached for his cell phone, but it went off in his hand with a familiar ringtone. "This really is like old times, us trying to call each other in the same moment."

"Hah! You trying to call me too? That happened a lot last year, didn't it, Daxman?

"Yes, it did. Okay, you jumped first. What's up?"

"I called to tell you that you were right about the FBI tracking down the source of the saxitoxin. It turns out to be from some small med school and research facility I've never heard of, a Huntington Heights Medical College somewhere in the middle of Connecticut."

"That's no surprise. A paralytic contrived to work as an anesthetic that would leave a patient unable to move or feel pain, but still be aware, and maybe in some fashion able to communicate, would be a major boon in many aspects of surgery, and especially for brain surgery where it's often quite necessary."

"Jesus, Dax, you're a pain in the ass sometimes, you know? I don't ever get to tell you shit about anything before you explain it to me first."

"Uh, sorry. So when did the theft take place?" he asked, changing direction to avoid more criticism of what he knew he often did without intent, coming off as a know it all.

"The theft was four months ago in early August. I was told that under the rules with this stuff, the lab techs have to inventory their supply every day. One day the numbers matched up, and the next day they didn't."

Dax stood to stretch his legs and instinctively began to pace. "I have to believe everyone who touches that substance has to sign for it each time, and that has to be an extremely short list, especially for any twenty-four-hour period. Any clues who took it and how much was taken?"

He heard the shuffle of papers across Janet's desk as she searched for the information. "That would be 4,580 ccs. The problem is they don't have any viable suspects. According to everyone's employment contract, if there ever is a theft of any substance, they all have to do the polygraph thing, but those tests revealed nothing. The problem stems from their security system breaking down majorly on just that one day, August 3rd. An estimated eighty medical students jammed into a presentation room to watch a demonstration of the saxitoxin being used on lab animals for what you just perfectly described to me, you shit."

"All right, sorry again," Dax said, more amused this time at her dig. "Were they able to track down all the attendees?"

"Hell, it turns out the Homeland Security people ended up reaming the ass of the head of the research department because he never arranged to have all students who showed up that day cleared. It appears the program had a half-assed registration table set up that anyone could have walked by without question. To add to the error, an e-mail invitation to this soiree was sent to all alumni and flyers were distributed on campus. Here's a line from the flyer. 'The positive applications in medicine of a known lethal substance.' How about that for a perfect invite to a crazed killer? It seems the researchers were looking to show off, and they let their guard down in the process."

"Did the flyer mention saxitoxin specifically?" Dax asked.

"No, but H.S. said after questioning the department folks that no one was keeping it a secret either. If anyone wanted to know, all they had to do was ask."

Standing still and shaking his head, Dax said, "I suppose that since nearly three generations have passed since this substance was initially declared a potential weapon, and it hasn't shown up anywhere as a danger or used illegally since, no one was thinking of it as a possible agent of destruction by a serial killer in the Bronx. Still, it's hard to believe post nine-eleven a research facility like this would let their guard down, but human nature is what it is."

"No shit, and the word is we're supposed to keep this on the down low so no one gets embarrassed publically. Of course keeping those kinds of secrets these days is pure folly. But something else. These med students, they're also in the age group that fits into one of the profile elements of our killer and this theft tends to maybe confirm that."

"The only problem," Dax injected, "is that without a definitive list of who those specific students were, we're left suspecting the entire student body, which is a much greater task. That also doesn't take into account an alumnus or non-student who may have slipped in under the radar. It sounds like a white coat and a stethoscope around your neck would have been the only required disguise to get in. What about security cameras? Were there any in place covering the demonstration?" he asked, switching his phone to his other hand and ear.

"Yes, but they weren't very much help. There were only two stationed in the back of the large room facing forward. Because the demonstration was on a raised stage in the front of the room, all we really got were the faces of the four presenters strutting their stuff.

Everyone else sat at tables looking forward, and all we can mostly see are the backs of their heads. While some milling around happened before and after the demonstration, not that many additional faces were retrieved. The few they caught and tracked down for questioning turned up a big fat zero."

"I'm sure our more-than-intelligent perp was smart enough to have checked out the room for any cameras and made sure he never turned in their direction."

"You know, Dax, from your own experience, and I can say the same from mine, universities and the like just don't take camera surveillance as seriously as businesses do, and these units went in years before nine-eleven. I was told they had recently upgraded the software for the entire campus with better picture quality, HD even, but no new cameras were added in that room.

"Well, my good lady, there's one thing nobody, including H.S., would have known to do back in August when this theft took place. That is, check out the alumni and anyone in the current student body who lives, or used to live, anywhere in or near the Mott Haven area of the Bronx. I'm sure they can sort for a good deal of that information in their student and alumni database."

"Way ahead of you on that. They're working on it for us now at my request. This is the best lead we've had so far. Got my fingers crossed. Hey, you were also trying to call me. It's your turn now."

"I was checking in to see if you had anything new to tell me, but I also had a rather unusual piece of information to share that I thought you'd find extremely interesting. This will have to stay under wraps until Dick and I gather a good deal more information."

"Yeah sure, so tell me."

"You're aware that the commissioner's wife was murdered eighteen years ago?"

"Yeah, heard it through the grapevine a couple of times and then read about it in Zurich's book about the family."

"Without going into all the details now, there appears to have been a major cover-up surrounding the whole event. The most intriguing detail being, that Mrs. Gallagher was wearing a nun's habit, veil and all when she was murdered."

"What the hell? Are you shitting me?"

"No, and she was stabbed six times, just like your victims, except five wounds were all to the chest; only one to the face, but that was in her right eye. How about that for a coincidence?"

"Holy shit on me. My head is spinning. What does all that mean? It fucks with everything we know. Like . . . like our perp is probably a very young man who would have been what, two or three years old back then? But Daxman, the guy who killed old lady Gallagher is already doing life in Sing Sing. Maybe there's no connection at all."

"That seems the most probable explanation, but you know what we say about coincidences involving murder?"

"Yeah man, there ain't no such thing."

"I've got Dick hunting down all the information on Margaret Gallagher's background. Maybe she was a nun at one time or the outfit has to do with some fetish of hers. We're just getting started down that road. The one positive thing about this discovery is that it appears the TV news reports on the murder of the nuns in your case may be the source of Teresa Gallagher's spells, a form of delayed response to discovering her mother's murdered body as a young child. I'm expecting Dick's research will tell us a good deal more." Dax said returning to sit at his desk.

"Wow, again," Janet continued. "Man, some people's lives get so goddam crazy, huh? And this reveal sure does cement how fucked up that family is. You're gonna tell me everything you find out, right? And even if it turns out to be no help on my case, I sure want to hear all the juicy details."

"I'll get back to you with all the news at some point. I have to be very careful now. You were privy to my last phone conversation with the commissioner."

"Oh yeah. Be really, really careful, Daxman . . . really careful."

CHAPTER TWENTY-FIVE

With all NYPD partners, individuals have quirks that tend to irritate the other. For Dax it was Daley's habit of barging through his closed office door without knocking. On one occasion, Daley came flying in with much-needed information he had been assigned to collect on a case while Dax was into a deep conversation between "Holmes and Watson" about the elements of it. It had been the only time he had been caught in the process since his mother had done the same once, barging into his bedroom. Only fourteen, he was employing his unusual skill to solve a string of murder mysteries he had been reading in several books at one time. In that instance, after being asked who he was talking to, he suffered only some minor embarrassment. In the event with Daley, a greater embarrassment caused him to lose his temper, ending in a series of apologies to his hurt partner.

Despite the results of Daley's interruption that day, his abrupt intrusions continued. Dax later decided to let the idiosyncrasy go unchallenged. He was never disappointed in his partner's total commitment to working hard at becoming the best possible assistant detective in his service, and how well Daley always handled being caught in the shadow of his celebrity.

Dax's revelation to Daley about how the Sherlock Holmes stories had stimulated his interest in joining the police department, caused Daley on his own initiative to read all four novels and fifty-six Sherlock Holmes short stories written by Sir Arthur Conan Doyle. Of late, like Watson, Daley had taken to recording in notebooks and on paper anything that Dax might reveal in their cases where the revelations involved observations or deductions that he felt other detectives would have missed. This morning was yet another storming through the door, though Conan Doyle's nineteenth-century characters were nowhere in sight.

"Man, you are not going to believe all the shit I found out yesterday. Jesus, Dax, I tried calling you till really late last night."

"Sorry Richard. Let's just say I was tied up and had my phone turned off. I realized it only when I got up too early to call you this morning." Dax made the statement with the kind of sly smile that said a woman was involved, which he knew would earn him Daley's complete forgiveness. While true about his encounter with Angela Gallagher, he took very few calls in the late evening if he could avoid them. It was one of his strategies at attempting to "turn off his head" to get any kind of decent night's sleep. While being blessed with an eidetic memory had its advantages, it had its curse side as well.

"Whoa there, partner. Someone good in your life, I hope?" Daley asked with enthusiasm, as he sat down across from him with an open manila file in his hands filled with printed Internet pages and e-mails.

Dax offered a confirming raised eyebrow, but asked a question to avoid any explanation. "What do you have there, partner?" he asked, knowing Daley would proceed with what he expected was by now a well-rehearsed presentation.

"Okay . . . Margaret Gallagher," Daley announced. "That would be one Margaret Elizabeth Gruner, born and raised in South Bend, Indiana. She graduated from a local Catholic high school and later attended St. Cecilia's College, a sister school of Notre Dame there in South Bend. Upon graduation in 1968, she entered The Congregation of Mother Mary, a convent in Ashland, Tennessee, to become a Dominican nun. Their specialty? Preparing nuns to teach in Catholic schools."

"So, you discovered very quickly she was a nun?"

"Besides the other research I was able to collect, I got very lucky reaching some folks by phone. You wanted to know the works on this woman, so I checked out her parents from her birth certificate. They're both dead now, but her father was a German immigrant who came here back in the early 40s and married Margaret's mother within a year of his arrival. Then there's a lot of this and that, nothing of any of importance to us, so I'll just jump to the best parts."

"There are best parts, Richard?" Dax asked, smiling.

"Oh, yeah. I found a ton of information the guy who wrote that book on the Gallagher family clearly missed. You remember he spent most of his time tracking down Gallaghers who live in mental institutions and searched out first and second-cousin marriages as the cause?"

"Yes."

"Probably, when he saw the commissioner and his wife weren't close cousins, he just moved on, never taking the time to check out their backgrounds beyond that. I'll start at a time several years after Margaret became a nun. Her chosen vocation name was Sister Mary Theophane. I know they pick the names of saints, but some of these names? Really, who ever heard of anyone named Theophane? I didn't bother to research it on Google to find out."

Dax laughed a bit and flashed a salute for Daley to continue.

"Okay, back in the late seventies, and this didn't lead to any press coverage until after the victims filed suits in 2008, there was a pedophile priest involved in dastardly deeds in the Chicago area, a Father Bennett, who served at a Saint Christopher's parish. He was accused of sexually abusing a large number of Catholic children over a number of years who went to public school and who attended his religious instruction classes each week. Sorry to be bringing that part up. Uh, because it was the same deal with Grace," Daley added, bowing his head.

"No problem, Richard. You can be sure I've read more than my share of similar cases since I lost my Grace. It's okay. Go on."

"This is where it gets interesting. Two of the victims, an older and younger sister, who filed a suit in 2008, said that back in nineteen seventy-seven, their parents vigorously complained to the archbishop about the abuse. The complaining got them nowhere. Their parents ended up pulling them out of the class and decided to move out of the Chicago area to protect them from any more contact with the priest or the church diocese. But here's the kicker. The two kids, as adults, claimed in their suit that the priest enlisted a nun as an accomplice to rape and sodomize them. Their depositions state that often the priest and the nun would have sex with each other and make them watch. Would make you want to puke, but guess who the nun was who was involved in all this. Our Sister Mary Theophane . . . Margaret Gruner, slash Gallagher."

"Holy shit, Dick, emphasis on the word holy. If I hadn't already had my own destructive experiences with the Mother Church, I'd have to admit to being stunned. The ramifications of this news could not only affect our issue with Teresa Gallagher, but--"

"What are you thinking beyond how nuts this is?" Daley asked in haste.

"Right now I'm rolling some things around in my head with no definite conclusions, but I suspect you're going to tell me more that will help."

"And you would be right about that," Daley said, grinning ear to ear and pausing a moment for dramatic effect.

Dax sat observing a well-established tic his partner exhibited when he had made any kind of material discovery on a case and had the opportunity to expound on it. His fingers twitched in an almost afflicted manner.

"The first thing I did was call the convent she attended to become a nun. I played it like I was a past student of hers, loved her work, and wanted to track her down so she could meet my kids. You know, the good nuns have that happen a lot. But the very young person I talked to in their office had little to offer. She took a few minutes to look up some basic records that showed her first teaching assignment was at Saint Christopher's in Chicago, but she had no records of where she transferred next or her current location. I could tell she had no idea about Margaret's checkered past or even that she was dead . . . and I didn't tell her."

"So next you contacted the diocese, the archbishop's office in Chicago?"

"Yeah, and I'll tell you, they didn't want to have anything to do with me. I spoke to a much older woman there, and she couldn't get me off the phone fast enough. She was rude as hell," Daley said with a protruded lower lip as a faux feeling of rejection, followed by a broad grin.

Dax leaned back in his chair to put his crossed feet up on and to the left side of his desk in an effort to not have the bottom of his shoes displayed in any impolite manner to his partner. He settled in, hoping to enjoy the guilty pleasure of discovering yet more incriminating news about their boorish boss, but still in full empathy with the destruction of the affected children. He folded his arms and waited for the next bullet item on the legal pad his partner had prepared for their meeting.

"I then called the school where Margaret worked, Saint Christopher's," Daley continued. "When I heard another elderly voice on the phone, I expected more trouble, but it went completely the other way. A Deborah Tierney, the lady I spoke with, kept referring to Sister Theophane as 'that woman,' with little gasps of disgust popping out every time she said her name. I could tell right away that whatever I wanted to know about that nun, this woman was going to tell me."

Before Daley could go on, a quick knock at the door was followed by the head of Captain Pressioso peeking in. "Dax, uh, Lieutenant, it's been a couple of days. What's the take on Teresa Gallagher? You haven't filled me in on anything," the captain asked.

"I apologize, sir, but this has been the very different case we both agreed it would be. Dick and I are going over where we are so far right now. As soon as I have something worth reporting, I'll get with you. Again, sorry for not checking in."

"Is everything okay? You and the P.C. getting along?"

"No worries there, sir. I can handle him," Dax said wincing inside, knowing the half-truth of his words.

Pressioso stared at Dax a moment longer. "I'll leave you to it then," he said, leaning back out and closing the door.

"Hey, Dax, and I'm not saying this like I'm feeling left out, but that guy really cares about you . . . big time," Daley said with overdone nodding for emphasis.

"I know, Richard. The feeling is mutual . . . but back to your report."

"Sure, let's see. Yeah, I was talking about Mrs. Tierney. After getting the big time vibe she was not a fan of our Margaret Gallagher, I indicated I was investigating her whereabouts. I didn't tell her I was calling from the NYPD, just hung it out there that she was being investigated. She asked me if I knew about her quote, unquote difficulties there at Saint Christopher's. I said I had some limited information, but if she had any details she thought might be helpful, I'd appreciate it. That's when she tells me the whole story about the pedophile priest and what I guess we should call a pedophile nun . . . the lawsuits and the whole history. She e-mailed me copies of the depositions taken by the attorney of the two sisters who sued the diocese. Those depositions filled in the important details I've just given you. In talking to Mrs. Tierney, I'll tell you, I was just trying hard to keep from sounding too surprised during the whole conversation. I was feeling like I was back in SVU with Janet again, digging up background on sex-driven nut jobs."

"I'll bet. Were you able to track down where our child-destroying nun ended up next?"

"Yes. Mrs. Tierney goes on to tell that the many sex abuse crimes by that priest and this nun were all brushed under the rug when any parent ever complained back in those days. Even though this particular case never reached the eyes of the public or the media, the staff members at the school, who heard about the abuse through the grapevine, were in a whirlwind of shock and disbelief. They were all pressured into signing a confidentiality agreement by diocesan lawyers and that included Mrs. Tierney, who had just started working there. There were also rumors back then that the archbishop had come up with cash to buy off the parents of the two girls to help defray their costs to move out of the city."

"Richard, you have no idea how many reports I've read of that same set of circumstances taking place all over the country during the decades before the issue came to light in Boston in 2002, and since then as well."

"Like a broken record for you, I'm sure," Daley said, but he moved quickly to continue. "Then something even more diabolical happened. As soon as this mess hit the fan, our Sister Mary Theophane somehow managed to disappear. Everybody, including the attorneys for the diocese were looking for her. Only it turns out she had stayed in touch privately with the archbishop. About six months after the family had moved away, Mrs. Tierney receives a personal request from the archbishop's assistant that all Theophane's school records be sent to his office. She complies, and a week later, the records came back to her with all references to the abuse issue redacted and a number of positive performance review-type things added. She was instructed to type up a completely new employee file with all the changes. The biggest change to her file? Every reference to her being a Dominican nun was dropped. The new file spoke only about a lay teacher, Margaret Elizabeth Gruner. Jesus, Dax, I could tell Mrs. Tierney was trembling on the phone with me, apologizing for being a part of it all. She told me she was so young and afraid of losing her job at the time, she just did it without question."

"You have to wonder, Richard. How many good people working at diocesan offices all over the country were wrangled into becoming part of these covers-ups with that same threat hanging over their heads? I suppose you're now going to tell me where our Ms. Gruner ended up."

"Oh, yes. Mrs. Tierney was then instructed to type a prescribed letter of recommendation to be signed by the top school administrator to accompany the new employee file, to be forwarded to an elementary school on the East Coast. That would be a Saint Aloysius Elementary School, and guess where that's located, Lieutenant McGowan."

"Holy shit again, Richard. Saint Aloysius on the island?"

"You got it."

Dax's feet flew off the edge of the desk. He leaned forward at a rapid enough speed to make Daley flinch. "So that gets her into Gallagher territory, and her somehow meeting up with our P.C. to then eventually get married."

"Yeah, but I haven't had the time yet to investigate any of the details of what happened after she was hired at the new school, or if she was ever accused of abusing anyone there. I was also going to check out the date of her marriage to the commissioner so I'd have an exact window of time to be working with. But, I also thought I should report all this to you before going ahead since I'd be contacting people so close to home around here the red flags would go up for sure."

Daley's point put Dax at a crossroad. His curiosity as to why the case file of Margaret's death was so drastically pilfered had now become a Pandora's Box. The P.C.'s wife had been a nun who had engaged in acts of pedophilia, but did her husband the commissioner ever know that? Had she revealed it to him before or after they married? Had he discovered it on his own? Was the cover-up of what she was wearing when she was murdered related to that set of circumstances, or did it involve covering up his motive to kill her, or both?

"At some time, it might be good information to have if we discovered she'd been abusing children at the new school, but you're right." Dax confirmed. "If we start making local calls, it's inevitable it will eventually get back to the P.C. Let me think on that for a while. We may already have all we need for now."

Dax leaned back with his elbows on the arms of his chair and his legs stretched out in front of him. His fingertips were pressed together with his gaze directed to the ceiling as the wheels of his mind ground down on the new information. After several moments that Daley let quietly slip by, Dax spoke. "Richard, my studies on pedophilia would indicate that because of the heterosexual actions between the pedophile priest, this Father Bennett, and Margaret Gruner, he would have been more likely to abuse female victims, and she, the boys in that school. While there aren't any studies to prove that definitively, do you follow my reasoning?"

"Yes, yes, I do."

"I haven't given you a report yet on my conversation yesterday with the commissioner's son, Jerry. I'll explain later how I was able to reach him, but he made reference to his father allowing things to occur in their house that should never have happened. While he wouldn't offer any details, based on what you've told me, we'd have to at least theorize that Margaret Gallagher may have sexually abused one or both of her sons."

"Oh, fuck! How much wilder is this all going to get? The P.C.'s wife abusing his kids? Is it possible the P.C. would have known about it and let it go on?"

"Possibly, and you're aware of young Michael Gallagher's problems during his short employment at both the NYPD and the NYFD."

"Yeah, he was tagged Mr. Violence. You know we all cover for each other when anyone gets a bit too testy with a perp sometimes, but the Gallagher kid? Hell, he was known to take swings at his fellow boys in blue at times over the slightest of provocations. Word was you couldn't kid with him about anything. He took it all as personal."

"And Richard, you also know from your own experience with Janet at SVU, his anger issues are textbook symptoms for a good many men who were sexually abused as children. That leads me to a point old detective Vovolizza brought up when I talked to him yesterday that I'd decided to put aside for the moment . That is until you just exploded everything we've learned so far with this new information."

"Jesus, what now?" Daley asked, the tremors in his fingers at full tilt.

"Well, partner, grab on to the seat of your chair. The ride is going to get uncomfortable. Vovolizza said he and his partner, Eddy Fitzgerald, were told by both the accused murderer, Diaz, and one of his employees, that sometime earlier, before Margaret's murder was discovered by her daughters, her husband, our P.C., had made an appearance at home. They heard what sounded to be a nasty argument between him and his wife, and then the P.C. left before any of the kids had arrived home from school. On top of that, Diaz has always claimed he came into the house and found Margaret already dying. He said he pulled the knife out from her eye and was placing kitchen towels on her wounds in a futile attempt to save her life at the same moment the two Gallagher girls walked in and saw him holding the weapon. This may be a huge leap, but if that story is true, and based on what you've found out about his wife, the P.C. certainly would have had motive to kill her if she was abusing their boys.

"There's more. After young Angela called her father to report the murder, he and his partner were immediately assigned to the case, and no one from the Southampton Police was notified. Vovolizza and Fitzgerald both were held to strict confidentiality about anything they saw out there, all required by the Chief of Ds at the time. Any guess who that was?"

"I have no idea."

"It was Shane Gallagher, the P.C.'s grandfather. Then someone, likely this Chief of Ds, made sure none of the crime scene photos ever made it into evidence. We already know a portion of the detectives' notes were torn out by someone who had a reason to. What do you think, Richard? Just how bad does all this smell to you?"

"But Dax, the P.C. could have just said he stopped home and she was alive when he left."

"Yes, he could have, but then why were the notes about his visit swiped, unless for some reason he didn't want anyone to know he'd been there? Based on the hate between Mrs. Gallagher and the landscaper, it may have been his plan all along that Diaz would easily be the first suspect chosen, whether they could convict him or not. As it turned out, we know that for some reason Diaz came into the house and was witnessed by the two Gallagher girls holding the knife. If the commissioner was Mrs. G's killer, it could not have worked any better than if he had scripted it himself. With that set of events already in place, he could easily claim any statement by Diaz or his employees that he had shown up there earlier was just a pack of lies."

"But . . . but something else doesn't make sense," Daley blurted with his finger pointed at Dax. "Why would the P.C. assign you to checking out his daughter's mental problems in the first place, and then agree to let us pull his wife's old murder case if he had anything to hide, like him being the real killer?"

"It could simply be all part of a pattern that eventually trips up people who commit murder, especially the ones with the biggest egos. To begin with, Gallagher rather naively looked at his daughter's issues as being something related to her present-day circumstances. Let's remember, he was convinced it had something to do with rookie hazing.

"As to pulling the old case file, I made it clear to him that my interest revolved around only one point, reading what the impressions of Teresa's state of mind were at the time, as recorded by the detectives on the case. I reminded him her mother's death could not be ignored because every professional psych doctor had at least brought it up in their notes. Some gave it a heavy emphasis. I had him in a tight spot. If he refused to let us check out the file, it would have been paramount to hiding something. Besides, and this is where the big ego comes in, both he and his grandfather believed they had done what was necessary to that case file to eliminate any incriminating evidence. But as sure as he was of himself, he couldn't avoid the temptation to admonish me not to treat his wife's murder like some old cold case that needed re-evaluating."

As Dax spoke, he watched as his partner's more positive hand tremors had converted to a full body trembling of what Dax knew was fear of where this was leading.

"Jesus Christ, Dax. We're not going try and pin that old murder on the P.C. now, are we? There probably isn't enough evidence to gather that would overturn a conviction of the other guy on a case that far back. If he really did murder his wife, I'm sure he'd have no compunction to figure out a way for old man, Vovolizza, to appear as totally incompetent, or worse yet, come up dead. Shit, Gallagher would find a way to get out of it for sure, and you and I would be entirely messed up forever."

"No, no, Richard. I'm not suggesting we take any action on that now. I'm simply sharing theories with you just like we always do, and--"

"Besides," Daley interrupted, "even if he did kill her, this doesn't have anything to do with our . . . er, your assignment to get his daughter fixed."

Dax caught the implied separation, but understood a married man with three children had to think in those terms. "Listen, Richard. You and I are only looking over the edge of that cliff we talk about getting too close to sometimes, and who knows, I might end up falling over it someday. But know this. I will never take you with me. You can count on that."

"I know. This is just scary for me. I have responsibilities you know. "

"Look, you're right. The case at hand is still Teresa Gallagher. We still have that as our first priority, and we've made substantial progress on her behalf. Let's get past that first. Once that's done, if there's any reason to pursue this old murder, I'll take it on by myself. I'll leave you out of it completely, I promise."

"Yeah, well, I'll be there for you." Daley said contritely and more in control. "This just got to me all of a sudden. Give me some time to munch on it more. I have to say, if we thought we had an ironclad case against the P.C., there'd be a lot of people in the department who'd be happy we made it."

"I know. We're talking unequivocally ironclad."

"Yeah, unequivocally ironclad," Daley repeated.

"One other thing, Richard, there's more to say in regard to Teresa's issues. Assuming one or both Gallagher boys were sexually abused, we have to wonder if Teresa was somehow exposed to it. It's not likely at her very young age she would interpret sexual things that easily, but if she had, it certainly could be an added factor in terms of her condition. We'd have to deal with the abuse if we determined it played a part in her issues, though it would certainly be a keg of dynamite added to the mix. There's one more step we have to take to either include it or rule it out."

"I'm afraid to ask. What's that?"

"We have to locate and interview Michael Gallagher. He's our only possible source to verify that information."

"Geez, Dax. I'd rather you talk to that nut case than me. I might ask him a question in a manner he'd think was the wrong way, and get on a plane to New York and beat the shit out of me," Daley said, managing the smallest of a jesting smile.

"Richard, I just found out last night he's back in the city. All kidding aside, I do want to be the one to talk to him. However, we have to find him first."

"Scratching my head, partner. How do you know he's back in New York, but don't know where he is?"

"His sister Angela told me, and now I'm a bit stuck. I promised her I wouldn't be talking to him anytime soon because of his mental state. She described him as being on the brink of a breakdown."

"What's the plan then?"

"First, we need to find out where Michael lives. I already know he isn't living at home with his sisters and the old man in the Hamptons. Maybe I can get Angela involved as a go between when I do interview him. The only problem with that, as you know, is that a third party can complicate the interview process. Angela would understandably be protective of her brother, and probably do her best to keep the conversation too sterile for our liking. In any event, I need you to track him down first; then I'll do the questioning. I'm already considering a plan how we might pull this off without getting any of the Gallagher clan in a tizzy."

"Great. You have any idea where I should start looking for him?" Daley asked.

"Yes, and I know just the place you can stake out where he'll eventually come to you."

CHAPTER TWENTY-SIX

Early in his career, Dax had taught himself various methods of concentration to block out the sounds of the many phones ringing on his floor at the Four-One and all the other ambient noise from just outside his office door. With his partner now dispatched to track down Michael Gallagher, he sat quietly reviewing all the new information Daley had managed to compile on Margaret Gallagher, a/k/a/ Sister Mary Theophane. The new intrusion of the sexual abuse of children into Dax's thoughts once more reignited a level of anger he was more than ready to entertain.

No one knew the depth of the research he had done into the subject of pedophilia after his daughter's death. It was not so much his expectation he would make great use of the information in his work, but because he had to know, had to learn the true nature of the evil to continue to deal with the destruction it had caused in his life. He leaned back, once more raising his feet on his desk, seeking a conversation where he could integrate this knowledge with the facts before him in Teresa Gallagher's case.

"Watson, it seems nearly every waking hour showers us with a plethora of unexpected, highly relevant information about the Gallagher family."

"True, Holmes, the word *avalanche* comes to mind, but what will you do should you discover from young Michael that he was abused by his mother? It would seem the open knowledge of that atrocity would only lead to yet another showdown with your unbalanced employer where the outcome for you could be a disaster."

"On that point, Watson, I am not in disagreement. However, there is more at stake here. Should we verify that Michael was sexually abused by his mother, it would imply even more elements of turpitude existed in that house."

"My God, Sherlock. I'm in fear to ask what you mean. I've been shocked enough from what we already know."

"It's the very nature of this depravity, Watson, this sickness, this evil orientation, or whatever science may eventually reveal as the proper title for it. Like anything in nature, there are degrees of such conditions. However, it often takes the form of an addiction that must be fed, and it has specific needs when it comes to the age of the victims these predators seek. It is most likely Mother Gallagher would have also sexually abused his older brother, Jeremiah, when he was a young boy. The pathology often involves the abuse of one child in a household until that child advances past a certain prepubescent age, where he no longer is desired by the offending pedophile. The enactor then turns to an available younger child to continue their sins of depravity."

"My word, Holmes. I had no idea. It saddens me beyond all convention that any mother might engage in such a practice in the first place, then to reject one child for another to perform these heinous acts because he is no longer young enough to suit her fancy? It sickens me beyond all tolerance."

"Indeed, Watson. If we are free to deduce that both boys were her victims, it would seem rather remarkable the commissioner was unaware of these goings on over the many years that were involved. Let's admit he was at the very least a detective at the time. He most certainly would have been alerted to something afoot, especially if his wife included the donning of her nun's habit as part of the ritual in these interactions with her sons. The desire, or at least the thought to kill any wife under those circumstances, would most certainly pass through the mind of even the most righteous of men, no less through the mind of a man such as P.C. Gallagher.

"The discovery of this abuse may change nothing in Teresa's case. The more I think on it, I'm convinced a child of her age at the time of her mother's death would not have been aware of such acts, even if she were to have walked in on their occurrence. She undoubtedly would have accepted whatever reasonable-sounding explanation was offered by her mother as sufficient. As I see it, the discovery of the possible sexual abuse perpetrated on these boys will only play a role in a later pursuit I'll take up when I pursue the P.C. as the potential murderer of his wife. As to Teresa, I see I am only left with the charge to discover the relevance of the number six with the assistance of Detective Daley, and then, for his protection, release him from any further connection to the Gallagher family issues going forward."

His conversation with Watson ended, Dax sat considering other possibilities. While convinced young Teresa may have been too young to be aware of the sexual abuse of her brothers, what of fourteen-year-old, Angela? He pictured a woman of her intelligence to be a precocious child more observant of her surroundings than other young women her age. He reminded himself that pedophiles were practiced masters of deceit in terms of all the people who were involved in their daily lives. Margaret Gallagher likely would have been successful in creating an acceptable story as to why she wished to don her old nun's habit at regular intervals. She could have described it as a remembrance she enjoyed while teaching children, or to better enter a state of mind to engage in serious prayer. He thought if he could devise such deceits so quickly in his head, surely Mrs. Gallagher was able to invent credible explanations for both her daughters.

On the other hand, if the more perceptive young Angela was aware of the devastation her mother was visiting upon her brothers, it would explain her constant need to be in contact with them to assess their psychological needs and her distress when she is unable to reach them. Her chosen career in the field of psychiatry and the research she was now engaged in was more evidence of that.

Pending Daley's ability to locate Michael, Dax knew it was time to check in with Teresa again as he promised he would, and to pursue a next step in questioning her memories. Meeting her in person would be essential.

CHAPTER TWENTY-SEVEN

"Welcome, Señor Dax," was Peeta's smile filled greeting at the Gallagher's front door. "

"Good day, Peeta. How are you and how is Teresa doing?"

"I am fine, thank you, but as I say when you called, little T, she struggles so much. She naps all day. She fears being awake mean more spells for her. She not go outside or watch TV. She say she is like in a cage. You have good news? Please say, yes?"

"Yes, I can report some progress. I don't have it all figured out, but I'm getting there. Is Teresa ready to meet with me?"

"Sí, I go to her bedroom to bring her down. You coming to the house make her smile and hope." Peeta pointed Dax in the direction of a large sitting room at the back of the house where he once overlooked a sun-warmed sandy beach whose shores were lavishly caressed by the waves of the Atlantic Ocean.

He remembered taking in the scene during an early summer evening cocktail party when he attended as a plus-one invitee of the mayor. Still standing in the elegantly decorated foyer, even at a great distance from the large floor-to-ceiling windows encircling that far room, he observed a different landscape. December produced a mixture of flattish gray and white clouds with scattered snow flurries floating down to a dark sea broken only intermittently by the passing flight of a hearty seagull.

To satisfy his curiosity, he once downloaded the registered architect's plans of the Gallagher home and researched the title and sale of the property. What he found was a portion of the history of the growing wealth of the family over a century's time. The land, this far out on the island, took nearly a day's travel by horse in the early twentieth century, only to be somewhat improved later by the automobile. With today's challenging traffic issues, the commissioner was required to reside in a Manhattan apartment for most of his workweek.

The original price paid for the land alone fell into what Dax knew to be a ridiculous number compared to its values in the twenty first century. Beginning in 1925, what began as an impressive home for its day of 5,000 square feet had over time been renovated and additions added to reach a 20,000 square foot imposing Mediterranean-style structure.

Dax calculated he would have time to scout out the kitchen before Teresa could be gathered for their meeting. He walked in front of the staircase to his left and through a large study that led there. The large open area that included two commercial stoves and two of the largest double-door refrigerators he had ever seen also housed a substantial half-circle breakfast counter. Beyond it was a formal dining table surrounded by double buffets and china cabinets.

Clearly, entertaining is a primary purpose for this mansion to exist.

He immediately focused on an open storage box for an array of large and small cutting knives and accessories. Just across from the cooking stoves, it stood on a massive stainless steel food preparation island containing two large butcher-block sections he was sure any premier chef in the city would be envious to own. He surmised that just to the side of it was where Margaret Gallagher had been attacked. If that wooden-sleeved storage box on the counter today was anywhere close to that same convenient spot eighteen years before, he knew he was correct in his speculation, as a similar blade to one he was now handling, was the murder weapon.

He stood for a quiet moment and turned around in slow motion and estimated the distance back through the study to the foyer and up the stairs to the family bedrooms. He deduced that if any noisy turmoil had taken place where he stood, it would have been well out of earshot of the Gallagher boys if they were up in their rooms as Detective Vovolizza had reported. He leaned back against the island counter. He pictured a fourteen-year-old girl, with her little sister in hand, having arrived home from school and coming into the kitchen where they expected they would find their mother maybe readying a midday snack for them. He closed his eyes, reached into the place in his mind that stored all he knew about murder, and pictured the whole scene unfolding. He did this exercise with every crime scene in an attempt to feel the emotions of all the participants, the victims, those who played the role of discovery and the killers. In this instance, he inserted separately both Miguel Diaz and P.C. Gallagher in that latter role.

A few hurried seconds later, he stood in front of the span of windows in the sitting room facing the ocean and heard two sets of footsteps coming up behind him across a brilliantly shined marble floor.

"Teresa, so good to see you again," Dax said, turning to greet her. "Peeta tells me your struggles with these episodes have been getting worse. I hope some of what I have to tell you will help."

"Oh, my God, Lieutenant, I hope so. I can't take this for much longer. I feel completely whacked out. Please give me some good news." Teresa said as Peeta with an open hand directed Dax to sit at the end of lengthy curved white leather couch with several matching large ottomans, all facing toward the beach. In anticipation of his report, Teresa and Peeta sat together on the ottoman just in front of him as if not to miss a word he had to say.

For Dax, a wave of Grace's countenance passed over Teresa's face. He flinched internally, and instantly knew its meaning for him. He took a deep, but well-hidden breath to overcome its effect, and began. "Let me start by telling you that I don't have a complete answer for you right now, and Teresa, I don't want to give you the specifics of any part of what I've discovered until I have this entire mystery solved. As a cop, I expect you can appreciate my reasons for that."

"Uh… yes," Teresa started weakly, "but I don't feel too much like a cop anymore. I have to get free of this before I can feel like that again. You get me on that?" she said.

"Of course," Dax responded, pleased to see her strength of person had not completely abandoned her. "I can tell you there are three factors in play to explain all the elements involved in your condition. I have already discovered two of them, and--"

"Really Lieu…I mean Dax? You have this two-thirds solved? Do you hear that, Peeta? We're almost there!" Teresa said, flailing her arms and smiling widely.

Peeta's look told Dax she better understood his words, and she had applied a more rational interpretation to them.

In an obvious attempt to help level out the extent of her charge's joy, but not quash it, she said, "Little T, he is a smart man. He will fix this for you, but he needs more time. It take longer for sure. Let him talk to us more now."

Her words reduced the breadth of Teresa's smile, dampened her physical reaction, and gave Dax a cue to proceed.

"Peeta's right, and that's why I'm here. I'm looking to fill in that last item that still escapes me. I want to broach a very sensitive subject with you, if you're ready. It's your mother's death. Do you feel able to answer any questions I might have about that day, when you were still only a little girl?" Dax avoided any reference to her being age six at the time.

Silence ensued for the next few seconds.

"Dax, really? That day is just a big blur to me. I feel really guilty sometimes that I don't cry or feel a bunch of emotional pain about it. But honestly, I don't remember being that close to my mother, more to my older sister, actually. I mean, it seems everybody just keeps telling me, even after all these years, how sorry they feel for me about losing my mother that way, but, I have a secret I've always held inside. I hate to say this, but I just don't care that much. Jesus, I've never told anybody that before, but if it helps you in any way, I'm owning up to it now. Well, I have told Peeta."

Dax's mind raced with a myriad of possibilities as to the meaning of what he just heard. A cop's automatic ask were his next words. "Teresa, just tell me what you do remember about that day. Angela waited for you at your school bus stop and walked you home. That was in the investigating detective's notes. Is that correct?"

"I think so. I mean, we did that every day. I don't remember that specifically."

"What do you remember happened next?"

"Geesh, I've tried to figure that out for years. I'm not sure. The first and only thing I remember is my sister crying and holding me. She was swaying me back and forth. She was in a terrible state."

"What did she say to you?"

"Uh, just over and over that everything would be all right. But, it's so far back now, I don't think I even knew what she was talking about at the time. There were these two detectives walking around. One of them asked me the same questions you just did. Hell, I'm only saying they were detectives because I know that now. I had no idea who they were at the time or what just happened. I remember going to the funeral, but I don't remember ever seeing my mother that day, and the wake and funeral were a closed-casket affair."

"So you have no memory of you and Angela walking into the kitchen and finding your mother's body with a man kneeling over her holding a knife?"

"No, I don't. I know I'm supposed to, but I don't. I mean, I guess I just blocked it out. People do that, right?"

Dax nodded his approval, satisfied he was correct in the supposition that Teresa would not have been able to count the number of stab wounds inflicted on her mother, and that her lack of memory of the incident, in addition to the family's desire to protect her, had precluded her giving any testimony at Diaz's trial.

"It was from my dad, when he came home later, that I first found out my mother was dead. I remember feeling a bunch of sadness right then, and again, some at the funeral, but like I said, not a lot. All I remember is that my mom seemed to only care about my brothers. My memories are that she pretty much ignored me. Hey, I was the youngest and got ignored by everyone a lot anyway, except by Angela. Shit, Daxman--that's what they call you sometimes, right? Does anything I've said help at all?"

"More than you might think," Dax answered. "Listen, I'm going to take what you've told me and apply it to what I've already discovered. Give me a few more days. There's something else I need to ask from both of you. Would you please keep my visit and this conversation just between us for now? I can't explain why in any detail, but it's very important. Can I count on you Teresa . . . Peeta? "

"Sí señor, no words from me."

"Hell yes, sir. Damn, I might not get any more sleep today or tonight for that matter, because of this conversation, and that would be a welcome change for me."

"Good. You'll know everything I know when it's ready to report. I had better get back to it."

Dax stood and slowly headed back toward the entrance door. He turned once more just before exiting to smile and wave. He wanted to be sure he left Teresa with the feeling that there was light at the end of the dark tunnel she now inhabited. The pressure was on. He had to deliver. He knew he was always at his best when that kind of pressure was on him.

As he drove out the extensive driveway to exit the Gallagher's property, he revisited Teresa's comments. Her reference to her brothers getting all her mother's attention was more confirmation that they were likely abused. Teresa's form of self-induced amnesia about the discovery of Diaz kneeling over her mother's body was not an unexpected barrier, and Dax felt he was eliminating one by one all the unknowns as he did in every case.

A thought hit him. His visit had taken him to the home where Angela lived and had him aching to see her again. He wasn't sure if his need revolved more around her phenomenal red-headed beauty, her intelligence, the discovery of the dramatically caring role she played in her family's life, or the remembrance of the wanting look on her face at their last meeting. He concluded it was all those things. Sure now of his next step to interview her brother Michael, he knew he would have to find some way to reconcile with her as to why he backed off his promise not to. Worse yet, what if he later exposed her father to be the man who really killed her mother? How would she react to him after that earth-shattering revelation? Was a potential meaningful relationship between them to crash into oblivion given his commitment to be the crime solver that he was? In a gut-wrenching wish not to foreshadow such results, he quickly decided to table those thoughts, but realized once again how much a role his emotions were now playing in his thinking and what a form of kryptonite they were to his Holmesian skills.

CHAPTER TWENTY-EIGHT

Thursday, December 14

The frigid air gripping the city had finally loosened to the point where the 9:00 a.m. temperature was above freezing for the first time in a week. The air still cold enough, Daley was forced to intermittently hit the Defrost button to keep his windshield clear. He was parked, binoculars within reach, in a construction-ravaged dirt area between two old warehouses in the process of a major renovation. His position was some fifty yards away and across from Angela Gallagher's office. Her red two-seater Mitsubishi was the only car in that parking lot. Taped over the radio controls in his car was an enlarged version of an NYPD photo of Michael Gallagher.

This kind of surveillance was always tedious. If and or when the intended subject would show was most often unknown. The time spent the day before had yielded no luck. Daley employed a number of methods for passing the time during these stakeouts. His favorite pastime of late was to continue his writing efforts, compiling notes on the cases he helped Dax solve involved Dax's special skills. While Dax was never one to boast about himself, Daley thought there was no reason he shouldn't on behalf of his friend and partner. He had devised a raised-level paper pad support that was rigged to his car's console just for times like this when he was doing surveillance work. It allowed him to write and still keep a watchful eye.

Only he and his wife knew that he had been taking online writing courses through Yale University's version of MOOC, Massive Open Online Courses that many major universities were now offering to the public free of charge. As Conan Doyle portrayed Dr. Watson chronicling the genius of Sherlock Holmes, Daley decided he would write a series of stories where Dax solved some of the more complicated murder cases in the city. He had ventured to his wife that as the partner of the famous Dax McGowan, he was sure newspapers, magazines and other publishers would have an interest in his first-hand knowledge as Dax's partner. While experiencing some guilt at taking advantage of his position, he found in himself a major satisfaction and an unexpected enjoyment in the art of writing. This morning, he had brought along his copious notes and the case file covering Dax's tracking down the pedophile priest who caused Grace's death. Daley's hand gliding across a white legal pad allowed him to relive the enjoyment of the clever trap Dax had set to catch the archbishop in a plan to have an important witness murdered.

As it turned out, he would be able to tell Dax this was one rare and lucky day. After only an hour and a half, at 10:30 a.m., he watched someone who appeared to be a bearded version of Michael Gallagher exit a city bus and walk an estimated hundred yards down the street toward Angela Gallagher's office. He wore heavy boots, a stained tan ski jacket, and a dark-blue knitted skullcap from which protruded long tresses of unruly brown hair. Enough mid-morning sun and the exceptional lenses in his binoculars made it easy for Daley to pinpoint enough of the man's facial features for a positive identification.

If Dax was correct, that Michael had arrived as a patient of his sister's, he figured there could be a possible wait of nearly two hours. Given the time of day and Michael's apparent financial condition, he would likely be fed lunch as well after his session with his sister. Daley returned his attention back to his legal pad, assured he had the time to finish a section of his latest story. Much like the survival technique of a grounded bird, he raised his eyes often to be sure he wouldn't miss any unexpected exit by the doctor's brother. Later, at 12:16 p.m., he watched as the commissioner's son boarded a bus going in the opposite direction he had come from earlier.

Daley followed as Michael's bus headed northeast into the Bronx. Shortly after crossing over the Harlem River, Michael exited into the densely populated area of Mott Haven. Daley watched him walk two blocks from a bus stop and enter a shelter on Willis Avenue. The sign above the door read Saint Vincent de Paul

Community Services. Daley quickly assumed, matching Michael's disheveled look and the familiar manner in which he walked the streets, he lived somewhere in the area. Parked across the street from the shelter for some time, Daley began again the process of working on his writing while darting frequent looks at the shelter's front entrance door.

About an hour after Michael's arrival, a figure emerged from a side door to an adjacent alley carrying several large black plastic garbage bags. The coatless, hatless, and longhaired man walked back toward a set of dumpsters to deposit them. As he turned back to re-enter the alley door, Daley easily recognized Michael Gallagher wearing what most certainly was an employee's apron. *So he may or may not visit or eat there, but this is where he works.* It was time to call Dax.

CHAPTER TWENTY-NINE

After a speed dial on his cell phone, "So Dax, as you predicted, Michael Gallagher did show at his sister's office, and I've tracked him to where he works."

"So soon? Good. I was hoping he was being treated by his sister more than once a week. By the way, I just spent a long lunch with our captain. He now knows everything we know. What's your location?"

"I'm parked on Willis Avenue in Mott Haven, but hey, you didn't tell him anything about your suspicion that the P.C. might have killed his wife, right?"

"No, of course not. Like I said yesterday, Richard, that doesn't exist for now."

"Okay, okay, just checking."

"What's up on Michael?"

"I'll tell you, it appears this guy who comes from a very wealthy family is now employed at the St. Vincent de Paul homeless shelter in Mott Haven. I'm betting he lives somewhere in the neighborhood. He certainly doesn't appear to be one of those people who shows up to do volunteer work. Let's just say he ain't dressed for the part."

Like coming up to the top of the water to inhale a much needed breath, Dax's mind burst into words spoken as his alter ego. *Watson, Watson, are you hearing what Richard is saying? We have discovered a rather young man who has been described as exhibiting all forms of psychotic behavior, who is now working in the very homeless shelter where the latest victim of our serial killer had been employed and was murdered. The tie-in to his childhood abuse at the hands of his mother while dressed in the same garb should tell us to throw out any idea of pure coincidence existing between our challenges with Teresa Gallagher and these murders. They are surely bound together.*

"Dax? Hey, are you there? Did you hear what I said?"

"Yes, Richard. What you said just set me back a bit. Listen, I'm sure you remember the last nun murdered in Mott Haven was a Sister Mary Barnabas. She not only worked at that shelter, but was murdered in the alley next to it you're likely parked across from right now."

"Holy shit! I was so focused on the Gallagher kid, I wasn't thinking at all about Janet's case. But . . . but hell, that has to make him a prime suspect for her, right? He sure has the violent past for it. He wouldn't be the first guy who had mommy issues involving sex abuse that turned into a murderer. We're supposed to be figuring out what's wrong with Teresa, but Jesus Christ, Dax, the more we dig, the more we find out about everyone else. Where the hell are we going to end up next?"

Dax stood rapidly, the legs of his desk squealed with a shrill as he pushed hard against it in the process. "It seems all doubt about whether I should be talking to Michael Gallagher has now disappeared. I know Janet had all the employees there checked out, but I suspect Michael, with a cop's background, figured out some way to avoid revealing his identity. His sister was very clear that under no circumstances was anyone to know that he was back in the city."

"Jesus, Dax something else. While we all knew him best as Mr. Violence, word was he was a highly intelligent guy, another reason that would make him right for these serial murders."

Dax's couldn't help but instantly think of how this development would affect his relationship with Angela. If it turned out that Michael was the Mott Haven serial killer and he was the detective to arrest him, on top of exposing her father as the real killer of her mother, it would certainly mean goodbye to that romance. Just as quickly, reason took over in terms of how to proceed. He reminded himself that Michael's guilt was at this point no more than educated speculation and played no role without hard evidence.

"Dick, I'm sure talking to him at his place of employment is out. It would draw too much attention to our line of investigation. We also can't bring him in for questioning for all the obvious reasons.

I'm going to have to create a circumstance where I can speak to him in a setting that will maintain our low profile, but also gives us some kind of an advantage. I also have to figure a way to confront him in a way I'd at least be able to determine whether he's a viable suspect in these killings without putting him or me in any danger, should he lose control of himself."

"Yeah, and we're not going to be able to call in any kind of backup, are we? But wait. We could check to see if the Gallagher kid was ever involved in any heavy crime scene investigation and his DNA is on file. Though that's likely a slim possibility. This is one time having everyone in the department's DNA would help. But, you're going to tell me that's not a good idea because if we searched for it and were wrong, we'd be toast having to explain why we did it."

"Yes Sergeant Daley. For now, we have to nail down his guilt beyond a shadow of a doubt before even thinking about that move. And Richard, it's important we keep up our surveillance on him, in case he has another victim already in his sights. Listen, I have a plan beginning to come together in my head on how I might approach him, but it will have to be at least tomorrow before I can pull together all the pieces of it. It might even present us with an opportunity to gather some of Michael's DNA.'"

"Sure glad that head of yours works 24/7 partner. Are you going to tell me what your plan is, or am I going to find out last minute as usual?"

Dax gave Daley a friendly laugh. "Sorry, Richard. Until I have it all set in my mind . . . well, you know."

"Yeah, I know. Sometimes the surprises you drop on me are worth the wait," Daley said with a smile Dax could feel over the phone. "So, okay. Since I'm already in the neighborhood, I'll just follow him home and take tonight's shift."

"No, my friend, you have a wife and three kids waiting for you. After you discover where he lives, I'll meet you there and stay the duration. Besides, I got plenty of sleep the last two nights." Before Daley could object, "Part of the plan I'm rolling around in my head would also involve Janet's help. I've already confided in her on much of where we are with the Gallagher family. We both know she can be trusted beyond any doubt."

"Yeah. Besides, she'd have our balls floating in the East River if she found out we didn't call her right away on this. Okay. I'll call you later when I find out where he flops tonight. This is just so insanely crazy. I mean as crazy as it gets."

CHAPTER THIRTY

Friday, December 15

Michael Gallagher was in a rush to finish disinfecting the last of forty large tables in the open dining area at St. Vincent de Paul's Shelter. It was 4:45 p.m., and a gathering crowd of famished clients was ready to sit and eat at the scheduled five o'clock hour. He was as hungry as they were. It had been a long day, and being given the assignment of cleaning up the adjacent alley floor earlier, after the profuse vomiting and eventual death of a frequent resident of the shelter, had put him well behind.

From somewhere back in the kitchen, a woman who could have entered only through the alley's side door, approached him while holding out a folded piece of white paper. The jeans she wore were tattered with swaths of dried mud running down her left leg, evidence her previous night's sleep may have been taken in the nearby park. She wore a thin green waistcoat, new enough to have been received after it was donated at some local drop box, but insufficient for the warmth current winter conditions required. Most of the mud on the left side of her face and short brown hair had been wiped off by hands too dirty themselves to complete the job.

"Here," she said. "Some guy paid me twenty bucks to make sure you got this."

"Uh, okay. Who was the guy?" he asked, avoiding any kind of introduction, a common practice for anonymity in Mott Haven.

"Hell, he didn't say and I didn't ask. Job done. I'm outta here."

He watched her head back toward the kitchen's alley door with a noticeable limp. Looking down at the paper scrap not more than three inches square, he read the penciled note: "You gotta meet me at Ezmerelda's at 5 thirdy. Ill buy. Sit way in the back so we can talk privit its important."

"What the fuck?" he said aloud. "Who is this joker that can't spell for shit?" *I don't have anywhere else to be,* he thought, *and that would sure as hell mean a better meal than I'm gonna get here.*

A few minutes later, two blocks away, a woman in tattered jeans and a thin green waistcoat had just reached the person she sought on her cell phone.

"It's done. I don't know if he'll show, but he got the message, and I can't wait to get home and get all this shit out of my hair and off my face. I went ape shit on this disguise so he wouldn't recognize me. Let's hope this works. If he's our man, once again you've come to the rescue, Daxman."

"Thanks, Janet. I'll call you as soon as I'm done with him."

CHAPTER THIRTY-ONE

Dick Daley was seated at a table for two in Ezmerelda's Diner. His chair faced across an aisle from a wall of windows looking out onto 3rd Ave. Lined under the windows was a set of five empty booths for other potential patrons in this favorite neighborhood hangout two blocks east of the St. Vincent de Paul Community Center. It was 5:15, and Daley had arrived early enough to be sure to secure a seat at this particular table nearest the booth farthest back in the restaurant. In addition to the expected clanking noises produced by food preparation in the kitchen, the low hum of the voices of several customers seated at the counter near the front door were the only sounds filling the air. Daley had worn his oldest jeans, a red flannel shirt, and a beat-up insulated jacket to better fit into the woodwork of the eatery's economically disadvantaged clientele. The heat from the fired-up kitchen ranges left it too warm to continue to wear his coat, but it was required to cover his belted badge and holstered gun, at the ready should they be needed.

Within ten minutes, he watched as Michael Gallagher entered the diner door. The young man peered in every direction like an animal on high alert of possible danger. It was clear Gallagher paid little attention to the bellowing male voice from the kitchen instructing him to sit anywhere he liked. Daley looked away, but kept the man within his peripheral vision to observe him walk slowly to the last booth in the back of the diner across from him, following the instructions in the note handed to him earlier. Gallagher chose to sit with his back against the rear wall with a clear view of the front door. Finally, with a pen in hand, Daley looked up from a crossword puzzle to give Gallagher the kind of disinterested half look Gallagher would be expecting from any other patron. Daley pretended to return to the task, occasionally sipping from a cup of coffee.

As the dinner crowd began to arrive and seat themselves, a patron entered who appeared to be an old sailor who had spent his life waging battle with unpredictable winds and ocean currents. While he had obviously survived them, his chosen profession had taken its toll on his anatomy. Deep, weather-driven lines on a permanently tanned face were accented by a long whitish knife-induced scar that ran from under his right eye down to his chin, several days' growth of a salt and pepper beard covering it only partially. He wore a medium-length black peacoat that displayed stains seemingly as old as the man himself, topped by a navy blue seafarer's skullcap. He looked in the direction of the back wall and headed his tall frame that way, slowed by the need of a carved wooden cane supporting his left side.

Daley expected the man to sit in the booth just before the last one Gallagher occupied, but proceeded past that to the commissioner's son's booth. Daley's heart raced. *Who the hell is this guy? Some friend of Gallagher's that's going to screw this whole thing up. And shit, where's, Dax?*

The old man removed his coat and placed it on a chrome hook that rose up off the back of the seat, exposing a tattered black plaid flannel shirt. For a split second, the aged sailor turned full face to Daley, winked, and then eased into the booth shifting side to side as any arthritically afflicted person might to get comfortable.

Daley could only interpret the wink to mean the interloper was somehow in on the plan, but why would Dax bring in a third party and not tell him? How could any outsider know what was going on? He attempted to look more closely at the man but was hampered by not wanting to cause Gallagher to catch on he had any particular interest. Then, it hit him. *Holy shit! That has to be, Dax! Wow!*

With his head lowered, Daley sat stunned for a few seconds. He reasoned the disguise made perfect sense. It was the only way the publically famous Dax McGowan could interrogate Michael without revealing who he was. If the encounter turned out to bear no fruit, no one, including the commissioner, would be any the wiser. Here was another brilliant display of Dax's talents, Daley thought, and then quickly reminded himself that his attention needed to remain focused in the event the conversation with the Gallagher boy turned volatile and unsafe for his partner. Unable to hear much, as Dax had begun the conversation in the furtive tones secret meetings were expected to be spoken, Daley accepted he would have to wait for Dax to tell him later what was said.

CHAPTER THIRTY-TWO

"You Michael Gallagher?" the old seaman asked. After, playing *his tapes* many times over in his head all morning, Dax remembered and practiced using the same hoarse and graveled qualities of the elderly Detective Vovolizza's voice as a perfect choice for the character he was now inhabiting.

"Yeah, and who are you, old man?" was Gallagher's mouthy response.

"That don't matter. I'm here cause a guy paid me two hundred bucks to deliver a message."

"Just what is that message?"

"He says you're the guy that's killing all these nuns around here, and he has proof."

"What the fuck?" Gallagher said in a hushed tone. "Listen, you crazy bastard. How about I take you outside, beat the living shit out of you, and you can give your friend the message that what you look like is gonna happen to him."

"Uh, I never saw the man. Some goon the size of a mountain comes up to me at the pier and asks me if I wanna make some good money. I sez sure and he tells me what his boss wants me to tell you," the old salt said jabbing with a pointed forefinger. "Hell, I got the big-time impression it was an offer I shouldn't refuse. You know what I mean? Don't take it out on me. I'm just the messenger here." Leaning over the table closer to Gallagher he whispered, "I got a feeling you wanna hear the rest too. This ain't nobody you wanna mess with. You know what I mean?"

Dax could see his prey's wheels turning, but continued the look of paranoia his ruse required. Seeing that Gallagher's look told him the fear of the unknown from a potentially dangerous character was having its desired effect, he waited on Gallagher's response.

"Okay. So give me the whole message so you can collect all your fucking money. That's what you want, isn't it?"

Cocking his head to the side, Dax sneered a smile. "It's this way, see? The guy says he knows your family is loaded and wants big bucks to stay shut up about it."

"Oh, really? And how many bucks does the bastard want?"

Gallagher's question was interrupted by a tall and rail-thin waitress bending over to deliver two plastic glasses of water and wanting to know if they had looked over their menus already stacked on the table. With a sweeping left arm, the ex-cop waved her off in an almost violent fashion. She left the table muttering in anger.

"Half a mil…$500,000." Dax answered.

Gallagher's high volume, "You crazy motherfucker," caused the eatery's entire clientele to go quiet, but only briefly, as that term spoken at that sound level was not all that unfamiliar at Ezmerelda's.

With both of his gloved fists pointing in Dax's direction, Gallagher continued. "There ain't any such fucking proof. Why? Cause I'm not the guy killing these nuns. Sure, there are nuns that need killing, but it ain't me."

Dax studied his face with all the skill he possessed. He was left with two opposing impressions in terms of Michael's guilt and decided to wait to hear what he said next, hoping it would offer some more definitive clue. Instead, he saw a seething anger rise up in Michael's eyes, and Dax could see he was stuck between wanting to say more, yet wishing to flee the conversation altogether. He chose the latter. Gallagher stood so abruptly that it caught the attention of most of the people seated nearby. They waited, wondering if a fight was about to ensue. Daley reached around his waist and fingered his gun.

Angry to the point of his whole body quivering, Gallagher slowly leaned over and whispered to Dax his exiting words, "You're one lucky bastard. Too many eyes on me here, or I'd be ripping your arms, and those fucking gimpy legs of yours, right out of their sockets." Later, Dax could only describe the heated breath hitting the side of his face as dragon-like.

CHAPTER THIRTY-THREE

After Michael Gallagher nearly unhinged the diner's front door during his hasty exit, Dax and Daley watched him through the array of street windows until they were sure he had walked well out of sight. Dax then rose and joined Daley at his table.

"Richard, I have it all recorded on my phone, and we can go over it in more detail later. However, I wasn't able to nail down whether he's our serial killer or not."

"Jesus, Dax, forget that for a minute. That's one helluva disguise. I was totally fooled until you clued me it was you sitting there instead of some ancient mariner."

With a sheepish grin that seemed well out of place on the face of a hardened seaman, Dax said, "I purposely didn't tell you about the disguise, Richard, because I wanted this to be a test. I knew that if I had you fooled, this whole disguise idea might work again for me in the future. More importantly, it was our best shot at me making an anonymous run at Michael's guilt or innocence, especially given our rushed timetable."

"That's okay. I've long accepted that, but I've been wondering all day how you were going to pull this off. The disguise worked perfectly. I have to say, you've just hit some new plateau in the sleuthing business, partner. It's all that Sherlock Holmes thing isn't it? And shit, I just realized I won't be able to brag about it to anyone, not for now anyway," Daley offered, receiving a sly grin from Dax in return.

That grin turned to a more serious face, "And as you probably observed, Richard, our conversation didn't last long enough for him to take even one sip from his water glass for us to retrieve any of his DNA. I was also hoping my words might make him sweat enough that his hands would deposit some of it on the table, but he never took off his gloves, either. He may be an angry loose cannon, but under that anger, I perceived plenty of the type of intelligence our very calculating and careful sociopath possesses. I believe he instinctively waited to sip his water or take off his gloves until he determined the gist of our meeting. Of course, my blackmail threat didn't ease his tensions one bit."

"He sure is a natural for this, Dax."

"Yes, he is. You'll hear the whole conversation from my recording later, but while his claim of innocence seemed at first to come off truthful to me, he did make a statement that there are nuns that needed killing, and it was more the way he said it that tended to erase that first impression. He also confirmed through his manic gesturing that he's part of the limited ten percent of the world that is left handed, as is our serial killer."

"That crazier-than-shit look on his face as he was leaving? What was it he said so quietly in your ear?"

"Just that if there weren't so many witnesses, he would have torn me limb from limb. His more exact words were he would be pulling my fucking gimpy legs right out of their sockets. No question he's a prime suspect, Richard."

"Shit. Not getting him to slip up is going to be a big disappointment for Janet," Daley said.

"I know, and I don't treasure the phone call I'll have to make to her, but our main goal still has to be to find a way to capture his DNA. I don't like it, but we may have to break into his apartment to recover something there. I'm sure there are plenty of strands of his lengthy hair there to be had."

Say, how long is it going to take to get you back to looking like my partner again?" Daley asked, with his arms crossed, and his face sporting a grin of pride.

"Part of that job involves me returning these hairpieces and some of this get-up to an old friend of mine. He's been a makeup expert on Broadway for a lot of years, a man named Zoran Ashe. Then, I'm headed home for a quick nightcap and to bed early. After being up all night staking out Gallagher until he arrived at work this morning, I spent five hours in Ashe's makeup chair getting ready for this. I need you to give me a ride to my car where it's parked in Manhattan. I took a cab over here; didn't think my Lexus would survive unscathed this long in Mott Haven."

"Sure, buddy. Old guys like you need your rest. Do we need to pick up any supplies along the way, adult diapers or anything?"

"Yeah, funny, funny. Just get me to my car, will you? I am totally beat. I'll call Janet to give her the bad news on the way. She won't be happy, and especially because she'll have to take turns with us doing surveillance on Gallagher every night until we can retrieve his DNA."

"This is crazy nuts, isn't it?" Daley said. "We probably have the right guy, and the three of us can't get a speck of help from anyone. Why? Because we can't trust our goddamn commissioner."

"It doesn't get any more ironic than that, Richard?"

The expletive-filled call from Janet's end of the conversation during the walk to Daley's car was as politely short as an exhausted Dax could make it. Only a few moments after he closed the passenger door of Daley's car, he slipped off into a deep sleep.

CHAPTER THIRTY-FOUR

Saturday, December 16

On the way into the precinct, Dax and his partner were met with a blustering winter storm. The result found them in Dax's office shedding their overcoats and shaking off a heavy dose of snowflakes that had attached themselves on the walk in from their cars.

"Jesus, Dax, we're going to have to get a mop in here to clean this melted snow off your floor. It's that bad."

Dax nodded, but before he could reach for his desk phone to ring maintenance, his intercom buzzed with a call from their captain.

"Dax? Sorry to interrupt, but the Hapberg murder Daley did all the legwork on, the one that's been reassigned to Roberts? Roberts and I need to talk to him, and he'll likely have to head out for a couple of hours to meet with a witness who says she will only talk to your partner. Can you spare him for a while?"

"Sure, Captain. We've hit a snag ourselves on Teresa Gallagher's issues, and I have to work on what our next steps need to be anyway," Dax answered, signaling to Daley it was the captain calling.

"The captain wants me?" Daley asked.

"Yes, he needs you to get with Roberts on the Hapberg case."

As Dax saluted in his partner's direction, his cell phone rang. It was Janet.

"Jesus, Dax. I just got a call from Homeland Security to tell me they came up with zero on any students or staff at Huntington Medical School having any ties to the Mott Haven neighborhood. Of course if it's the Gallagher boy, that doesn't matter anyway, but I was hoping it would turn out to be someone else, just so we wouldn't have to deal with all the shit that'll come down on us if we finger the commissioner's son."

"Hey, Janet. Yes, that would have been nice. Anything else?"

"My captain wants me at yet another press conference this morning to update the media on our otherwise nonexistent progress. This is a helluva fix. Here I am working with you and not telling my Captain what I really know are the facts . . . again. No complaints, man. I know it has to be this way, but now I gotta lie to the whole world on television too. Are we gonna break into Gallagher's place today while he's at work or what? Hell, even if we get a good hair sample and a rush on the test, it could easily be a couple of weeks before we get the results. Do you have any ideas on what I could bullshit about today to keep the media off my back till we can nail Mr. Violence with something concrete?"

"Sorry, my friend. I'm as frustrated as you are. The answer is yes on breaking into—Wait, I have another call coming in," he interrupted while viewing the Caller ID. *Whoa, this can't be good.*

"Janet, it seems the only time the commissioner wants to talk to me is when I'm already in a conversation with you. I'll get back with you later." As he pressed the "Take" prompt on his phone, he heard her say, "Oh shit, not him again."

"Yes, commissioner? I assume you'd like an update on Teresa's issues," he said hoping to gain at least some control over the direction of the conversation.

"That would be right, Lieutenant. What do you have to report? I'd been expecting some form of communication from you at least every day, and I'm not happy I have to be calling you."

Dax expected the usual display of arrogance, but also detected a sinister underlayment in the eerie degree of calmness in his superior's voice. His instincts told him the commissioner's voice and manner meant that danger lay ahead. Caution tempered his next words.

"Commissioner, I was waiting until I might report something to you I could claim with certitude as the cause of Teresa's spells. While I've made some excellent progress, there is still more to learn--"

The commissioner interrupted. "So, what you're really saying, Lieutenant, is that you don't have this figured out yet, and you're stalling me with things you've labeled under the still-more-to-learn category. I get that bullshit all the time from all you peons who work for me."

"That wasn't what I meant in any shape or--"

"Shut up, McGowan. You can quit trying to pull that tough guy shit with me. You got away with it last time, but you're a fucking dead man now. It seems our retired Detective Emanuel Vovolizza is very unhappy that some of the notes he took during my wife's murder investigation went missing. Do you want to explain to me why all these years later he has a renewed interest in that case?"

Ouch!

Dax was certain the P.C. already knew the answer to that question. Dax could feel his face go flush, his heart pound and his neck began to feel like a garrote was about to squeeze the life out of him. The physical reactions didn't prevent him however, from deducing that the aged Vovolizza had probably begun to stew on what had happened to his case notes. The old detective reached a point where he couldn't help himself and made inquiries that eventually reached the commissioner. Dax also had to assume that his theory proposed to Vovolizza, that the commissioner could be a potential suspect for his wife's murder was somehow drawn out of the old man, whose once held skills at deception had long faded. Dax was certain his fate had already been determined. The only weapon at the ready was his McGowan version of Holmes.

"I've already told you, Commissioner, that I leave no stone unturned when I've been assigned a case. I follow every lead wherever it takes me, and frankly, if you're unhappy with any discoveries I've made, you have only yourself to blame. You know my reputation. Did you really think you could intimidate me into staying away from certain aspects of your family issues, when family issues are the crux of your daughter's problems?"

"Listen, you motherfucker, I expected you to follow my orders to the letter. Yes, I expected some delving into personal matters, but you were to report everything to me, and only me. All I wanted was my daughter back on the job with you keeping your mouth shut about whatever you learned in the process. But no, you had to track my wife's already fully prosecuted murder like some old cold case, which I specifically instructed you not to do, and then, you had the audacity to imply I might have been involved in her death? Here's how it's going to go down. I've got two of my staff on the way over to see you. You're going to turn over your badge and your gun to them."

Dax could already hear his captain outside his door boiling over with expletives he was certain were aimed at the commissioner's emissaries who had already arrived. He knew they would be armed with written instructions from the P.C. that his captain would have no choice but to obey. He now had to be sure there were no more casualties beyond himself. He hoped his partner remembered his previous instructions, that should the shit hit the fan, he was to claim he knew nothing but only followed orders and that his involvement was limited to tracking down the more mundane elements of Teresa's case.

It was clear the sounds of his captain's objections and the two men's insistences were moving closer to his door as the commissioner went on with his tirade in the manner egomaniacs employ when experiencing delight in the pain they were inflicting.

"And you will not touch or remove anything from your office. You will also be frisked and empty all your pockets, turning over their contents to these officers. They will return to you only your house and car keys and escort you from the building. If you resist any of these actions, they will immediately arrest you on breach of precinct security charges. Are you perfectly clear on these instructions, Mister McGowan? Let me emphasize the word mister, because as of today, you no longer have any status in the NYPD. And if you think you have any recourse through your union, think again. I have more friends there than you do. Oh, and I can't wait. The press is going to have a field day with the whole fallen-hero thing. Are you getting all this, McGowan? Do you completely understand what I've just said to you?"

"Yes," was Dax's only answer as he ended the call before the P.C. did. He immediately unbuttoned the top button of his white shirt, slipped his cell phone between the back of his neck and its collar, and tightened his tie to secure it in place. Knowing a search warrant was normally needed to rummage through the data on his personal phone, but the P.C. would disregard that technicality, Dax couldn't allow it to be taken and potentially use the record of his calls back and forth with Janet which could potentially put her in harm's way.

The next half hour of humiliation was more than anyone, even a man able to take on the most stoic qualities of a Sherlock Holmes, might ever endure. The entire precinct had come to a halt. Detectives and office personnel stood still as if captured in a state of distress in a photograph. Unanswered phones took on the status of nonessential background noise.

In addition to Dax struggling to control the appearance of his extreme discontent, there were points in the process when Dax thought he might have to prevent his captain from drawing his own gun against the intruders. Through his open door into the outer office he could see Daley's look of total despair, accompanied by the concern on his face that he may be personally drawn into this avalanche of professional death.

As Dax's office was searched, enough time elapsed to allow him to begin to think of what lay ahead. While he had broken no laws, he was anticipating what methods the P.C. would employ to account for firing him. There would be a claim that the famed Dax McGowan had let his detective skills go to his head. Tired of the day-to-day work of solving ordinary murder cases, he had concocted a ridiculous premise based solely on false conjecture that the equally famous police commissioner was the murderer of his wife eighteen years earlier. So desperate was Dax that he had based his case on the rantings of a retired detective whose sketchy NYPD record contained its own set of well-earned reprimands. He would be portrayed like the hero fire fighter who was caught setting fires, in order to create events where he could be seen as a hero yet one more time. Yes, Dax thought, no one was a better master manipulator of the media than Jeremiah Gallagher.

As Dax's escorting from the building was about to take place, he was able to regroup himself with the thought that he still had a host of facts and clues to pursue on the P.C.'s family. Cop or no cop, going forward he would never give up until the commissioner was exposed to be, as his own son named him, the super prick that he was in conjunction with any crimes he could legitimately nail him with. *This egomaniac bastard chose the wrong kid from the Bronx to pick a fight with.*

With a hand on each of Dax's upper arms, the anticipated perp walk out the precinct door was about to begin. It hit him hard knowing that once they exited, he would be met by a pre-arranged group of press members to witness and record his extraction.

Gallagher's diabolical destruction of him was welled planned. He chastised himself for not being adequately prepared for what "*Watson*" had warned him was bound to happen. For now, he could say or do nothing. His only remedy would be not to lower his head in any kind of shame, as all might expect he would, but to peer directly into the eyes of the many media people he knew so well, to mildly wink and offer them a look that said, *To those of you who know me, hold on. There is more to come.*

CHAPTER THIRTY-FIVE

Knowing his home would be crawling with paparazzi, Dax decided heading there was a bust. He would also have to avoid any of his usual haunts such as Coogan's cop bar, where he often granted interviews. In addition to the media, the questioning would be even more intense from his fellow officers of the law. He told the commissioner's henchmen when they searched him that he had mistakenly left his cell phone at home that morning, knowing his house could not be searched without a warrant. Fortunately one of the officers who showed up to do Gallagher's dirty work winked a message to Dax that he didn't buy the story of forgetting the phone, but would say nothing more about it, evidence of his displeasure with the assignment.

Thinking and planning as to his next moves was critical, and Dax sat once again in the secluded maintenance area of Central Park looking for quiet.

"Watson, I find myself in quite the dilemma, and it shall take the very best of my skills to extricate myself from it."

"Holmes, I find your attempt at describing your current state of affairs in such a matter-of-fact fashion not the least bit entertaining. I warned you of the dangers you had exposed yourself to with this man, but you wouldn't listen. Now you find yourself in a hole so deep it may be impossible to climb free, I fear."

"My dear doctor, it may be impossible for a man to flap his arms like a bird and fly; however, in the realm of human interaction, the word *impossible* rarely applies.

"Sherlock, you may have more faith in the human spirit than I, and under normal circumstances I would bow to your skills. Even as your best friend, though, I must say there appears to be a no way out of these circumstances. Should I even ask? Do you have a plan at the ready?"

"Yes, but best described as in formulation. I will begin by stating there is only one result any plan must achieve if I am to successfully return to my position within the NYPD. It must involve the taking down of Police Commissioner Gallagher. I can picture no scenario where both of us may remain in our current positions at the NYPD at the same time. To accomplish that, Gallagher must be publicly exposed as the tyrant and enabler of wrongdoing that he is. That accomplishment will not be sufficient on its own. It will also take a credible case to present to a grand jury regarding the murder of his wife."

"But Holmes, you're going to have to produce a substantial amount of evidence for that to happen, and it most certainly will involve a good deal of time to gather, to say nothing of how difficult it will be because it involves a murder that took place so many years ago. Whatever your plan, my friend, it seems to me that you must strike while this iron is hot before the public and your peers begin to believe these scurrilous charges against you could be true."

"I could not agree more, Watson, and let me present to you the status of my current thinking. In the landscape of my mind, I have pictured a series of lines that extend like tree branches representing all the Gallagher family members in terms of two major events. The first involves the total dysfunction of their family revolving around the crime of pedophilia, leading, it would appear, to the matriarch's murder, and more specifically, influencing Teresa's episodes of disorientation. The second event is the apparent connection of Michael Gallagher to the serial killings in Mott Haven resulting from his childhood abuse at the hands of his habit-clad mother.

"I must focus, and discard any thoughts not relevant to tying those tree branches back to their central core, the tree's trunk, if you will. There lies the most relevant and most elusive clue that will expose the reason why all these events are related. As from the very beginning, my instincts continue to tell me that the clue is in discovering the meaning of why the number six sets Teresa off into these spells that plague her."

"I am sorry, Sherlock, but it also seems possible that whatever the connection Teresa has to this number six, it may turn out to be some other childhood fear playing a completely different role in her life, manifesting itself more openly now as a result of many current day reminders of her mother's death. Even then, my friend, I have listened to you one by one eliminate all the possibilities where that number might have played its part in all of this. What is left to pursue?"

"What you state, Doctor, brings me to a position that I had not yet considered. Based on all the facts before us, I have placed all these tree branches in what would appear to be the appropriate places. The facts I refer to describe the roles of all the players in this story of familial destruction. It may be that I need to work backwards, so to speak. I'm now wondering if I have not been able to deduce the critical play of the number six because there is no place where it fits based on the roles I have assigned all the players. If I experiment with changing their roles in any new way, will new possibilities also reveal themselves? I then have to ask myself why I hadn't considered these role changes beforehand."

"What could those changes possibly be, Holmes? I'm unable to--"

"Of course, Watson. I see it now. I must admit to succumbing to a weakness I have fallen prey to yet once again. I am distraught at the implications now involved, and I must act immediately not only to save our distressed friend, Teresa Gallagher, but, also in the same line of action save myself."

Dax sat still for several minutes. His thoughts travelled down several roads of logic based on the new possibilities he was considering. He purposely "took off ramps," as he recalled them to test whether his latest conclusions were solid enough to pursue. Each "exit" refined further which road made the most sense. Each new consideration on that path only led to a final inescapable deduction, and the only possible meaning for the number six. He chastised himself yet again at missing a most primary clue, and then proceeded to formulate his plan.

He released the airplane-mode function on his phone to reveal a host of voice mail messages, most from what appeared to be every media reporter he knew. As expected, there were also several from people close to him to which he had to respond. From his partner,

Dick Daley, to Janet, Angela, and sadly, Teresa Gallagher, whom he knew would feel abandoned based on the actions her father had taken against him. His mind made an immediate list of phone calls in the order for them to be made and the research necessary to follow his newest train of thought to the end of the line. He would then make what he knew would be his most important call of all.

CHAPTER THIRTY-SIX

Two Days Later, Monday, December 18

Dax's phone read 9:08 a.m. as he sat sipping coffee while seated on a brown vinyl sofa in Janet Meehan's small Cape Cod home, six blocks east of the forty-fifth precinct where she was stationed. Looking around, he smiled at how his friend, a hard-charging, street-wise detective could also be such a fastidious housekeeper. *You could eat off the floors in this place.*

The day before, Sunday, had allowed him some limited freedom to travel about the city to complete the pieces of the research he needed done, because a good deal of the search to find him by the hot chasing media people was at a more minimal mode. He was also able to reach the mayor at home, to set up a special meeting two days hence on Wednesday morning. He would host the event that would include all the important players in the mysteries surrounding the Gallagher family. One invitation was to be surreptitiously made by the mayor's office to keep the invitee unaware of the meeting's other attendees.

Teresa, on his first call, had said, "Lieutenant, uh…Dax? Is what you've just told me really true? Oh, my God, I hope so. Can't you tell me now? I'll burst if I have to wait until Wednesday."

"Yes, Teresa, it's true. I have the answers as to what causes your condition and what sets you off, but all the facts must wait until Wednesday's meeting. And please, as I asked, it's imperative that you keep this meeting confidential from every other human being in your life. You may, of course tell Peeta, but she must be held to the same promise of confidentiality. If you don't, I may be restrained by your father from ever revealing to you what I've discovered. Do I have your word?"

"Yes, yes, of course. My whole future depends on it."

Part of his next call:

"Richard, just checking in. Are you all set for Wednesday?"

"Yes, partner, I've got it covered. I'll be ready for whatever happens that day, but, Jesus Christ, you never cease to amaze me. My mind is still boggled at what you've told me."

"I had to boggle my own mind first before I could re-look at this entire case and tell you what I'd figured out," Dax said with a small laugh invading his words. "I was thinking I'd better purchase another burner phone. I've received calls from some people who just might be questioned as to my whereabouts and forced to give up this number. As a second precaution, it's been difficult running all over the city to make calls pinging off different cell towers, so I can't be tracked down here at Janet's place."

"Extra burner phones are a good idea," Daley agreed. "I have to tell you, everyone in the precinct is scared shitless, and no one is talking to anyone else right now. The captain, he's hardly left the confines of his office. I think he doesn't want to mistakenly smile in front of anyone about what you've told him. Good thing you did. He was a mess before that."

"Yeah, taking the pressure off him means a lot to me. I also explained to him I would have made this meeting happen sooner, but I had to be sure everyone involved would be able to attend. Anything else I need to know?"

"Well, as far as walking out the precinct doors these days, with all the crazy reporters camped out there, I had felt like a guy who's bleeding and been thrown into a stream with hungry piranha. There is one other thing now. There's a rumor going around the P.C. wants to arrest you on some trumped-up charge of mentally abusing his daughter so he can better make his case to both the press and the mayor's office that he did the right thing in suspending you. You better stay as out of sight as much as you can until the last minute Wednesday."

"Will do, Richard. I'm not surprised he's working so hard at building up his defenses. He's going to need them come Wednesday.

And listen, partner, I totally appreciate the pressure you've been under these last few days, but if all goes well--"

"I know, man, I know. I believe it will."

Hanging up and taking a long sip of his coffee, Dax remembered his call to Janet from the Central Park maintenance area on Saturday following his conversation with "Watson."

"Janet…Janet, calm down. I've got this all under control. Listen, before I explain why, I have to ask if I can bunk at your place for a few days. I'm sure you can imagine what I'm up against now with the press. Where do you hide your extra front door key?"

"Jesus Christ, I hope so. Fuck, the NYPD can't afford to lose you, man. Hell, I can't afford to lose you. You're my best friend in the whole damn department; you know that?"

Dax heard tears in her voice.

"Uh, along the brick walk on the right side of the house, there's a key under the third brick on the left side of the walk," she finished.

After relating to her the basic outline of his latest deductions, Dax went on. "Janet, because I have more work to do on it today, I'll get into all the details of my plan going forward when I see you at your house tonight. You'll know everything then. You're such a damn good cop, Janet Meehan. Also my friend, would you please bring home the DVD copies of the security tapes of the people attending the saxitoxin presentation at Huntington Medical?"

"Sure, but I thought we already decided they were no good to us."

"Maybe not, but I'm thinking differently now. I won't know until I can view them again to verify what digging deeply into my memory bank tells me what I think I saw."

Part of another call to Angela:

"I have to do it this way, Angela. I can't allow this set of circumstances I'm in with your father to get in the way of helping your sister. I'm fortunate to still have a strong enough connection in the mayor's office to have this meeting set up with you, Teresa, and your father with the mayor present. Sternberg said he'll see to it that I can at least finish my assignment for Teresa's sake and then let the commissioner and me work out our difficulties from there, if that's even possible. It's not just the news I have for Teresa and her needing you there for how it might affect her when she hears it, but it should also put you in the best position to make an immediate determination of what kind of treatment she'll need going forward."

"Of course, but Dax, why can't you tell me what that news is now?"

"Angela, my partner will tell you I often don't reveal information even to him I believe is correct until I have verified it beyond any doubt. I should have all the answers I need by Wednesday morning. Your being there, you sweet and beautiful lady, will surely make all the difference for your sister. Please, just trust me for now."

Dax was sure Angela was turning all the possibilities over in her head as her silence went past a comfortable set of seconds.

"Okay, Mr. Detective. I'm sure I can wait to hear what you have to say, and my father is not going to like that I kept this from him. I'm sure he doesn't want you anywhere near my sister now. Maybe I've just been too close to my sister and missed seeing some things you've gleaned from your investigation. We psychiatrists aren't perfect, you know.

"And Dax, please, please don't think that the things we've talked about--what we might pursue personally later has changed. You're one of a kind, Dax McGowan. I'm sure the story my father has made up about you is a complete fabrication. From having grown up in the politically charged environment that is our family home, I've all too often been privy to hearing such false stories, he and his cohorts made up about any number of his various political competitors. You can count on me."

"Thanks, Angela. I'm feeling much safer now about Teresa's needs, and frankly, I was concerned any future you and I might have was a dead issue. I'm glad to hear that's still open."

Other calls followed.

CHAPTER THIRTY-SEVEN

Two Days Later, Wednesday, December 20

Although it was 8:50 a.m., one of the smaller conference rooms in the mayor's office suite had begun to fill as early as 8:15. The mayor's aide who set up the logistics of the meeting reported to Dax and the mayor everyone was arriving close to the different times they had been requested to show up. Dax and His Honor Mayor William Sternberg were still standing in the mayor's private office finishing a conversation.

"So you've got this, Dax? No qualms, you're sure of all your facts and ready to go?"

"Yes, sir, ready to go," was his smiling reply. Dax knew the mayor to be a gutsy guy, but there was no mistaking a tinge of fear in his voice.

"Okay. I won't mince any words. This is a major political move we're making here. Any glitches, and Gallagher, who right now has the press eating out of his hands with these crazy charges he's made against you, could turn my life into a shit storm. I'm betting big you can make all these accusations stick?"

"All set, sir. You've seen me do this before, and right now, I need to get into that room before the P.C. shows up, though, he'll likely arrive late, so he can make one of his entertaining dramatic entrances. Are you ready to stand your ground, your Honor?" Dax asked with a kidding sternness.

"Yeah, I am," was the emphatic response. "As you know, I've

been looking for the opportunity to deep-six this prick for a long time. Let's go push all my chips into the pot of this poker game you've got me into," Sternberg finished, exuding a smile of complete commitment.

Dax quietly entered the meeting room through its door, positioned very close to its right-hand wall. He slid well to the left along the back wall and made himself appear overly busy with his iPad to give the impression to everyone present that he wasn't to be disturbed. The room went silent for a moment at his entrance and then continued with the conversations previously engaged. When he had the opportunity, he peered down the room's main table that normally seated only a dozen people, with two end captain chairs and five others on each side. The table was considerably narrower than most conference tables, which provided a closer proximity for its meeting attendees. The room itself was laid out across a plain white marble floor with a four-foot-high sculptured, dark wood wainscoting and a medium green, rough-textured wall matting that rose from the wainscoting to a ten-foot ceiling. On the wall to the left hung three large street-side, eastward-facing windows that ran from the wainscoting to the ceiling and were blanketing the entire room with early morning sunlight.

As planned, the mayor's assistant had left the head chair at the front of the room vacant and directed arriving guests to assigned seats. From Dax's point of view in the back, the first seat to the right of the head chair in the front was occupied by Dr. Clinton Hogarth, the department's forensic psychologist. Next to him to his left was Teresa Gallagher with her former nanny, Peeta Sanchez, seated to her immediate left. Left of that head chair, directly across from Teresa sat her sister, Angela. She and Teresa were engaged in a clasped hands-across-the-table conversation. For a brief second, Angela caught Dax's eye and offered a wink that he sensed had a slight sexual taste to it. He responded with a boyish grin.

Seated to Angela's immediate right was his partner, Dick Daley, sitting in a slouched position, apparently well involved in the latest novel he was reading. Standing behind Daley, leaning on the sill of the middle window against the left wall, was Janet Meehan. She also exchanged a wink with Dax, but one of a different kind.

Beyond the head chair, against the front wall, was a raised eighty-inch high-tech viewing screen currently empty of any content. Just below it sat an NYPD technician. He was busy hooking up a laptop and other equipment to wiring leading back to the wall below the screen.

A new attendee entered the room, and Dax waited to observe an expected look of astonishment on Angela's and Teresa's faces to see their older brother, Jeremiah Junior. The legs of Angela's chair screamed across the floor as she stood attempting to reach her brother in haste. Seeming confused at first, Teresa followed her sister to his side. The hugs and tears among them were profuse. The questions about his surprise appearance ran at a quick pace.

"I heard you were hurting pretty badly, Teresa, and I wanted to come and see you, among other reasons for being here. That guy over there invited me," he said, pointing to Dax. "I caught a red eye and literally just took a cab here from LaGuardia."

Dax noticed that Jerry was very much a younger version of his father, though taller, thinner, and lacking gray hair and just as square jawed.

"You really are something, Dax McGowan," Angela offered across the length of the room, forcing a small bow from Dax in return.

The greetings done, the attendees all returned to their assigned seats, Jerry sitting immediately to Peeta's left, and across from Angela. Since Peeta also stood, momentarily vacating her chair for his greeting, he had first attempted to take her seat next to Teresa, but was met with a stern look from the nanny he had never met, telling him he wasn't going to sit there. He smiled and quietly acquiesced to her unspoken claim to the chair.

During the commotion of Jeremiah's entrance, Captain Pressioso quietly stepped in the door, and with an air of claiming his attendance only as an observer, moved halfway along the right wall to stand alone behind those seated on that side of the table, his arms folded. Dax nodded across the room in his direction, and his captain returned the same.

Enough time with nothing happening elapsed, and Dr. Hogarth looked in Dax's direction with a when-does-this-thing-get-started look. Angela and Teresa joined in the visual request a few seconds later. Soon after, with the exception of Jerry, all the others present suddenly became still at the sound of the well-known walking cadence of Police Commissioner Jeremiah Gallagher heading down the hall in their direction. He had embedded in the heel of all his shoes a small metal heel plate that echoed off the mostly marble floors of the city's municipal buildings where he trod. All knew that the stern face he employed as he stalked through the corridors of government hid his inner reveling at the fear he knew the sound visited upon anyone within its earshot. However, his well-practiced visage of superiority went to total confusion when he saw the makeup of the persons present in the room. After a moment to gather himself, he stared particularly surprised to see his son from California, who returned a look nothing short of loathing.

Dax wondered how long it would take the commissioner's peripheral vision to pick him up standing just back and off to his left.

"What the fuck are you doing here, McGowan? This is the most fucking stupid thing you could have ever done, and why the hell is my family here? I'm here to meet the mayor. It so happens I have two assistants downstairs that I'll summon who will gladly come up and arrest your ass for--"

"Commissioner," the voice of Mayor Sternberg began in high volume, "Lieutenant McGowan is here at my request."

The P.C. turned around to see the diminutive mayor standing just inside the door behind him.

"What? First thing, I decide who is, and who isn't a Lieutenant around here, not you," the commissioner claimed defiantly.

"Yes, and I decide who is and who isn't the police commissioner around here, don't I? I suggest you take a seat at the table and with the rest of us listen to what Lieutenant McGowan has to say."

"Wait a minute. I'm out of here. I'm not sitting through some crazy shit you've cooked up, Sternberg. I make my own decisions about what meetings I attend and don't attend."

"Sit your ass down, Commissioner," the mayor commanded as two exceptionally tall and muscled uniformed police officers entered the room, closed its large wooden door, and stood as assigned sentries in front of it.

In full belligerence, the P.C. walked over to the officers, neither one he had ever met, looked up, and raised his index fingers to their faces. "By the end of the day, I'll have your badges."

The officer whose nametag read Morliano towered menacingly in return. "You heard the mayor. Sit your ass down. Now!"

The palpable tension in the room was broken only by the

squirming and unintelligible fear-filled mumbling of Dr. Hogarth. For Captain Pressioso, the reaction was covering his mouth in an attempt to stifle his own personal amusement.

In a clear no-win situation, the commissioner turned back to the blank faces of the other guests and began his own mumbled words, something about hell to pay later. He chose the isolated captain's chair that was closest to the door, his look expressing an attitude that he wasn't recognizing anything that might transpire in the coming proceedings.

Sternberg then moved to the front of the room just ahead of the large screen and the technician seated there. "Ladies and gentlemen, thank you all for being here on such short notice, and let's get right to the reason you were invited. For that, I turn things over to Lieutenant McGowan. Dax?"

"Thank you, Your Honor." Dax nodded as the mayor moved aside for him to take his place at the front center of the room. Dax stood still to take a few seconds to look into the eyes of each person as he summoned all the Sherlock Holmes in him to rise to the surface.

"Thank you again for your presence here, especially you, Jerry, who had to come so far," he added, exchanging a plain-faced nod with the Hollywood screenplay writer.

"As you all know, I was originally assigned to discover the cause of Teresa's devolvement into these spells she endures," he opened, realizing a bit of the Basil Rathbone was seeping into his speech. He decided to let it flow, as it both seemed appropriate and reduced the tension he was experiencing.

"I'll begin back to a time and place eighteen years ago when the elements of an event causing these spells took place, the murder of Teresa's mother, Margaret Gallagher. I was first alerted to clues concerning it in a phone conversation with you, Jerry. You said there existed some rather terrible goings on in your household during your childhood. You offered no details, but they did lead you to leave the state to seek a college diploma, and a career that left you virtually out of touch with your family ever since. I didn't find it surprising that your family operated at a high degree of dysfunction having had more than my own share of encounters with your father."

Daley erupted with a chuckle after hearing a desperate, "Fuck you, McGowan," from the police commissioner.

"However, in my attempts to gather more information on Teresa's condition, I interviewed one of the detectives that handled the case of your mother's murder. I discovered that on that very hot summer afternoon, she had been wearing a nun's habit from her former days as a Dominican nun.

"Teresa, I want to bring up something that I believe you had no knowledge of, and based on our discussion about your relationship, or I should say lack of a relationship with your mother, I hope this won't be too stressful for you to hear. On further investigation, in violation of your father's orders, I'll add, Detective Daley and I discovered that your mother, in her earlier profession, had been sexually involved with a priest. While that alone would not be relevant to the issues before us, she and this priest, as a pair, committed horrendous serial acts of pedophilia on young children."

Dax paused just long enough to allow for all the expected gasps and other reactions he knew the revelation would produce. Jerry first raised his head and then lowered it in a manner of accepting Dax's words as the truth. Teresa clearly struggled in disbelief. It was also clear to Dax that Angela wanted to appear surprised but was unable. Her expression showed that the statement was not news to her. Fear, disgust, and sadness then followed on her face. While Dr. Hogarth's state of confusion was of no importance to the proceedings, Dax did extract a touch of enjoyment at what he saw as the doctor's realization that he was producing the kind of discoveries Dax had predicted a detective like himself would eventually reveal.

Dax continued. "As a result of my daughter's death at the hands of a pedophile priest, Teresa, my education into the pathology of pedophilia led to the logical assumption that your mother had visited her sexual addiction upon both your brothers. First Jerry, until he became too old for her pre-pubescent interests, and then Michael. The original phone conversation I had with Jerry last week then took on a whole new meaning. My second conversation with him this weekend confirmed my suspicions."

"Wait, Dax. This is nuts! My mother was a nun? A pedophile? Oh my God. Jesus, Jerry, is that really true?" She asked with both hands over her eyes looking through her fingers in his direction.

Jerry reached past Peeta, his eyes asking for Teresa's hands in return. She offered them, but held on tight in a manner hoping the answer would still be no.

"It's true, Little T. Listen. McGowan here gave me quite a few details about your condition, which was my main reason for showing up today. But he also said today's meeting had the chance we could get this whole abuse thing out in the open. I don't think I ever realized how much I've wanted that to happen until he created this opportunity for it. Please, don't let it upset you. I'm okay now. Well, as much as I can be. I have days, when . . . just don't feel bad in any way about something you had no idea about. You were just a little girl at the time, and it all started even before you were born."

"Where's Michael, then? Why isn't he here if this happened to him, too?" Teresa asked, sobbing.

"I have a good many answers for you about Michael, Teresa. I'll be offering them soon," Dax answered. "In the meantime, it's important that you try to gain control of yourself for what I'll be revealing to you next," he added, catching the commissioner sliding around in his chair like a child who had just been confronted about telling lies.

Teresa was now in the throes of a complete bear hug from Peeta, and continued to sob softly. After a noticeably directed whisper in her ear from her former nanny, she quickly wiped her eyes. "I'll be all right," she offered confidently. She sat more upright in her chair but maintained a look of both hurt and confusion.

Dax took a split second to peer in Angela's direction hoping to determine her reactions. He immediately looked away from her returning glance with the picture in his head of what he had just observed. Shock.

"It was also clear, Teresa, that your father here was well aware of your mother's crimes. Not only had Jerry implied that fact to me in so many words, but the old detective who investigated your mother's death also described the many extensive lengths your father and family reached to cover up what your mother was wearing the day she was killed. I'm sure he feared the press would eventually make the same inquiries Sergeant Daley and I made about your mother's past. By the way, commissioner, over the weekend, we invited Detective Vovolizza into the prosecutor's office for a taped interview about how you kept the Southampton Police out of the loop on your wife's murder investigation until it was too late for them to gather any meaningful evidence. He also gave us a good breakdown of what notes he and his partner took at the scene, stating that anything less than that found in the case file would mean the file had been tampered with. And frankly, there was also physical evidence in the case file of the detectives' notes being ripped from their spiral binders. Mayor? Anything you'd like to add?"

Standing in the back of the room now and to the right of where the P.C. was seated, the mayor turned to him. "This blows my mind to even be saying this, but as we speak, we are searching your office, P.C. Gallagher, and have a warrant to search your home for any and all we can find that was missing from that case file. With the taped interview and the signed affidavit we have from Vovolizza, along with the remains of that file and a statement I expect we'll be able to procure from your son here, how shall I put it? You are toast."

Dax observed the transformation of his soon to be fired boss now stuck with his lips clenched for more than a few seconds, but then the P.C. replied in a most expected fashion.

"Fuck you, mayor. Fuck all of you. That case is so old, and it'll be my word against some old worn-out detective whose past as a detective is rife with breaking the rules and being stupid. Same thing where my son is concerned. Who's gonna believe some liberal-ass Hollywood freak about some sad-sounding stuff he decided to make up to gain his career more attention? Just wait. You'll see who everybody in this city believes. What are you going to do, arrest me, you stupid shits?" the commissioner asked, glancing at the two officers guarding the door.

"No, Mr. Gallagher, we wouldn't think of doing that," Dax injected, "at least not this very minute, or I would already have my partner reading you your rights. Let's wait until I finish my presentation and we see where that takes us.

"I'm sure we'll be facing some statutes of limitations on the potential charges we might bring against you, such as obstruction. But realistically, how do you think any police commissioner could possibly survive the release of this information to the media backed up by a statement from your own son who you never protected from these crimes your wife perpetrated on him? Think ahead, you fool. We still have your son Michael's statement to retrieve as well. He's back in the city now, you know. It looks like a cut-and-dried case of the fallen hero, doesn't it, Mister Gallagher? Emphasis on the word, *mister.*"

Gallagher's façade of arrogance was nowhere in sight. Dax

watched a variety of emotions flash across the P.C.'s face. Fear, caged animal, and rage on the verge of explosion led Dax to gesture to the mayor to move away and allow the formidable officers on hand to step forward. They moved barely in time to grab Gallagher's right hand as he reached under the lower part of his pant leg for a small-caliber pistol strapped to his ankle. Dax always wondered later if the disgraced P.C. had murder, suicide, or both in mind. He was sure the first bullet would have been meant for him.

The officers handcuffed the P.C. to his chair at the mayor's request. Allowing for a trail of angry diatribe exiting the P.C.'s mouth to play itself out, Dax moved on.

He turned to his right. "For you, Angela, life must have been tough. You were both astute and old enough to catch on to the abuse that was going on in your house, weren't you? I'm sure your mother's continuous donning of that old habit, and the unmistakable reactions of your younger brother Michael, couldn't have escaped such an intelligent and observant mind such as yours. It must have played hard on you. It led you eventually to play the role of the matriarch in the house after your mother's death, always watching out for your sister and brothers."

The room went quiet as some facial expressions exhibited disbelief. Coincidentally, the low hum of the heated forced air coming through the ventilation system stopped suddenly adding an eerie texture to the mood. Angela, who was focused on her clasped hands in her lap, raised her head to look at Dax. "My God, Dax. It seems you've set this meeting up to help me as well. You've just revealed the contents of a nightmare I've been carrying all these years. I was so young myself and had nowhere to turn before my mother's surprise death. I tried once to approach my father about what Michael was suffering at her hands, but he'd have no part of it. His look told me he'd known about it all along. My mother was very controlling. It may be hard to believe, but as ferocious as my father can be, he was as afraid as the rest of us of my mother's wrath. I was always at my wit's end about the abuse. It's why I've dedicated my life to discover ways to help abused children, and, I hope adults like my brothers who carry the aftermath of that abuse. Thank you for allowing me a chance to unburden myself of this awful secret. I thought I'd have to carry it to my grave."

Dax bowed toward her and then turned to the technician behind him.

"You ready?"

"Yes, sir," he answered.

Teresa stood in a hurry. "But Lieutenant, these . . . these, my spells. I'm crazy sorry about my brothers and anything my super sister had to endure. Really, really I am. I can't imagine what they've suffered. But...but you said you had my problem all worked out. I know this sounds selfish, but what about me?"

"No fear, Teresa, I was just getting to that. I know what I'm about to say will give you the information you want, however, I must prepare you that what I'll be telling you may be extremely jarring. You have Peeta sitting to one side and the man to your right, as you know, is Dr. Clinton Hogarth. I arranged the seating this way so we can afford you all the help you might need. Are you ready?"

"Jesus Christ. Put me in a straitjacket if you have to. Hell yes, I'm ready."

"Doctor, are you ready?" Dax asked, and Hogarth nodded.

"I'll start by saying, that as much as you believe you don't remember anything about your mother's death, it is the single most critical cause of you devolving into these near unconscious states that have been plaguing you. I'm sure your first question would be, 'Why now? Why after all these years; why in just the last four months?'

"The reason lies in your being constantly barraged by the media regarding the serial murders of all the habit-clad nuns in the Mott Haven area of the Bronx. I know you've followed the stories since their beginning."

"Sure, of course, who hasn't? Jesus, pictures of dead nuns, pictures of them everywhere," Teresa responded, but she began to tremble at the content of her own words. She collapsed back into her chair. Peeta put an arm around her again, and Dr. Hogarth reached in his briefcase for a syringe.

"Teresa, I became convinced it was the TV animation versions of these nuns wearing the old-fashioned habits that set you off because you saw your mother donning a similar dress at the different times during the week she abused your brother . . . that, and she was wearing it the day she was murdered."

"But, Dax, I don't remember ever going ga-ga after watching the news on those murders. It doesn't do anything to me that I know of, does it, Peeta?" she asked turning toward her.

"Yes, Little T. Sometimes you do the spells, sometimes no. But you always shake when we watch. I shake too at those stories, but you are worse."

"There's a reason these spells occur when you watch those story on the news at times, and why you don't at other times," Dax offered. "Just understand that you were significantly affected by those news reports more than you know, though it was something else that triggered your spells, a catalyst, if you will. Teresa, with the thoughts of those murdered nuns constantly in your head, your extreme spell reaction to them was always set off whenever you were also directly confronted with the number six. It was likely when the 'Six O'clock News' banner was shown on TV during the news about these murders that you went into full spell mode. It would also have occurred when you viewed the number in a large font on a clothes rack in a store, a place Peeta told us early on where you suffered episodes. It also happened when you encountered six boisterous uniformed police officers in the hallway at One P.P. the first time we met. The longer these reports have been in the media, the easer it's become for that number, in any form, to push you into that state, which is why your condition has continued to worsen."

"Wait a minute. What?" Teresa asked, more severe body tremors causing her voice to quiver. "The number, what? The number . . . Why can't I say it? I can't . . . " Teresa's head gyrated. Her eyes rolled up into their lids, showing only white.

"Hold her tightly, Ms. Sanchez," Dr. Hogarth ordered as he injected her arm with a mild sedative.

At the sight of the doctor's action, Angela rose quickly but was stopped by Dick Daley holding onto her right arm.

"Let go of me, you fool! What the hell are you doing?" she said, yanking her arm in an attempt to free herself.

"Angela!" Dax yelled. It's important we wait until Teresa comes out of her spell and you remain where you're seated. Please, trust me on this."

Angela peered hard at Dax.

"Please, Angela, please stay in your seat. It's very important," he repeated in a calmer tone.

"Okay," she said weakly and re-took her seat.

As Dax had observed during the spell Teresa experienced in their first meeting, she began to come out of her lost state quickly, more so with the help of the calming sedative in her veins.

"Teresa, my friend, I deduced early on that this particular number has always been a thorn in your side ever since your mother's death. What I had to discover was the reason why. While you've always had what we might call an allergy to that number, it's only been that number now tied to the deaths of these nuns, stabbed much like your mother was, that have put you over the edge.

"Allow me to ask you something. Did you ever know how many times your mother was stabbed?"

"I don't think I ever knew that," she answered in a whisper. "Like I told you before, my recall of that whole day is very fuzzy."

"And even though you and your sister walked in on Mr. Diaz leaning over your mother with the weapon, the knife in his hand, you have no memory of that as well. Correct?"

"Yeah, a big nothing, and as I told you, I must have blocked it out."

"It seemed logical to me at one point the fact that your mother had been stabbed six times was the source of your problem. However, at every turn, I could find no proof that you were ever informed about the number of stab wounds your mother received."

"Jesus, Lieutenant. It sure appears I don't like that number one bit. I . . . I'm totally lost now."

"Well, Teresa Gallagher, I eventually figured it out. I was reminded by an old doctor friend of mine that once you eliminate all the obvious possibilities, you must begin to look at potential solutions that even the evidence in front of you would not support. You see, once I was satisfied that your mother's death was the basic cause of your problems, I concluded that the only potential circumstance left under which the number of times she was stabbed would have any meaning for you would be if you were an actual witness to her murder."

"But I wasn't! I told you, I don't remember a thing."

"There's a reason for that," Dax said, watching everyone in the Gallagher family for their reactions and catching the one he most expected. "You were in a state of hypnosis at the time."

That sentence being a prearranged signal, Dick Daley slowly turned toward Angela as Janet Meehan's heavy shadow from the morning's sunlight moved like an angel of death to encapsulate her. Janet swiftly pulled Angela's left arm back, applying one handcuff to her wrist. Daley restrained her right wrist and both were then securely attached to the leg braces of her chair.

"Teresa, I'm sorry. It was Angela. Yes, fourteen-year-old Angela who murdered your mother," he announced to the room.

"I'm totally lost. Peeta? Help me, please? This can't be . . . how? How?" Teresa swayed as if entering a spell state again. Although she was shocked in total dismay, Dax could see her fighting heartily to gain control of herself.

"Teresa, Teresa," Dax yelled. You want your life back? You want your job as a cop back? Grab it all back. Right now!"

The fluttering of her eyes slowed with each of his entreaties and commands.

Like a tiger mother's attempt to shake her cub loose from danger, Peeta grabbed Teresa's hair on both sides of her head to gain her full attention.

"Little T, he is right. He knows what is wrong. Now we fix it. Hear me, Little T. You and me, we fix this."

Teresa went limp in the manner she always had, as the fatigue of a spell ended. Peeta looked up to Dax. "Señor, it is over, so soon. This is good. Sí?"

"It's a start, wouldn't you say, Dr. Hogarth?"

"Yes, Lieutenant, maybe a very good start."

"Then you'll see she gets whatever treatment she needs so she can get back to work as soon as possible, with you the guy signing off on it, right?"

"Yeah, sure, McGowan," the doctor said in a clear attempt to sound like a nice guy.

Dax turned to his right again. "Nothing to say, Angela? Thought you had me well within your control, didn't you? You had me off my game for quite a while. I have to admit to being under a totally different form of hypnosis. There is no doubt that you're extremely good at diagnosing the needs of the people you meet and then employing whatever kind of manipulation you deem best to control them. And damn, part of it for me was that flaming red hair of yours."

Angela's face reflected a look of total command. "I guess, Lieutenant, reading about your exceptional skills in the newspapers never prepared me for what it meant to end up being one of your victims. Are you going to tell us how you came to create this outlandish story of lies?"

"No lies, Angela, just the truth. Once I deduced the only way Teresa could be so adversely affected by the number six was for her to have witnessed her mother's death, it led me to make sense of all the other facts surrounding the entire case. First, it's certainly not inconceivable that a precocious fourteen-year-old of your intelligence could concoct such a clever plan to commit murder, especially when her motives were so strong. While your older brother Jerry's abuse took place when you were younger and more naive, you undoubtedly observed the severe emotional damage tearing apart your younger brother, Michael. With your father's knowledge of the abuse, but no inclination to help, you became desperate to save your brother. Here's how I see that day eighteen years ago.

"Jerry and Michael always arrived home much earlier from school than you and Teresa and quickly retired to their bedrooms. No doubt Michael was under orders by your mother to be in his room so she could visit her addiction on him at that specific time of day. Believe me, I know from my daughter's experience that pedophiles like to count on a certain schedule of time when they will commit their heinous acts. You, Angela, already knew your brother would be abused by your mother from the time he came home until you and your sister arrived later. You also knew it was the same day Mr. Diaz and his crew would be there for weekly lawn maintenance. The bad blood between him and your mother was a perfect fit for your plan, but the timing was tight. Your mother would normally have come down to the kitchen to greet you as if nothing had happened after abusing Michael, still dressed in her habit. But you still had to worry there was a chance Jerry might also show up from his room at any time. You had to kill your mother the moment you arrived, but the problem was what to do with Teresa whom you walked home with every day from her bus stop? There was no time left to dispense with her. For you, the easy fix was to hypnotize her on the walk home.

"You'd been studying the process in detail for at least four years by then, after reading a book gifted to you at age ten by Dr. Theodore Sarbin. Remember? I remarked to you at your office about how young you were when you received a signed first edition copy of it. You stabbed your mother with a great degree of rage, the thrust through her eye likely the climax. You immediately hugged your mother profusely to cover any potential blood spatter evidence on your clothes. You hugged Teresa as well, for the same reason. You then dispatched Teresa to call out from behind the front door to Mr. Diaz that your mother wanted to see him in the kitchen. You were sure Teresa would never remember that either, since she was still under your control. You only released her from the hypnosis when you saw your father heading in the front door later after the detectives had already questioned her. Of course, the last thing they would think is that she was hypnotized when she was unable to give them any kind of coherent response. It was a brilliant plan, except for one thing. Clearly, murdering a young girl's mother in front of her, no matter how deep in a hypnotic state she might be, had to have some long-lasting effect on her. You wouldn't have known that at age fourteen, but you know it now."

"Holy fuck, Angela!" Jerry blasted. "Jesus, you were constantly trying out that hypnosis stuff on all of us back then. I hated that shit, and you always had Teresa dancing around performing ridiculous antics like some cheap hypnotist's audience volunteer."

"Thank you, Jerry." Dax bowed. "It seems all that practice on Teresa worked. However, I imagine she was a lot like my daughter, Grace at that age, an avid *Sesame Street* fan. She learned to count everything in sight, as the Muppet Count Dracula instructed kids to do. Except for poor Teresa, that day it was one, two, three stabs, and then four, five, and a horrific sixth stab to the eye. Hard to totally block that out for anyone, especially an impressionable six-year-old girl. That number has haunted her all her life and laid in wait to eventually reveal you, Angela, as her mother's murderer."

Throughout his discourse, Dax watched Angela's eyes darting as she considered thought after thought of how she could escape his accusations.

"I hate you, Dax McGowan. You led me on that you were romantically interested in me, always looking up my dress. All the time you were planning to pin my mother's murder on me so you could come up with some reason for my sister's mental health issues. I told you not to expect to solve her case when the psychiatric community had already failed. It appears you don't want to have to admit you can't solve every mystery, and I find your attempt at using me as your scapegoat as abhorrent as any sociopath's story I've ever heard. I'm sure my father will tell you that stories don't make murder cases. It takes proof, and what proof could you possibly have with the convicted murderer of my mother already sitting in prison?"

"Yeah, you're really fucked on this bullshit, McGowan," the elder Gallagher chimed in, grinning broadly.

After Angela's challenge and a true-to-character addition from her father, Dax's mind went to the thought of how satisfying it was when a well-planned trap worked so well.

"Angela, the basis of your defense might play well to some folks if it weren't for you living out some of your own sociopathic fantasies. There's another twist in all this that I still have to offer. You see, these serial killings of nuns in the Bronx have not only been the source of Teresa's memory being jogged, but also their similarity to your mother's death created for S.V.U. detective Janet Meehan and me, the type of coincidence that could never be ignored. Your father would know exactly what I'm talking about when it comes to such coincidences," he said, nodding toward his new ex-boss, who returned an expression of revile.

"After pegging you for your mother's death, I had to consider the leap that you were also responsible for killing these nuns that all live in Mott Haven."

"My god, you can't be serious. Is everyone listening to how sick these ridiculous statements are being made by this conceited cop? Why in heaven's name would I be involved in killing those unfortunate women? This is pure insanity."

"On the pure insanity issue, I agree. Why would you, Angela? Because Michael lives there now. Yes, we found him. While he buses to your office for counseling sessions, I'm sure we can verify with the staff where he works at the Saint Vincent de Paul Community Center that you made visits there to check out his surroundings. Surely, the trips you made to that neighborhood would have brought you in contact with any number of habit-clad nuns who are often found working in those economically depressed areas. You must have panicked at the sight of them, especially when you met one of Michael's coworkers, Sister Mary Barnabas, your latest victim, who had just started working there the week before. You would have seen her as an immediate danger to your troubled and previously sexually violated brother. Taking into account the desperation of a fourteen-year-old killing her mother in a fit of cold, calculated rage to protect her little brother once before, deducing you might repeat the offense given similar circumstances in the future was a path worth pursuing. It's clear that your brother's return and living circumstances re-awakened your imbalanced mothering instincts. You had to keep killing these poor women not only to protect your brother from some imagined dangers of abuse, but also to prove to yourself you did the right thing eighteen years ago. It was all part of a sociopath's process of validation. Frankly, Angela, once I took that track of thinking, the evidence I sought became quite easy to produce."

Angela's face became like a reflection in a distorted clown house mirror as her cheeks and lips wavered between quivering in fear and tensing with hate. She raised her eyebrows as if to speak, but no words came from her mouth. A moment later, she finally managed, "There is no proof that I ever did such a thing," though her halting voice evidenced the weakness of her denial.

Dax ignored her and went on. "When Detective Meehan and I first discussed the serial killings, we came to the immediate conclusion that all the aspects and traits involved provided a profile that didn't fit any one single type of serial killer. However, once I injected you as the perpetrator, Angela, it all fit. Here are the critical elements.

"First element. The killer stalked all the nuns for the clear purpose of finding the ideal isolated place to kill them and leave them at the scene. Why? Lugging bodies to a dumpsite requires the strength of a man in most cases. Some of these women easily outweighed you by twenty pounds or more. For you Angela, leaving them at the scene of the crime was a must.

"A second element involved your medical knowledge. Two things were at play here. The first was your choice of saxitoxin as a paralyzing agent. By the way, for all of you who are not aware, saxitoxin was the substance Angela used to disable her victims so she could perform her ritualistic killings without their putting up a defense. The killer had to be able to understand the nature of that complex substance. Another critical key at play relates to you being able to learn just where to make the exact slit in your victims' aortic arch to produce the slow bleeding death you wanted them to suffer.

"Finally, a most important third element. I have to admit, we detectives will always use the pronoun *he* in cases like this, unless it's clear in the rarest of cases that a woman is involved. In this case, I'm sure you expected that our finding semen inside these women, would guarantee we would continue to seek out a male perpetrator. I had to think on this issue a good deal to figure out how you pulled that one off. The first thing I did was verify with the M.E. that despite the post mortem vaginal damage from sex, she was unable to retrieve any skin cells of the perpetrator from the genitals of any of the victims. Even with the use of a condom, it would be extremely rare to avoid at least the deposit of a minute number of skins cells in at least one of the four cases. There being none, it was easy to assume you had used some form of sex toy to create the bruising and a baster to inject the semen. But where did the semen come from, and why didn't it match up with anything in any DNA base we searched? I contacted a friend who works at Columbia where you're conducting your research and retrieved a copy of your grant. I read that as part of your study you collect semen samples from all the young men to check for potential genetic changes that may take place over time from the therapies and drugs you administer to them. You also have complete background checks done on your subjects. That would alert you to which subjects never had any trouble with the law and therefore didn't have their DNA in any database the police would be checking. You are one brilliant woman, Angela Gallagher, I must say.

"Your grant also states that you freeze these samples as a means of storage. That explained to us why the sperm count of our so-called young male perpetrator was so low. It's a side effect of the freezing. We have a warrant in the works to capture samples of the all the semen you have stored in your lab. I expect we will eventually find one that matches the semen found in all our victims. So Angela, how am I doing so far on the issue of proof?"

Despite the visage of near uncontrolled rage that Dax observed just below the surface of her face, it was her father who spoke on her behalf.

"McGowan, all you have is a bunch of circumstantial evidence. Hell, even if you find one of those boys over there matching up on the DNA, for all we know, he's the one killing those women. Those kids in her study are all a bunch of whacked-out loonies to start with. A good defense attorney would have a heyday in court with the possible alternate suspect theory. Give it up. You're going nowhere on this."

Dax looked at him and raised his right eyebrow in smiling disbelief. The P.C. had just spoken like he still had his job and was admonishing one of his minions. "There's more, Mr. Gallagher," Dax said turning and nodding again to the computer tech behind him.

On the screen appeared a security camera's view of the backs of a number of relatively young people, many in white lab coats, and some with a stethoscope around their necks. The scene was paused.

"As everyone can see," Dax began again, "the security cameras at this Huntington Medical School research auditorium filmed a group of medical students, virtually all with their backs to the cameras. It was determined by a group of Homeland Security investigators that a substantial theft of the dangerous agent saxitoxin had occurred during this demonstration on August 3rd of this year, roughly four months ago, just before these killings first started. Let's zoom in on one of the women in this shot," Dax said, nodding again to the tech. "Sure glad the school upgraded to HD this last year.

"Does anyone notice anything unusual about this woman with long black hair whose face we cannot see?" he asked rhetorically. "Notice the lab coat she is wearing has folds in it you'd see only on such a coat just after it had been purchased and removed from its wrapper. This coat is as pure white as they come right out of the box, but also notice the curvature of her left calf muscle. There is a thick uniquely shaped one-inch scar at the base of her calf just above the Achilles tendon, apparently from some previous injury. I use the word unique because it perfectly matches the scar on your left leg, Angela. And the next view, please?

"On this same woman please look at the lower part of the nape of her neck. Observe where the black hair of this apparent wig is separating as her head is in a leaned forward position. Notice the streaks of fiery red hair floating underneath. You see, Angela, your hair is quite a beautiful and overpowering trait. It appears it just can't be kept silent, despite any means to cover it up."

"So I was there that day," Angela offered. "So what? I attended the demonstration and went disguised so I wouldn't be recognized and set upon to be asked a million questions based on my celebrity as a leading doctor of psychiatry."

"Thanks for admitting that in front of witnesses," Dax said. "We checked, and there was no other proof you were signed in that day. You were one of a fair number of folks who passed by without registering. I presume you made an immediate drive up there after receiving the e-mail sent out to all the alumni of Huntington Heights that a demonstration of the positive use of a lethal substance was going to take place. You did attend Huntington Heights Medical School to gain your M.D., PhD, am I right? All you would have had to do was make a call to a friend on campus to find out the substance was saxitoxin. Someone with your knowledge and maniacal intentions would have found that opportunity all too enticing to pass up.

"In any event, none of this will be as crucial to our case as the results we'll obtain from the warrants being executed to search your office and your home that will turn up the rest of what we need. I suspect we'll uncover the saxitoxin you've saved for use on your next victims and the knife and scalpel that matches what the M.E. reports are involved in these murders. Proof, Angela, mounting mountains of proof. Really, is there anything you have to say in your defense before we read you your rights?"

"I'll just repeat what my father said, McGowan. Fuck you."

There it was. Dax wondered when he'd see it, when it would come to the surface. Well-hidden it was until that moment. The Hannibal Lecter look was sliding up from her chin through her forehead like a theater curtain rising on a play about death. Next came the smile; that most dangerous of smiles was the completion of the transformation. Knowing sociopaths held the need to be appreciated for the genius of how they planned and executed their crimes, Dax hoped this might be the right moment to bring in his final revelation.

"And Angela, as you and Lieutenant Meehan will be reviewing more of the details of your case, I'm sure she'd be quite impressed to hear how you expertly caused the demise and disappearance of your father's ex-assistant, John Zurich, who wrote that book about your family. Of course the news of his disappearance only led to a spike in its sales; though I imagine that you reveled in the thought he wasn't around to enjoy it."

The broadening of her sick smile assured Dax she would welcome the opportunity to have her superior intelligence stroked all-the-more by detailing the author's demise.

Her extended silence and the computer tech blanking the screen and standing to accumulate his equipment had the effect of calling the meeting to a close. Peeta, with the assistance of Doctor Hogarth, accompanied Teresa toward the meeting room door. Just before her exit, Teresa turned to look in Dax's direction, appearing to want to say something to thank him, but was unable. He understood she might never thank him, given the destruction he had just inflicted on her family. His only satisfaction came from the grateful face of Peeta who engaged in a profuse bow to him. He bowed in return.

Following behind were the two giant police officers accompanying the defamed police commissioner. Dax and Daley had moved over to the window side of the room to watch the processions including the final twosome of Janet and her handcuffed suspect heading to Janet's precinct for booking.

She turned to Dax after a couple of steps and jerked Angela to a stop so she could speak. "A twofer, eh, Daxman?" she said with a short laugh. "God, you didn't hear me say this, but I am so looking forward to the next press conference on this case. I'm going to have to avoid celebrating too soon and showing up drunk for it. Thanks, my friend. We'll talk later, eh?"

"Sure. How about at Coogan's with Dick and me after your press conference. Save the drinking till then?"

"Oh yeah. We be doing that for sure."

"And Janet? Don't turn your back on that one. She's dangerous."

"Hah, Daxman. Don't worry. She'd be the one to regret any move like that."

A final salute from Dax to her was followed by seeing both his captain and the mayor coming from his left to greet him.

"Well, Dax, I can't tell you how happy I am to finally be rid of that son of a bitch. Maybe the whole Gallagher reign around here has finally come to an end," the mayor added with one hand on Dax's shoulder and the other in their handshake.

"Let's make sure of that, shall we?" was Pressioso's response.

"I agree," Dax said. "You know, Your Honor? You might be standing right next to the man to take Gallagher's place, a man who would work hard to make that happen by ridding us all of the Gallagher lackeys in the department.

Dax's prompt had the mayor turning to the captain. "You know, John, you've always been on my short list to replace that turd. Let's talk again before day's end. I'm going to have to appoint an interim P.C. right away. You up for that?"

"Yes, sir. I'd be honored," Pressioso said, showing a wide-eyed expression at the offer made so quickly after Dax's suggestion.

"Gentlemen, we'll leave you to it," Dax said. "I now have to track down Michael Gallagher to prepare him for what's about to happen. I think Angela may have been making some progress with him on his abuse issues, but he's obviously going to have to find someone new for that help. I know some expert local people for pedophile victims I can refer him to."

At the offer of an "Amen" from their captain, Dax and Daley turned to leave and headed out the door. Once down the corridor and out of earshot of anyone, Daley stopped Dax with a request he was finally ready to broach with his partner.

"You know what's going to happen, Dax, with the press stories on this? They'll filet the P.C. open from head to toe. They'll have a field day with the scandal of his being married to a pedophile he knowingly allowed to abuse his children, to say nothing about how much the public will be blown away that Angela was the serial killer that's had the Bronx in a grip of fear."

"Right you are, Richard. I suppose we shouldn't engage in too much celebration about those discoveries. This whole affair is also going to give the entire department a major black eye we'll all have to work very hard to overcome."

"That's true, and I'm all in with you on that score. But, what will get lost in all that uproar will be the masterful way you applied your skills in solving two sets of murders eighteen years apart. Oh, they'll give you the basic Dax McGowan hero stuff again, but the details of how your mind worked through this will get lost in the process. Jesus, Dax, really, what other detective on the force could have figured out so quickly Teresa's aversion to the number, six? Even then, they would have likely just written it off to her somehow discovering the number of stab wounds her mother received and let it go. They would never have gone to the lengths you did to nail down the real reason she knew that number, much less deduced her fourteen-year-old sister was their mother's murderer."

"Thanks, Richard, but don't forget the important work you did on the case."

"Yeah, yeah, and a thanks back to you," Daley nodded. "But something else to think about. In listening to you lay out each step in Angela's life that brought her to the point of murdering her mother and eventually becoming a serial killer, it made me think about something I would never have considered otherwise."

"What's that?"

"Jesus, Dax, in her own way, Angela was a victim in all this as well. She only killed her mother to protect her brother from what she could see the abuse was doing to him. I mean, sure, it was screwed up, but who knows what any of us might do at age fourteen under those circumstances with no help from the father?"

"Just from my own experience, Richard, I can tell you that pedophilia affects everyone connected to the victim in a most serious and scarring way. Beyond all the people in the room we just left, think of all the Gallagher clan who jumped through hoops eighteen years ago just to cover it up. Yes, in a very real sense, next to the boys who suffered from the abuse directly, we could easily consider Angela as the next most affected family member, followed by Teresa of course. I'm not meaning to create any sympathy for her, just stating the reality of how trapped she felt as a result of the pedophilia, ultimately making a bad decision to stop it, a decision creating major damage to her psyche with huge long term consequences."

"That would make an interesting storyline by itself," Daley began, "if it was somehow made available to the public, and that gets me to my point. Unless someone informs the public about all the aspects of these two cases and just how talented you are and the lengths you'll go to uncover the truth, no one will ever know what really happened."

"Richard, that's fine. I'm not looking for any pats on the back."

"Of course I know that, but think about this. How are all those young kids out there, you know, all those potential detectives ever going to be inspired to join the NYPD without some kind of model to emulate? Listen, I need to tell you something. I've been taking writing courses online, and I've already recorded a substantial amount of notes about the details of some of the cases we've worked on together. I'd like your permission to submit some of those stories to our local newspapers and magazines, and maybe to a publisher for an eventual book. Would that be okay with you?"

"Whoa, Richard. I had no idea this was going on, and for some time it appears. Maybe I'm not such a good detective after all. You're really serious about this, aren't you?"

"Yes, dead serious."

Dax stood ruminating on his partner's suggestion and in a state of enjoyment at his enthusiasm. He turned his head to look out the corridor window at an all-blue, but cold December sky to allow him to concentrate on the specific point about inspiring the next generation of detectives. His smile began to widen as he thought of his own inspiration drawn from Sherlock Holmes as the trigger for his own career, albeit a fictional character.

"You know, my good friend, for the single reason alone that your stories might encourage some new blood for the department in this fabulous city of ours, I have no major objection to your idea. You realize you'll have to write these stories in a manner that the public doesn't think you've now become my publicist. There'll be some people who will claim it anyway."

"I know, I know. I've already thought of all that. So I'm good to go on this?"

"Yes, my dear fellow. You may proceed," Dax answered, smiling broadly again, his right eyebrow raised and applying a full Basil Rathbone tone to a choice of words he knew the iconic Holmes would surely have uttered himself.

THE END

My Dear Readers,

I hope you enjoyed this fast-paced Dax McGowan mystery, and if you feel it deserves your time, please go to Amazon and place a review there. Reviews are very important to me and my success as an author. You can access the necessary link through my website, www.jackharneyauthor.com.

If you would like to know more about Dax McGowan's history, I invite you to read my first book, *The Millstone Prophecy*. In *Millstone,* Dax attempts to track down the pedophile priest who caused his daughter to commit suicide. A citywide investigation soon turns into an international manhunt approaching the gates of Vatican City and beyond with startling results. An intransigent hierarchy, a wimpish legal community's response, and his own conscience thwart his efforts, as Dax's own life becomes imperiled in the process. Some readers have called it a mix of *Law and Order, Special Victims Unit* and *The Da Vinci Code*. You can link to its location on Amazon as well through my website, and an option to contact me personally if you'd like.

Thank you again, Jack Harney

ACKNOWLEDGEMENTS

While writing a book, that is by its nature a rather solitary endeavor, it's rare for any work to ever reach the eyes of readers without the efforts of a solid team backing up its author. This book is no exception.

I want to thank my long time writing partner, Julieanna (Jules) Blackwell, a well-published short story writer herself, for her patience and expert review of *SIX* in its many stages of development. At the point of a raw first draft, Heather Awad, Barbara Hipsher and Lena Woltering who provided excellent beta reader input, both positive and the, "Jack, this really needs work," kind of constructive criticism.

I was also fortunate that Oksana Hopkalo brought her unique editing skills to this work to address style and content issues needing attention. To my professional editor, Roberta Bobbie Christmas, I say thank you. You offer a great deal more than showing writers where their commas are misplaced. Bobbie is known nationally as, The Book Doctor.

And then there is the person I believe is the best book cover designer in the business, Victoria Landis. The minute I begin to show anyone the creations she produces to exhibit the heart of my stories, the oohs and aahs just keep on coming.

Finally, I owe the many victims of child sexual abuse and their families I've come to know, my gratitude. They opened my eyes to the real story about the effects of pedophilia on the human mind. Beyond that, I also owe them for allowing me to witness their kind of courage, the kind that stems from the depths of the human spirit.

ABOUT THE AUTHOR

Jack Harney grew up in the Mott Haven area of the Bronx, still one of the poorest and more diverse areas of New York City. Irish born, it was no surprise he chose his main character, Dax McGowan, to have a parallel background. It is also no surprise Harney's lifelong interest in everything Sir Arthur Conan Doyle and Sherlock Holmes, Dax would employ a similar skill set in his work as a detective. Spending most of his adult life in the world of business, and despite being known for applying a creative flair in those pursuits, Harney describes those years as his Left Brain Period. Five years ago, he entered what he now calls his Right Brain Period, doing what he has always desired to do most, write.

If you would like to contact the author, he can be reached at www.jackharneyauthor.com.

Made in the USA
Charleston, SC
26 February 2016